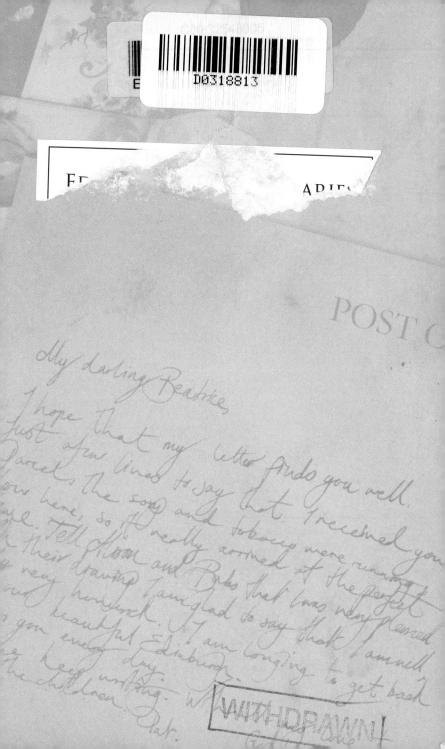

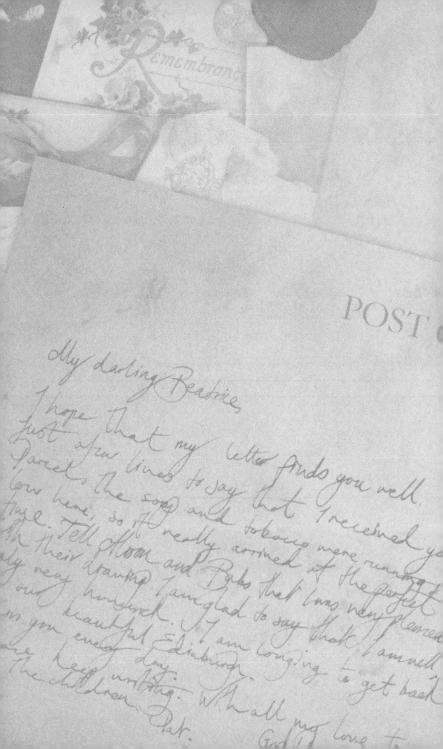

Remembrance

POST O

My darling Beatrice,

I hope that my letter finds you well.
Just a few lines to say that I received ye
parcels the soap and tobacco were runn—
low here, so it really arrived at the perfect
time. Tell Fiona and Babs that I was very please
with their drawing. I am glad to say that I am well
our our homesick. I am longing to get back
in your beautiful Edinburgh.
one keep writing. With all my love to
the children. Pat.
                                        God

'Life is a thing too glorious to be enjoyed.'

— G. K. CHESTERTON

THE
GL🌺RIOUS
THING

CHRISTINE ORR

-m-
MERCHISTON PUBLISHING

Generously supported by the Edward Clark Trust

First published by Hodder & Stoughton 1919

This edition published in 2013 by Merchiston Publishing
Merchiston Campus, Edinburgh, EH10 5DT
www.merchistonpublishing.com

**Edited, designed and produced by
Edinburgh Napier University
MSc Publishing students
2013**

Morgan Amer, Bree Bauman, Char Bennett, Erin Bottomley,
Áine Flaherty, Lindsay Flannigan, Sarah Glidden, Mark Goodwin,
Joe Harris, Emma Holak, Rebecca Laycock, Keren McGill,
Adam Mulholland, Niamh O'Brien, Sally Pattle, Juliane Schmidt,
Thomas Storr, Louise Thirion, Emma Wilson

ISBN: 978-0-9576882-0-9

Printed by Bell & Bain Ltd, Glasgow, G46 7UQ
Typeset in Adobe Caslon Pro 11/13 pt

Contents

Acknowledgements

We are grateful to both the Cadbury Research Library: Special Collections, the University of Birmingham, and the Society of Authors (as the Literary representatives of the Estate of John Masefield) for permissions. Also to the Edward Clark Trust for funding this project.

Special thanks to Yvonne McEwen, Honorary Fellow, the Centre for the Study of the Two World Wars, the University of Edinburgh, for the introduction and her invaluable assistance throughout. To Dr. William Kelly, Honorary Research Fellow, the Scottish Centre for the Book, Edinburgh Napier University, for assistance in proofreading the text.

Our gratitude also extends to Catherine Walker, Librarian at Craiglockhart, Curator of the War Poets Collection; to Lizzie McGregor of the Scottish Poetry Library for her help at the start of the project; to the Laycock family for use of their family heirloom; and to Gwyneth at the Dress Fabric Company. We are also grateful for the help and opinions of Edinburgh Central and Leith Library Book Groups, and the ladies at the Far From The Madding Crowd Reading Group.

Introduction

—YVONNE MCEWEN

Christine Orr's *The Glorious Thing* is not a novel about men going off to war, it is a much more subtle study of conflict. The novel is primarily focused on the personal battles and inner conflicts individuals and families faced on the Home Front during the Great War. The book, in part, is the story of a physically injured man's return from the Western Front, and his struggle to overcome the limitations his disability placed on him. David Grant spent two years at the Front where eventually, if not inevitably, he became a casualty of the war, but with avowed determination he was not prepared to be its victim. Christine Orr describes his regeneration:

"Now he had to find his way back into the ordinary life of the world; he had to make a beginning. That sense of beginning again was a curious one; he felt as though he had grown old, and died, and come back, conscious of the process all the while. Yet it was a beginning without exhilaration, without fresh strength."

However, it was more than physical injuries that ailed him. He was disillusioned with the prosecution of the war and the price it exacted on lives and communities. The war was in its third year and, for David Grant, great sacrifices had been rewarded with great failures. He knew there had been "petty gains and losses on both sides, and little obvious progress". His disenchantment led to depression and "shattered nerves". He found his salvation in old established relationships, new acquaintances, books, and Marion Sutherland. The Sutherland family consisted of six siblings. The eldest was Patrick, his age being nearer thirty when he volunteered for war service. Billy, aged sixteen, was still at school. There were four sisters, Nannie, Effie, Marion and Jullie, and all six lived with their long-suffering uncle Alexander, an Edinburgh builder whose business was damaged by the continuation of the conflict. As the war entered its third and bloodiest year, their middle-class life became increasingly more difficult. As Orr explains, "They lived in a quiet street in an unfashionable part of Edinburgh, and had not as much money as they would have liked. After the war began they had less than ever". Despite her own emotional frailty, Marion Sutherland carried the burden of holding together an economically challenged and emotionally charged home, but as Orr writes:

"The Sutherland household suffered from too many mistresses. Nannie was the official head, but she worked and played at her own sweet will so that the other sisters had to make up for her deficiencies according to their time and ability. In consequence they were always tripping over each other in domestic duties, and not a day passed without a storm in their tempestuous family teapot. More and more Marion was letting the burden fall from her shoulders, more and more Effie was taking it up. But the general result was not a happy one."

War can change people and their circumstances, but it can also transform places. The Edinburgh David Grant knew prior to the outbreak of the war was not the Edinburgh he came home to. Almost daily, the vicissitudes of the war brought changes to the emotional and economic fabric of the city. By 1916, Edinburgh was a hive of activity in support of the war effort. Fashioned after real events and places, Orr's book has some wonderful vignettes of Edinburgh life during this period. For example, on 22 March 1916, at St. Cuthbert's Hall, King Stables Road, Dr. Elsie Inglis and Dr. Alice

Hutchinson gave a lecture to a packed hall on their work in Serbia. According to *The Scotsman*, Lord Salvesen presided over the gathering, which was hosted by the National Union of Women's Suffrage Societies. In his address, Lord Salvesen said the women had earned the admiration of all Scotland for what they had achieved. Clearly influenced by news of the Scottish Women's Hospital work in Serbia, Christine Orr has Nannie Sutherland involved in organising a fundraiser for the Serbian Relief Fund. However, while having tea and cakes in Jenners' Tea Room with her co-organiser, Mrs. Gerard, she discovers the event will be a Scottish pageant and all donations will go to the city of Edinburgh's regiment, the Royal Scots. According to Mrs Gerard: "It will be a Scotch thing for a Scotch Regiment". Disappointed, Nannie responds, "Won't Scotch things be rather stale… I have a topping oriental costume I once wore at a fancy ball." Mrs. Gerard's response is swift and comic, "My dear, you couldn't blend Eastern things with a pipe band."

Christine Orr's use of Edinburgh's buildings and places brings the war on the Home Front vividly to life. Craigleith Poor Law Hospital (the Western General) became the 2nd Scottish General Territorial Hospital in 1914. It had 520 beds set aside for military use. By 1916, there were 1,300 beds occupied by sick and wounded soldiers. Orr uses the hospital as a backdrop to resolving Effie's domestic dilemmas. Fed up with being taken for granted and feeling like a slave in her own home, she enlists for war work at the hospital. "There was a satisfied sparkle in her eyes as she laid down some parcels on the bed, and flung off her scarf. 'Well it's settled,' she announced… 'I'm going to cook at Craigleith. This day week they want me.'" The National Gallery is where David Grant first sees Marion Sutherland, and where "there were several wounded soldiers, who were admitted free and thought the thing a pleasant variety from a picture palace".

The Home Front activities in the City of Edinburgh are well illustrated, and the book is a fascinating combination of fiction and social history. Christine Orr writes beautifully, sympathetically and humorously about the city and people.

The reprint of the book is timely as next year will be the one hundredth anniversary of the outbreak of the First World War. Some historians have argued that the literature of and on the war has skewed or corrupted historical facts. There are those who bemoan that our knowledge of the war comes primarily through literature and not history. It has been described as a literary war because of the prodigious output of novels, poetry, memoirs, and war literature in general. Others maintain that the literature of the time, written by participants in, and witnesses to, the events on the Home and Fighting Fronts should not be dismissed as mere literary froth. No doubt the arguments will continue well beyond the centenary. Yet, as demonstrated by the 19-year-old Christine Orr who published her book in 1919, the prism of the witness is a potent force; in fact, it can be a glorious thing.

—Yvonne McEwen, Honorary Fellow,
the Centre for the Study of the Two World Wars,
the University of Edinburgh

THE GLORIOUS THING

One

I wasna the man I had been,
Juist a gangrel dozin' in fits;
The pin had faun oot o' the warld,
And I doddered amang the bits.

—JOHN BUCHAN

I t has been said that there are a few simple recipes for happiness which never fail, and one of them is: "Take a book, a good fire, and a singing kettle." But David Grant had not succeeded in achieving the desired result although he possessed all the ingredients. There certainly was a generous fire burning on the hearth, and crackling in cheerful duet with the little clock on the mantelpiece; at one side of the grate a small kettle struck up a preliminary humming; and on his knee lay a book of Chesterton's, one continuous switchback of surprise and paradox and startling delight. And he was not happy.

From his face you would have judged him to be a man who took his pleasures soberly. He would have been handsome, his sister was wont to say, if he could have carried it off with an air; but airs of all sorts were foreign to him, except a certain air of reserve, half unconscious, and purely by way of self-defence. He was clean-shaven, and very fair-skinned, indeed too pale, although the red glare of the fire concealed that.

His mouth had humorous lines about it which broke into a quick, appreciative smile now and then as he read. His eyes were grey, the eyes of an honest boy, puzzled with life, and at the same time of a man who has been hurt in it, and ready to turn cynic. One hand held his book, the other rumpled his already untidy hair. Occasionally, at some noise or movement outside, his eyebrows would contract and he would look up with a little nervous gesture; his whole attitude was one of strain as though he had suffered pain so long with his body braced for endurance that he had forgotten how to relax now that relief had come.

After a while he threw down the book, tired with the effort of concentrating his mind on it; it was almost the first he had read consecutively for two years. His weary body sank back into the wide, shabby armchair with a feeling of luxury. He might not be happy, but things were undeniably comfortable – and quiet. He almost missed the sound of guns, as one who lives by the sea misses the sound of the waves when he goes inland. Oh it was all very comfortable; and yet he was not content. The last sentence he had read repeated itself over in his brain, an irresponsible paradox, apparently, and yet patently true – "Life is a thing too glorious to be enjoyed."

Now that the kind and pleasant things of life were his to enjoy again was he hankering after some of the glory – a very different matter? He had been vegetating here for several weeks, after coming out of hospital. Health was coming back to him; it was possible to breathe freely again without a knife-like stab of pain at his side; it was even becoming possible to think sanely. But he knew that he was still very helpless, and the knowledge made him angry and bitter.

"A good sign, Will would say," he supposed, "but I'm getting an old wife. Not thirty yet, and a wretched body like this to carry on with. Oh I dare say it's undiluted self-pity, but – life a glorious thing?"

David Grant's two years of the war had been hell unmitigated. He was not made for soldiering. From the beginning he had been a dreamer of dreams; he had played with words and thoughts, had seen both sides of every argument with equal sympathy, had sought beauty before all things. Ready action did not come very easily to him, but he had enlisted as a private some months after the beginning of the war, and gone roughing it with the rest. All the while, he had hated the hut life, and the coarseness of the other fellows, the uniform, and the drill, and the half-cooked food, the atmosphere of stale cigarette smoke, and the very sound of popular songs. In the trenches he did not feel it so much; one became very primitive and it was too cold to think. He had no time to be afraid till the shell which buried him and several others had exploded; and then it was too late.

After that came hospital, which was worse than either the trenches or the huts. The memory of it remained with him like a hideous, pain-haunted nightmare, pervaded with the stink of chloroform.

The business of the surgeon, and indeed any sort of pain, had always made him shrink; now, he lay more than once in a cold sweat at the thought of a coming operation, and when they told him before the fourth, he fainted clean away. But that was over… he was at home again; and it was golden autumn weather in Castlerig, with a haze above the Pentlands and the distant spires and ridges of Edinburgh; and the crab-apple trees in the garden were laden, and the wild geans burning like flame.

Now he had to find his way back into the ordinary life of the world; he had to make a beginning. That sense of beginning again was a curious one; he felt as though he had grown old, and died, and come back, conscious of the process all the while. Yet it was a beginning without exhilaration, without fresh strength.

The stillness of the country helped him, and its beauty; he could have caught and held that beauty like a material thing lest he should lose it again. But even the stillness and the beauty were marred for him by a persistent sense of failure.

The war was in its third year; there had been disappointments and blunders, petty gains and losses on both sides, and little obvious progress. The people at home were grumbling; the politicians were muddling along as was their wont. Some men doubted whether the war had ever been justified, others talked openly of a patched-up peace, a peace which should leave the world in a slightly worse condition than before, bankrupt, restless, hard pressed for food. And for this, he had come through the two years of hell, and he had only done what hundreds of other men had done before him. It seemed all no use.

He realised that his depression was the result of ill-health; he had paid the penalty which the war exacted from highly-strung men – shattered nerves; and a wound, low down in the back near the spine, had left him stiff of one side, and limping. But it seemed that not only had the strength of his body been sapped, but the strength of his will and soul as well, and in its place there remained only a futile anger with himself.

As he sat there, the garden gate swung open, creaking. David heard it, glanced at his wrist-watch, and muttered "Post." Then he got up slowly, and dragged himself over to the window. In the gloaming, a man was coming up the garden; when David saw him, the quick smile came to his face, and he tapped on the pane.

In another minute the parlour door opened unceremoniously, and the visitor came in. He was short and wiry, and sunburnt of face; the cheekbones high, the light blue eyes steady, and a small moustache on his lip. You would have guessed him to be a Border farmer, but in reality he was an overworked country doctor. He looked fifty, but was several years younger.

"I just caught the post girl on the brae," he remarked. "Here's your mail, man."

David took the two letters he held out. "That's Minnie," he said, inspecting a London postmark.

"Good business! And this…" he tore it open… "is my uncle."

William Ross took a chair, uninvited; he seemed entirely at home in David Grant's parlour.

"You don't need to be thinking of the office yet awhile," he said decisively. "Do ye hear me, David?"

"Havers, Will! The uncle needs me badly. They're chock up with girls; in fact there isn't another man left in the place but old Romanes, the head clerk."

"You aren't fit," said Ross stolidly. "As your physician…"

"That's an insult." David slid from his seat on the edge of the table, and stood erect, with a little laugh which hid the fact that he caught his breath painfully for a moment. "See how straight I'm getting. Jenny thinks I've grown, poor lamb; although it's only the effect of a gradual unbending from my former wilted position. When's our next jaunt to be, Will? I'm as keen about learning to walk as I used to be about learning tennis with Alicia for a teacher."

The Doctor propelled him carefully into a chair. "Sit down and don't be a fool," he said. "You can't go back to business for two or three months yet. If you behave yourself, I'll maybe look in and take you for a daunder on Sunday, but that leg doesn't want to be used too much as yet."

David stirred the fire, and set the kettle, which was boiling, on the hob. "You're infernally professional tonight, Will," he complained. "Do be a human being, not a walking medical text-book. Medical text-books always give me the creeps. I mind Cousin Jessie had a perfect library of them. "What to do till the doctor comes" style of thing… and the things they told you about your inside I – by the way, talking of insides, stay and have a bite of supper. Jenny's just bringing it in, I imagine."

"I would have liked to, fine," said Ross, "but I can't spare a moment."

"You're a nice one," David reproached him. "Before you

came, the blue devils were fairly dancing all over me, and when I saw you at the gate, I thought now for a crack and a smoke and a general cheer up. You're a broken reed, Will."

"Minnie's letter ought to cheer you up," the Doctor told him. "I would stay willingly, but Castlerig seems to have fallen under the pestilence. I never was so busy in my life. I've just come from Oxgangs Farm, and the poor bit pony's fair run off her feet. The wife there is in a bad way. They have some fine Wyandotte pullets I saw as I was leaving. Would ye care to take three or four, David? I'm thinking of a few myself. It's a grand laying strain."

"I'll not bother the now," said David indifferently. "Jenny thinks she has as much as she can manage; and so she has – with me. Perhaps in spring…"

"Well, I must be off," said Ross, rising. "I just ran in to see how you were. Sleeping better?"

"Imphm."

"Which means no. You'll need to start that drug again. I insist on you getting sleep."

David made a wry face. "It shall be done," he said sub-missively. "There you go again, Will – text-book! At least wait and hear Minnie's news. I was keeping her letter till you went, because it feels like a long one. However, if you're going to pop off…"

He opened it, read the first page, and laughed.

"A week's leave! Well wangled, Min! She's coming down on Friday."

"How's she liking it?"

"Oh, first rate. I think she imagines the WAACS run the war. She was in great excitement when she first went into khaki."

When the Doctor left him, David took up his sister's letter and read it over again. Her writing was like herself, vigorous, clean, full of character. Minnie was his twin, a jour-nalist in London; young, modern, agnostic, independent, and withal a true, leal woman. There were but the two of them, without father or mother; and they had been brought up in Edinburgh by a good, narrow-minded cousin, who died just when they had grown to manhood and womanhood. Minnie had gone to London at the age of twenty, bent on her career, in spite of a number of obstacles; it was like Minnie to let nothing stand in her way. David had had his ambitions too; but in those days, Cousin Jessie was ill, and growing elderly, and so he stayed at home, rather as a matter of course, and before the war had been junior partner in the firm of his uncle, Duncan Traquair, a rich Edinburgh lawyer. Then, for him, came the fighting. Meanwhile, Minnie had worked her way up successfully, and now she had qualified for the post of administrator in the Women's Army; he could picture her, highly pleased with herself, busy and efficient, glorying in the khaki which he had loathed.

She had been in Scotland after her period of probation, but this was her first regular leave, and David was glad she was going to spend it with him, for he had not seen her since he came out of hospital. The two were close friends, although as different from each other as night from day. They had quarrelled systematically and fiercely from the age of eleven to twenty-two. Then one night, in much stress and sadness at the time when Cousin Jessie died, Minnie saw her brother's character in a new light, and that made a difference ever after.

Now as he read her letter again, Jenny, the servant, came in to light the lamp and bring him his supper. She was a stout, rosy Scotswoman, near sixty, but still marvellously nimble. She had been with Miss Jessie from a date unknown; and had nursed and scolded and adored the twins through all the vicissitudes of their life in the dull town house. When Miss Jessie died, Duncan Traquair offered them this cottage in Castlerig, a village on the northern slope of the Pentland Hills, about five miles from town, which was still valiantly holding its own against the encroachments of suburbia. He had bought the little house once as a plaything for his beautiful and petted daughter, Alicia, and she had tired of it. Brother and sister alike hated town life; and David was for accepting the offer without hesitation, for he had the gift of yielding graciously, which Minnie considered a defect in his character. But she put her foot down. "We shall be debtors to no man," she declared with mock solemnity. "We pay a rent for the Shieling, or we stay here!" So they paid a modest rent, and emigrated to the beloved village which had been their home in old days, when their father was parish minister there.

On the same principle, Minnie dismissed Jenny. "We can't afford to give you the wages you deserve, so we just mustn't have you," she said regretfully, and prepared to do the housework herself. At the time, Jenny was glad to go, for her sister had turned ill; but when Minnie could stand the restraints of domesticity no longer, and fled to London, she came back to look after her laddie.

"Jenny," said David, waving the letter, "we're going to have a visitor."

"Losh sakes, Mr. Davie, and me wi' the clothes on the pulley, which same isna workin' and the ironin' the morn!" gasped Jenny breathlessly. "When's he comin'?"

"Oh, not tomorrow," said David, referring to the letter. "Friday, I think she said."

Jenny caught the pronoun. "It's no' Miss Minnie?" she cried, with a complete change of expression. "Blessin's on her, it's no' the lamb hersel'?"

"Ay, it is Jenny," David told her laughing. "She's to come in uniform too. What an honour for two humble bodies like us. You'd better give her room a clean."

Jenny pursed up her lips. "It'll no' be breeks?" she inquired disapprovingly. "It wadna maitter between oorsels, for she was aye fit tae wear them, but I wouldna like the village tae tak' a scunner at her."

"Smart khaki costume with bronze buttons," read David

reassuringly. "It sounds nice. Jenny, you'd better shift the cracked mirror out of her room, and give her my quilt – it's warmer than her old one. Will the crab-apples be ready for jelly before Friday, eh? And oh, woman, bake! – luscious, crumbly, brown perkins with tins of treacle in them, and shortbread… home wouldn't be home to Minnie without your shorties, Jenny!" He watched her, smiling, as she set plates and silver on the table, and drew down the blind.

"Hoot, ye needna flatter, Mr. Davie," she retorted, well enough pleased. "And is it you that's mindin' this hoose, or me? A man boady shouldna meddle wi' sich concairns. Is the kettle bilin'? Come now, and tak' this bonnie omelette I've made to ye. The young hens is layin' brawly, and it's as weel, when the Doctor's aye girnin' at me tae fatten ye on eggs."

David looked round from his chair by the fire. "Jenny, you're a saint, but I couldn't touch an omelette," he said. "A cup of coffee'll do me. Just give it me here. I wish you hadn't bothered setting the table."

Jenny looked at him sharply. "Cup o' coffee? Pack o' blethers, I say," she declared. "There's nae nourishment in a cup o' coffee. If ma memory's no failin' me, the which it is often nooadays, I've heard that coffee's a slow pison in yer inside, forbye it'll keep ye from sleepin'. I'll mak' ye gruel rather."

"Heaven forfend," said David hastily.

Jenny looked pathetically at the omelette, then brought it over to him. "Wull ye no be temp'ed? What *would* ye eat, then, Mr. Davie?"

David smiled up at her whimsically. "Eclairs," he said.

"In war time!" She flounced to the door with vexation. Before she shut it she saw him lie back in his chair, obviously tired with talking, and her heart was anxious as she went back to the kitchen. "Puir lad," she muttered to the omelette, "this world's a sad world from what it used to be. Gin I wasna a church member I wad be temp'ed tae blaspheme whiles."

David, left alone, drank his coffee, and looked into the fire, thinking of Minnie's letter, and of Minnie – Minnie who had never said, "It's no use," who had made life a glorious thing by sheer strength of will. By some philosophy of her own she had always managed to get the best out of it. Cousin Jessie, he remembered, had never been able to subdue her altogether; and Cousin Jessie, with the best of intentions, had made his own childhood miserable. No, it was not the war which was to blame, it was weakness in himself.

His eyes wandered from the fire. The parlour was a pleasant room, in that state of moderate confusion which is the secret of true home comfort. He and Minnie had taken a pride in it in the old days. The pictures were all well-known friends, each with a story and association unlike the dull, expensively framed prints of rich folk; an article of Minnie's had bought that little copy of a Turner, and he had to stop smoking for a long and tedious time before they could afford the etchings over the fireplace. There was a piano, with "Songs of the North" and a pile of tattered music lying on it, although neither brother nor sister would consent to perform alone in public. There was an ancient mahogany sideboard with their one treasured silver salver in the place of honour, flanked by a carafe which had never held wine, and Cousin Jessie's great family Bible with dusty red markers. The mantel was laden with photos – stiff family groups; snapshots of Minnie's London chums; a beautiful girl with grave eyes, who was Alicia Traquair; a thin-faced lady in puffed sleeves, who was Cousin Jessie; a scowling little girl with a huge lace collar, and a solemn little boy in an ill-fitting sailor suit, who were Minnie and David themselves, once upon a time – Minnie had painful memories of that photograph. Beside his chair was a table with new novels on it, a week-old *Punch* left by William Ross, and the morning's *Scotsman*. It was all familiar and well loved, and it made David remember… He began to see things in pictures. That was an incurable habit of his. His thoughts about life were not so much a matter of reasoning, as a succession of drab or vivid tableaux. It was always the colour of a scene remembered or imagined which appealed to him.

He saw again the evenings they had spent here, all in the rich glow of lamplight; the suppers Minnie had cooked, and Ross and the others had helped to eat, and the whist and music afterwards, when he jingled the piano, and the company shouted student songs. There were all the New Years they had brought in, all the Christmas Eves, and birthdays, and little domestic festivals to celebrate an accepted story or some similar piece of good fortune.

He called to mind when the house was still his uncle's, and haughty Aunt Margaret had snubbed him, and cousin Isabel, the cheeky flapper, had tried to teach him to waltz; and Alicia, laughing, had scrambled eggs on that very fire, while he, eighteen and extremely bashful, had stood watching her with adoring eyes. That was a firelight scene, warm and rosy like a boy's first love; for he had been very much in love with Alicia then, although he never told anyone about it, in case they should laugh at him. In those days, David was always imagining that people were laughing at him, although he realised now that they had probably taken no note of his existence.

Still older remembrances returned to him. There was the day he came upon *The Lady of Shalott* in his uncle's library – it was the first great poem he had ever read, and it cast a spell over him. He remembered yet the thrill of that spell, as he lay face downwards on the hearthrug clutching the big book, living as a knight with Lancelot, and a courtier at the Palace of Camelot. He remembered too how the spell had been broken when Alicia and Isabel came in, beautifully dressed as usual, like children in a picture by Gainsborough; and Isabel, with the pout she always wore, said in a loud whisper: "Tell him not to! Mother says these common children have such dirty hands. He'll spoil Papa's book." And he had sprung up, and stood silent and miserable, a knight no longer, but a common little boy with dirty hands, and big boots, and tears that would come welling up in spite of his twelve years. That was a remembrance which began in all the colours of the rainbow, and ended in a blur of shame.

There were the drab weeks of school, with long dreary Sundays in between, drabber than the rest. There were quarrels with Minnie, and punishments from Cousin Jessie. Looking back, he fancied that he must have been a timid, uninteresting child; Alicia might be beautiful, and Minnie clever, but his was always the shy and stupid part – although he had loved fair and splendid and brave things as much as any of them. He had suspected dimly that life was going to be a glorious thing, but he had not yet succeeded in proving it so. Or else perhaps the paradox was true, and it was very much too glorious to be enjoyed. There might be a kind of hidden, mystical, unfulfilled glory in a child's loneliness, and a boy's perplexity, and a man's pain; there certainly was not happiness. Perhaps there was not meant to be happiness. David wondered… Then his thoughts came back to the present, and with a revulsion of feeling he wished that Minnie were not coming on Friday in her khaki and buoyancy and gladness of success.

Two

Be this a fable; and behold
Me in the parlour as of old,
And Minnie...
—A Child's Garden of Verses

Minnie arrived punctually on the Friday evening. She had to find her way up to the Shieling alone, for David could not manage the station brae. He was waiting for her in the hall when she swept in like a gust of fresh wind, raindrops on her rough coat, and eyes bright beneath the khaki hat.

"Hello, Tousle!" It was the chief of her many nicknames for him.

"Assistant-Administrator Grant!"

Kisses were rare things between them, rare because he was shy, and she strictly unsentimental; but at that moment Minnie forgot her principles, and held out her arms to him. They were both rather red in the face. She was self-conscious in her uniform, and he knew that she had not seen him out of bed yet. He tried to take the stairs with agility, but it was a failure, and Minnie rushing on ahead, turned back, and gave him her arm.

"Isn't the house braw?" he asked her. "Jenny's had a perfect redding-up in your honour."

"My own wee room?" she cried. "Blessings on it! A fire! Oh what luxury in war time. And you don't mean to say the tea roses are still going strong? I never smelt anything to beat

Castlerig tea roses." She buried her nose in them, then flung off coat and hat, and fumbled at the lock of her case. "Lost the key, of course! What a character for a government official!"

David produced some bunches of keys from his pocket, and eventually found a substitute. She dragged out a pair of slippers, a nightgown bag, and a comb, and tossed them on to the bed. Then she posed before the glass, tugging back some rebellious wisps of hair, and straightening her khaki tie. "Aren't I swanky?" she asked thoughtlessly, executing a war-dance with her skirts held out. "First-rate pockets – I can laugh at the fashions now, and blow my nose as much as I like. Green shoulder straps tone awfully well with my complexion, don't they?"

David turned to the door. "Come down when you've washed your hands," he said with his back to her. "You won't trip in the passage now. We've had grand new linoleum laid."

Minnie stared after him, taking in the situation. "Oh what a great pig I am," she said blankly; and was very quiet when she appeared at the supper table, ten minutes later.

When they had finished, they drew their chairs close up to the fire. "Got a cigarette?" inquired Minnie. "Oh, only that old pipe? Never mind. I have just one left myself. Give us a light then."

He struck a match, and held it out to her. When she had lit her cigarette, she leant back, balancing it between two brown fingers, the other hand deep in a pocket and her legs crossed comfortably. He remained silent, watching her; and she asked suddenly, "You don't object? I never know quite what your views on things are, Tousle. Not that it would make the slightest difference..."

He gave his quick smile. "No, I was just thinking that you suit a cigarette. Some girls don't."

"Is that a compliment?"

"It is... to you."

She pulled her chair nearer to his, and rumpled his hair

affectionately. "Drop that *Bystander* attitude," she ordered. "You look just now as if you were studying a picture, or observing human nature, and I'm neither. Are you preparing to put me in your novel?" David's novel was a standing joke between them; it had never been written yet.

They both laughed. "The rôle of bystander's rather a pleasant one," remarked David meditatively. "Cowardly, of course; one's exempt from the burden and heat of the day. But I feel rather like that just now... as if I were looking at the world from the outside, like a newcomer."

"And what's your impression?" she asked curiously.

"Rather a gloomy one... Look here, we'll not talk about me. We'll talk about you. I want to hear your news, my dear."

"I like the way you call me 'my dear'," she said. The sort of thing a nice old-fashioned husband would say to his wife. David, I believe you're an anachronism. I don't know what century you've walked out of... you, and Jenny and the Shieling bodily, yes, and all Castlerig. Oh, it's such a rest to come back here away from Zepps and politics and revues."

"Think so? I wish I did. What's life in London like just now?"

"Well, of course, we're exceedingly preoccupied with the war – Zepp raids and things. That goes without saying. And rations. It's all an unmitigated bore, but we just have to stick it out. We must win eventually – we've got to. I'm no vain optimist. I only say that because there isn't any other way out of the present muddle. It'll cost a lot, but we must win."

Minnie leant forward, and flung away the end of her cigarette. She rested her chin on her hands, and looked into the fire with grave eyes. David looked into the fire, too, his head turned away from her.

"And when we win," he said, "the men will be all killed off, and the women's strength drained, and the kids starved, which is a bad look-out for the next generation; and Germany will hate us like the devil for ever after, and someone will go and start a squabble in the Balkans just to keep things lively."

"Well, it would be worse if we stopped now," said Minnie quickly. "David, you surely haven't turned a pacifist?"

It was the second time that night that she had put her foot in it. He coloured up.

"Just now," he said, "I'm for whatever will bring us straight out of this cursed business, and afterwards I'll be a pacifist till the end of my days."

"Well, the thing that will bring us straight through is victory, of course," cried Minnie. It was so clear and easy a matter for her.

"Will it?" said David, raising his head suddenly, and really asking the question. "If it would, God knows one wouldn't grudge anything. But it doesn't seem likely... it all seems... no use..."

He was ashamed of the words as soon as he had spoken them, but they made Minnie see at last. She sprang to her feet impetuously, and perching on the arm of his chair, she linked her arm through his.

"Oh, I don't know," she cried. "It may be victory and it mayn't; but I'm absolutely sure that nothing that was bravely and worthily done or given could ever be of no use. You know I'm not given to gush, David, but I do believe that with all my heart."

He looked up, and their eyes met; and both were a little confused and apologetic, for they rarely gave each other so much confidence.

"I'm a pessimist and a fool," said David.

"I've no earthly business to be chattering about victory like that," declared Minnie. She thought that he was looking very tired, and her heart smote her. "Oh, let's forget the war... How faded this wall paper's getting... David, *do* you remember when I tried to paper the parlour all on my own?"

"I should think I did. It was about as successful as my attempt at laying a tennis court."

"The two don't bear comparison. Tousle, you were an old lunatic." And so they dropped into kindly reminiscence, and the evening passed.

After she had said goodnight to him, she went into the kitchen to pay Jenny a visit on her way up to bed.

"Let's see ye, let's see ye, my lamb," cried Jenny, catching her arm, and turning her round in the middle of the floor in the flaring light of the lamp. "Braw's no the word... ay, I'm glad it's no breeks. Sic a bonnie badge... nae petticoats, forbye, that'll be tae save the washing. Dearie, Miss Minnie, I'm prood o' ye!"

"Thank you, Jenny," laughed Minnie, straightening her skirts and taking a seat on the edge of the kitchen table. "It's lovely of you to be so nice, and it *is* lovely to be home again."

"And div ye think we've keepit the hoose weel? Sic a scrubbin' an' scourin', an' Mr. Davie wad gie me nae peace. Na, it had a' tae be spotless for fear ye'd find a flaw in it. Did ye like the supper? I doot the rabbit was tough... if ye ask me it was an auld stirk, and nae mistake, but what could ye look for frae Noble's?"

"You and the butcher still squabbling? Really, Jenny! And tell me about your own folk."

"Hoot, they're nae subject for conversation. Tell us aboot the wark ye do in London, dearie. Hev ye tae manage the hussies that leaves dacent situations tae mak' munitions and sic like freevolities, a' tae get a glint o' the khaki? My, if I was you I'd mak' it warm for them."

"We're only too glad to get the hussies, as you call them," said Minnie. "It's the like of them that are going to help win the war, Jenny."

"Aweel," said Jenny dourly, "I wish ye'd hurry up aboot it. I'm no daein' wi' this war ava'. The Boer War was a kind o' interest in the papers, and so forth, but it's changed times, I doot."

"You old sweet tooth, you're missing your sugar," chaffed Minnie.

"Ay and mair than my sugar. I've lost twa nephews. Ye'll mind the wee callant ye used tae play wi' at my sister's at Corstorphine, when I took ye oot on Saturdays, unbeknown tae the Mistress? Aweel he's gane, puir lad."

"I'm sorry," said Minnie quietly. Then after a minute's hesitation she added, "Jenny, David's not looking well; he's looking worse than I expected. What do you think of him?"

"He canna be weel seein' he neither sleeps nor eats," said Jenny defiantly. "And him alane a' the day. That's nae life for a human crater. It's a peety but what he was mairried wi' a douce bit wifie tae cheer him up."

"Don't, Jenny," said Minnie irritably. "He'll never marry, you know. Oh, it's me again. I ought to be here at home, instead of gadding about in uniform. What's the use of a woman who doesn't like staying at home? She's a mistake."

"I've nae doot yer services are valyable tae the country," said Jenny, bitter for a moment. "But what for should he no mairry, supposin' he was a wee thingie lame? I tell't him lang syne I wad box the limmer's ears that turned up her nose at my laddie, and I mean it still."

"He's not the marrying sort; he's too reserved with women," said Minnie, musing. "That was Cousin Jessie's fault again; she kept him down so. Jenny, why *is* life so difficult for the nicest people? It isn't fair. I always got on far better than he did, and there's a hundred times more in him than in me. No, don't lay on the butter; I'm not fishing. I grant you freely I'm very much on the spot, with plenty of show and sparkle, but you know these dull proverbs about all that glitters, and still waters. They're true. I'm just beginning to realise what a *brave* thing it was for him to join up – knowing what it's meant since, and how he used simply to loathe pain of any sort."

"Ye're richt there," said Jenny. "I ken what it's meant to him. But ye mauna misca' yersel', dearie."

"Don't worry; I'm aware of all my virtues," Minnie assured her. "But David's different. He's complex of mind, but he's so awfully single of heart. Yet people don't see these things because he's shy... it must be funny to be shy, such a nuisance..."

The door opened, and David came in. "Can I have a fresh candle, Jenny?" he began. "Hello, you two look like conspirators over there!" Jenny was bending over the fire knitting, and Minnie sat very close to her on the corner of the table, her short skirts bunched up and her legs dangling. David pulled the wisp of hair that curled over her right ear. "You bit crater," he said teasingly, "you look like ten perched up there. What were you talking about, eh?"

"And they say men aren't curious," remarked Minnie, jumping down. "We were discussing your vices, my son. Come away to bed like a good child, and I'll see about the fresh candle."

So they went, he leaning on her arm; and Jenny, watching them go, sighed to herself.

Three

In a world of flying loves and fading lusts
It is something to be sure of a desire.
                                        —G. K. CHESTERTON

It was four o'clock of a February afternoon, and the light had begun to fade. A few belated visitors were drifting through the vacant rooms of the Mound Gallery, where a society of young Scottish artists was holding its annual exhibition. There were several wounded soldiers, who were admitted free and thought the thing a pleasant variety from a picture palace; some elderly women in black; a couple of smart girls; and three men who seemed to know a vast deal about art and went from picture to picture, criticising, disparaging, laughing, and very occasionally praising.

David Grant watched them, and felt rather more interest in them than in the pictures, when all was said and done.

Three months had passed since Minnie came first, and she had just had another short leave for New Year week. They had had lunch in town together, and he saw her away at the Waverley Station, coming in to see the Exhibition before he caught an afternoon train to Castlerig. He could walk now, steadily, although a little slowly still, and had returned to work.

He had bought a catalogue, but he did not look at it much, for the names of the artists were strange to him. The few young fellows he had known were out in France, more than one killed, and those who remained were for the most part women.

An art gallery in war time is a curious place, a sort of backwater, belonging to a different world. David had not been in one since 1914, and he came expecting many things. He had looked, to begin with, for a host of war pictures, and he was disappointed, for war is not romantic nowadays. He had looked, too, for a new strength and beauty. He had read when he was in France – with raised eyebrows – a magazine article which stated that the war had purged our national life and brought the big things to the front, and made us nobler in character. He admitted to himself that it was difficult to believe, with two men cursing each other at his shoulder, and a drunken row going on outside. But perhaps it was true among the homefolk.

As a matter of fact, he found very much what had always been there. The skillful studies of still life with exquisite, minute details, the lurid impressionistic apples and oranges glowing as no earthly apple or orange ever glowed, the naked women, the idyllic children, the quite pretty fishing villages, were familiar, and strangely out of place, ineffective, remote from the current of tragic life.

And being young, little more than a boy and at the stage when a boy's ideals begin to seem as dull and futile as tinsel and spangles away from the limelight, he was very sorry and indignant too. He thought of Greece and Italy with their wonderful form and colour, and he doubted whether his own country knew anything – or cared either – about art. Then with a change of feeling, he felt a sort of pity for the men and women who painted these pictures. Doubtless they were real lovers of beauty and worked hard at their art; doubtless they were at pains to set down the part of beauty which they had made their own according to the clearness of their vision. It seemed cruel that they should work away, caring so much and achieving so little. He wondered whether, after all, it was a whimsical fate that dropped genius on a few, and left the others to fight along; or whether it was indeed the fault of those others. Had they looked long enough, and cared deeply enough? Perhaps they had been too hurried and easy-going; not like the old Italian painters, who toiled all day till they were weak from lack of food, not like the Greeks, who were for making not only their sculpture but their cities, their bodies, their laws, their commonest things beautiful from beginning to end.

He rose to go out, and looked round. There were one or two good things, but for the most part it all seemed – no use. The thought slipped out almost before he was aware. "No use again," he reproached himself bitterly. "This damnable depression of mine spoils everything. Criticism's a poor dodge, and yet the faults are there."

Going down the steps before him were a man and a girl, evidently brother and sister. David watched them, for brothers and sisters interested him, and he was curious to see their faces. Once the man turned. He was in officer's uniform, over six feet, with sturdy shoulders; his face was young and sunbrowned, and his eyes twinkled beneath dark brows. A curious feeling, half envy, half self-contempt, came to David; this fellow looked so thoroughly a man from head to foot. It was just such a man that he had longed to become when they were small, and Minnie and he quarrelled. He had vowed to grow up big and strong and brown, to play golf and shoot – though he had hated games then – and jingle money in his pocket, and be very proud and great; he even decided to grow a fierce-looking beard if it would stop her from calling him cry-baby, and despising him with all her might. That was at eleven; he smiled as he thought of it. And now? The place was hung with mirrors, and he caught sight of himself as he passed. He was tired after the extra long day in town, and every line in his face showed it; the motion of going down a stair still wrenched his side a little, and that showed too – not a pleasant reflection.

David could not see the girl's face; she seemed nearly as tall as her brother, round-shouldered and lanky; she was clad in a drooping burberry coat, and her hair was untidy beneath her old velour hat. She let her brother do most of the talking.

Most men would have dismissed her as a commonplace person. Not so David, who hated smart women because they invariably made him feel a fool in their presence. Besides, he had always been attracted by commonplace people. He had a kind of sympathy with them, realising that he must seem very commonplace himself, and wondering if, within their hearts, they considered themselves as interesting as he considered himself in the vanity of his youth. It was a pleasant thing to imagine the world full of princesses and princes in disguise; oneself, of course, a prince of the highest order. Was this girl a princess, or an impostor under her disguise?

He was glad when she too turned her head, as they came out of the Gallery. Her skin was colourless, and there was a weary look on her face. Yet her complexion was clear and smooth, and she might have been very beautiful if she had taken a little trouble with her clothes and her health. As it was, her eyes were the only fine thing about her, dark and large, with a rare gladness of laughter in them as she looked west along Princes Street.

It was dusk in the town. A yellow light lingered after the sunset, fading into weird green above the misty streets where folk passed like shadows. Through the gloaming, the shaded lamps flashed a vivid blue. And all this was framed between two of the great, sombre pillars round the Gallery, which rose on either side of the girl like the pillars of an Egyptian temple.

"There's the real thing," she cried to her brother. "It makes all that look drab compared with it. Oh, things are far more beautiful than anyone ever painted them."

David heard her. So she had felt it too! The world of a sudden seemed to him to be full of friendship. He felt an insane desire to speak with her, which was absurd, since they could say nothing important or interesting to each other there on the crowded pavement. But things were happening like a fairytale that evening. The chance to speak was granted him. The girl had a muff, and she had apparently taken off her gloves while indoors, and thrust them carelessly into it. One fell out as she and her brother stepped over the threshold, and David bent, rather stiffly, and picked it up, fearing all the while that they would have disappeared among the crowd before he reached them. But they were walking slowly. He came up behind her.

"Excuse me," he said.

She turned round abruptly, and he met her look of surprise steadily.

"You dropped it, I think," he explained, holding the glove out to her, and raising his hat.

"Oh, thanks awfully," she said. "I am stupid."

That was all. She gave him a distant little smile, and answered her brother's call: "Coming, May?" and the two crossed the street and disappeared. But David followed them with his eyes, and wondered who she was, and marvelled that she could seem shy and dowdy and beautiful all at the same time. And so he turned to take his own way along the quiet side of Princes Street.

Meanwhile brother and sister mingled with the crowd on the further pavement. "I see them," said Marion Sutherland. "I hope they haven't been waiting long." She nodded towards the door of a tea-shop just ahead of them.

Two girls were waiting there, and as Marion and Pat came up, one of them caught his arm. She was a slight creature, and her head hardly reached her brother's shoulder. Her face, half hidden by heavy black furs, was small and pink, with a fair curl placed fashionably over one ear. Her grey hat matched her silk stockings and suede shoes, and there was a faint feminine odour of scent about her. "You've been a perfect age," she said quite crossly. "Come along, do, and let's get some hot tea before we all catch cold."

The girl beside her laughed a welcome to Marion, looked Pat full in the face with a friendly nod, and led the way. She walked with a good long step, her slim ankles and brown shoes very neat below her brown fur coat. A little brown hat was set straight on her head, and the face below, although the features were irregular, was gay and kind. She looked young enough to be Pat's wife, and ridiculously young to be the mother of two high-spirited children whom she had just deposited at a party, to be called for three hours later, when they should have had their fill of cake and crackers and blind-man's buff.

Beatrice Sutherland, in her right of married woman, poured out tea. Pat sat opposite to her, making jokes and looking happy as a young husband and father on leave ought to look. Marion spoke rarely; Nannie yawned, and polished her nails, and complained of the sandy taste of the wartime cakes, and the poorness of the tea, and told them what a boring afternoon it had been, and how there wasn't a decent hat to be got in Edinburgh. After tea, Pat and Beatrice set off home to their flat, while Nannie and Marion turned in the other direction.

The Sutherland family were six, all told, ranging in age from Patrick, who was about thirty, to Billy, the schoolboy of sixteen. They lived in a quiet street in an unfashionable part of Edinburgh, and had not as much money as they would have liked. After the war began, they had less than ever. They were orphans, living with a mild, middle-aged uncle, whose business, a builder's, was heavily hit. Pat, the hope of the house, had to leave the business and join up; and it so happened that none of the others were at the moment fit to earn their living, with the exception of Marion, who was in her uncle's office.

The two youngest were still at school, Nannie stayed at home under the impression that she was keeping house, and Effie, a blooming maid of twenty, was at a college in Atholl Crescent preparing to teach cooking and household economy.

It was Effie who opened the door to them on this particular night, for Nannie had left the latchkey in her handkerchief sachet. She was as tall as Marion, but, although younger, more mature in figure. She had Nannie's fairness, and twice Nannie's energy, with a vivid, capable manner of her own. Compared with her, Marion seemed washed out and shabby.

"Well?" she said. "Aren't you half dead with cold? Come in and get roasted. Got a hat to suit, Nannie? Uncle Alexander's slipped on a bit of ice, and bumped himself black and blue, poor soul. Billy's been getting into a fine row over that Latin you did for him, May. There's a letter come from Noël."

She chattered on as they came into the dining-room. Nannie ran and flung herself down on the hearthrug, shivering. Marion began to take off her hat and coat, and left them each lying on a different chair, for Effie to pick up later on.

There were two young people engaged in an altercation on the window seat, and these, presently disentangling themselves, appeared to be Billy, the baby of the family, a fat, jolly boy, red of hair and face, with nice eyes and freckles; and Jullie, a year older, with a long dark pigtail, mischievous eyes, and arresting tartan stockings, who came forward, a shorthand notebook in her hand and a pencil stuck jauntily behind her ear. The family circle was shortly completed by the entrance of Uncle Alexander, who put a nervous head round the door, entreating them: "Not so much noise, children, if that be at all possible!"

"Bring me Noël's letter, someone," commanded Nannie, perched on a hassock, with her coat thrown back. Effie tossed it over to her.

"He's coming home on leave," announced Nannie in a moment. "What great luck!"

"Everyone's home on leave just now," remarked Jullie.

"We can't put him up," said Effie with decision. "Are you aware, friends, that Lizzie has given notice? She came to me this afternoon, and said she was tired of muddling through here, and she thought she'd fancy munitions after all, in spite of being delicate, and we might have a month to find a new one. Condescending, wasn't it?"

Nannie shrugged her shoulders. "Let her go," she said calmly. "She was a little fiend. You'd better go to the registry, Effie."

"I can't possibly go tomorrow," said Effie. "It's my heavy day at laundry work."

"Well once and for all *I* can't," retorted Nannie. "It's high time I began to see about that matinee. I've put off and put off, and I must run round to Mrs. Gerard's tomorrow. Then you know Dorothy Watson's brother – the Flying Corps one – made me promise to take him over the sights while he was in Edinburgh, and I can't disappoint the boy. And that'll mean a picture house and tea into the bargain. How things do mount up!"

"Don't they!" said Marion with suspicious sympathy. "Well, I won't offer to go after what happened last time."

"I wouldn't ask you," said Nannie tartly, returning to her beloved's letter.

The Sutherland household suffered from too many mistresses. Nannie was the official head, but she worked and played at her own sweet will, so that the other sisters had to make up for her deficiencies according to their time and ability. In consequence, they were always tripping over each other in domestic duties, and not a day passed without a storm in their tempestuous family teapot. More and more, Marion was letting the burden fall from her shoulders, more and more Effie was taking it up. But the general result was not a happy one.

Four

The play's the thing.

—HAMLET

It was always a wonder to Effie Sutherland that she managed to rise at all on the winter mornings. The very sight of Jullie, slumbering deeply, her dark head a rumpled mass on the pillows, had often well-nigh sent her back to her own blankets. But she was usually stirring before seven, and after Lizzie left, she rummaged out an old alarm clock, and set it at six, much to the annoyance of Jullie, her roommate, who at first would rouse up in sleepy wrath, demanding: "Was that the gong?" Gradually, however, she became able to sleep through the shrillest of alarms, and on this particular morning, Effie left her breathing quietly like a child, when she went to light the kitchen fire.

She had a full programme before her. First there was the breakfast at eight; then, sandwiches to make for Uncle Alexander and Billy, Billy himself to be started schoolwards at half-past eight sharp, and Jullie to her classes at nine; finally there were the dishes to wash and her own room to dust before she was due at Atholl Crescent at ten. The rest of the housework she had perforce to leave in the hands of Nannie and the charwoman. But Nannie, who did not usually appear downstairs until the end of breakfast, was good for nothing before eleven, and the charwoman had only three hours to spare them. Nevertheless, Effie, in spite of a heavy day of laundry work behind her, and another of cooking before, had plenty of energy for the task. With her hair twisted round her head in two plaits, to be combed out and dressed later, and an overall covering her fresh blouse, she set to work in the kitchen, kindled a fire, and put on the porridge pot; and later, when the hall was dusted and the dining-room table set, she came back to make the toast. Seated on the edge of the kitchen table while the kettle boiled, she remained idle for a rare moment, swinging her plump neat feet, in the old down-at-heel slippers she kept for working, and surveying her hands with a little frown. They were not pretty hands, though shapely enough; red with many washings in greasy water, cut and blistered in little domestic mishaps, the nails broken and irregular. They were not in keeping with the girl's face above her overall, and the rebellious bits of hair curling out of their plaits like a golden halo round her bent head. Alone there in the silent kitchen with the vacant dull light of a winter morning beginning to creep through the window, she might have sat for the portrait of Cinderella, or indulged in some comfortable moments of self-pity.

Being Effie, she did nothing of the sort, but only made a mental resolution to buy cold cream and a pair of manicure scissors on the way home that afternoon, and frowned a little more crossly, wishing that the kettle would be quick.

Then as she stood up to place the toast in the rack, a paragraph in the newspaper which she had spread on the table caught her attention. It was headed "A Girl Heroine". Effie glanced through it, biting her lip. It was about a munition worker, who had suffered from contact with a highly poisonous gas. She read the last words twice over: "Between her sobs and gasps for breath she managed to whisper, 'It's not fair that the boys should have everything to suffer!'"

"My beastly hands!" said Effie aloud, suddenly. Then she took the teapot and toast, and went upstairs, rather slowly, to sound the gong. She heard Uncle Alexander coming down, and Billy behind him whistling; Jullie was running the bath water in a tremendous hurry, and she burst into the dining-room a quarter of an hour after the others, her slippers and cuffs unbuttoned, no brooch fastening her blouse, and sleepy cheerfulness upon her hastily washed face.

Marion followed her, yawning. "Nannie's just wakened this minute," she remarked. "She wants her breakfast up."

Effie rose without replying, seized a tray, and dumped china onto it quickly. When she was halfway upstairs, Nannie, leaning over the banisters in a frilly dressing-gown, commanded shrilly: "Bring the apricot jam, not the marmalade!"

"Take what you get and be thankful," retorted Effie, completing the ascent. "Of all the lazy dogs, you are the laziest."

"How cross you are," said Nannie, who had by this time subsided among her pillows. "I had a fiendish night. My bottle's leaking, and I'm convinced the mattress is swimming. I hardly slept a wink."

"If my mattress was swimming, I wouldn't stop at convictions," said Effie, leaving the room. "Didn't you look, silly?"

She arrived downstairs again in time to stuff sandwiches into the respective pockets of Billy and her uncle. She had also presence of mind enough to shout a message to Marion, who was already half-way along the street, and who turned a conveniently deaf ear.

Jullie was the last of the family to be tidied and admonished and hustled out onto the doorstep; and from the dining-room window, Effie watched her tartan stockings and pigtail vanish round the nearest corner. Long after they were quite invisible, she continued to gaze out on the street, and drum with her fingers on the pane.

She was wondering whether they, and all the other families like them, commonplace and selfish, were worth that munition girl's painful gasping for breath, and worth the sacrifice of the men whose task she had tried to share. "And anyway," cried Effie, in her heart, "it's a scandal that three of us hale and hearty women should be eating our heads off at home; no, four, with Jullie. They're not so precious busy at the office – goodness me, I wish they were – that Marion couldn't spend more time indoors, and even if Jullie is a kid, people grow up quickly nowadays. It's no use expecting anything more of Nannie, but the two of them could make things rub along if they put their backs into it, and I —"

Her train of thought ceased for a moment. Effie was practical above all things, and it seemed foolishness to cut short the training to which she had already given more than a year. "I've got to earn my living," she reflected, "afterwards. Well no, I haven't," she added impetuously. "I've got to do my bit."

Then she turned away from the window. It was not in her nature to soliloquise, and she reproached herself for wasting time, and made haste to mend matters by clearing the table with energy.

Crossing through the hall, burdened with a tray of dishes, she found Nannie at the hall table. "About time," she remarked.

Nannie looked round quickly. "No letters for me?" she asked.

"None at all, except business ones," said Effie shortly.

"What a bore! Mrs. Gerard promised to write. The matinee's to be an Old Edinburgh pageant, you know, and we'll have the dickens of a time getting up the dresses. I suppose I'll have to run round sometime today, and I don't know when I'll have time." Nannie pouted, meditating.

"Such a waste of time and money," said Effie. "Let me pass."

"But it's for the war, you wet-blanket."

"Well, if you call that war work, I don't. You just play yourselves."

"Well we can't all go to the front. Some of us have got to stay at home," protested Nannie, with a rueful smile which admitted the weakness of her logic. She seemed so pretty and inconsequent, in her old checked skirt and soiled blouse, with her hair bundled into a would-be Grecian knot, and an absurd blob of powder on her nose, that Effie laughed instead of preaching.

"You'll have to stay at home in earnest when I go to cook in a hospital," she threatened, and went on into the pantry, admitting to herself that Nannie was hopeless, and yet confessing that she would take a ticket and enjoy the pageant with the best of them when the time came.

And so with her laugh, Effie forgot her morning thoughts and the munition girl, and she had not time to remember them all day. She was not given to heroics, and rarely had an introspective moment.

Nannie, left alone, sat for a while by the dying fire in the dining-room, pondering on life in general. She was deaf to the queries of the charwoman about dinner, and areas, and washing; at last she roused herself to inspect the larder, and dust the drawing-room in her own perfunctory fashion. After that, some time was spent deliberating between the black hat with the cerise ribbons, and the plain white; and finally deciding in favour of the white, she enveloped herself in a fox fur, snatched up gloves and bag, and departed to shop and call.

Mrs. Gerard was a woman whom no one had ever surprised without her hat on. When Nannie arrived, she was wearing coat and gloves as well, and was dividing her parting caresses between two great dogs and her little boy.

"My dear, how entirely nice of you to come!" she said, sliding the child from her lap, as one might brush away crumbs. "And when I owe you a letter too. I'm just going out – do you mind? Walk round by Princes Street with me, won't you?"

"You must excuse such an early call," said Nannie, "but I really couldn't go on with anything until I heard what arrangements you had made."

"I tell you what," said Mrs. Gerard. "We'll go and get patterns for the costumes at Jenners, and have some coffee or buns or something, and discuss things."

At the mention of buns, the little boy began to prance round her. "Oh do take me," he begged. He was a pretty child, in a blue tunic, but his hands and cheeks were marble cold, for it was one of his mother's fads to keep him with bare legs and sandals in all weathers.

"Peter, sweet, you can't possibly," said his mother airily, and sailed out of the room with Nannie, while the sweet Peter set up a disappointed howl, stamping his feet, as spoiled children will, to keep time with his sobs.

"The first thing, of course," said Mrs. Gerard, "was to get together a committee. You can't do anything without a committee nowadays. I got my sister, and that entirely nice child Madge Wallace, who recites so cleverly. She belongs to two amateur acting societies, and she ought to be some use. Then I wrote a Mrs. Woodward whom you don't know. She's an artist – studio out at the South Side, had a little picture hung last May, although neither Jim nor I could quite make out what it meant – still she's clever, and ought to help with colour schemes and posing, you know. But my greatest find – Nannie, congratulate me – you'll never guess!"

"Some professional?"

"Not a bit of it. You're quite on the wrong tack. It's a man, my dear, and such an entirely delightful one. Jim knew him long ago somehow or other. When he had leave last, he got me introduced, and had him to dinner. He's colonel in a Royal Scots regiment out at a camp in Midlothian, and we ran into each other at the West End yesterday. My dear, he's promised me the military Pipe Band! Think what an attraction. And quite a lot of the younger officers out at his place are keen to help us if they can. Such a find! Men are so scarce just now for theatricals, and all the others, on the Committee, I mean, are simply delighted."

Nannie preserved a silence which savoured of the sulks, but Mrs. Gerard's next remark changed her expression.

"Of course, I should have said at the very beginning, only Colonel Cadenhead put me off, that they want you to be treasurer, my dear," she said. "They have insisted on me being president, though I'm sure I didn't want to; such a labour and worry. We're to meet at my sister's on Friday, with ideas."

"Yes, do tell me," began Nannie, who had been striving to get a word in. What's the scheme of the thing? Is the Scotch idea still going strong?"

"Well, yes, oh did you see that officer who passed? I'm so short sighted. Did you see Royal Scots on his shoulder? It wasn't Colonel Cadenhead? But you don't know him! Oh, quite a young man? My dear, I assure you the Colonel isn't old, still I know what you mean. Yes, I want to be out of the common. People are fed up with revues and so on, and fairy plays are run to death. Something national and distinctive, don't you think? And when it's for the Royal Scots…"

"I didn't know," interrupted Nannie innocently, "that it was for the Royal Scots. I thought it was for the Serbian Refugees."

"Ah but I changed my mind," laughed Mrs. Gerard. "After I saw Colonel Cadenhead, you know. Nannie, look at that woman in the sables! I'm certain she's one of those munition workers who are making fortunes, such a coarse face! My dear, I heard a quite entirely absurd story about a grand piano being seen going into a tenement in the Cowgate! Did you ever? Yes, it'll be a Scotch thing for a Scotch regiment. I mean to make it a pageant of Old Edinburgh with all the notables appearing, and specially romantic scenes enacted, such as bits of Mary Stuart. Of course the dresses will be the main thing there. Then I thought for part two, we might have a one act play, Scotch, of course, perhaps one of Barrie's. Isn't there one called *The Sentimental Minister*, or perhaps we could dramatise *A Window in Thrums*?"

"Won't Scotch things be rather stale?" asked Nannie. "I have a topping oriental costume I once wore at a fancy ball."

"My dear, you couldn't blend Eastern things with a pipe band," reproved Mrs. Gerard. "Come, here we are. Such a squash! We'll go right up. Yes, the window table. Coffee and cakes for two. (The cheek of these waitresses nowadays!) I said coffee! Nannie, look at the colour of that sugar; it makes one ill. They'll be asking us to eat sand next. No, I don't recommend the sponge cakes. They're made with some nasty egg substitute and taste like india rubber. Everything's different, I know. These things bring home the war to one, don't they?"

Nannie sipped her coffee and reflected. "I don't really see how I could be treasurer," she said. "I'm a fiendish muddier at accounts."

"The best thing," said Mrs. Gerard, with the air of a dictator, "in a big affair like this is to get some lawyer friend to take charge of the accounts and expenditure, hiring of the theatre, advertising and so forth. But what about your uncle?"

"Uncle Alexander," said Nannie frankly, "is a perfect loony. He's so slow. He'd take a day to grasp what it was all about, and he'd let himself be diddled on every side. He never was any good as a business man."

"And there's your clever sister."

"Marion wouldn't thank you for the compliment. She's a little fool, and quite disobliging. She'd say she hadn't time, and she'd make an utter mess of things. If Pat was at home, I'd ask him, of course."

"See what they say anyway, and do try and get someone to help you," encouraged Mrs. Gerard, who hated business matters herself.

"I might beard old Mr. Traquair in his den," mused Nannie. "He's rather an old dear, and always fearfully polite. It seems almost a shame to bother him."

"Mr. Traquair?"

"Uncle's lawyer, I mean. We've known him since we were kids. He's a good sort. Has two kids himself. You must have seen the girl's picture somewhere. She was presented at court, and married in great style. She's supposed to be a great beauty, but I think she looks uninteresting. She got an awfully wealthy husband down in England, and a big property."

"Traquair? Ah… Oh yes, I remember. Mary Traquair, wasn't it?"

"No Alicia. Such an ugly name."

"Oh, then it can't have been the same. But my sister sat behind a Miss Traquair at the opening of the Usher Hall, and said she was perfectly lovely, and everyone looked at her. She said it was *the* Traquairs, but there must be some others. Well, do get Mr. Traquair; get someone, anyway, and come to the meeting of committee full of entirely fascinating ideas, won't you? You can be so original when you like, you know."

With which piece of flattery Mrs. Gerard left Nannie not ill pleased, and seeing herself, in imagination, cast for Mary Queen of Scots.

Effie was reminded again of her vaguely formed plan before night. Jullie had gone up to bed early, and in the middle of brushing her hair, she had stopped to sew buttons onto a blouse which she had newly run up on the machine. Effie found her at this when she entered the room.

"You careless brat!" she said. "You've simply dashed through that. Look at that wiggly seam down the front. It's not fit to wear."

"No one's going to take a microscope to my seams, thank goodness," said Jullie. "Mind I'm not a professional dress-maker like you."

"You're a great one for big checks, but that purple suits you," commented Effie, standing back, her hands on her hips, to criticise, as Jullie slipped on the offending garment, "It suits you just fine; but I told you not to make a V neck like that. The square ones are more in now anyway, and the doctor said you were *not* to wear such low necks if you want to live to the age of twenty. You know your throat's not strong, and it would kill a hippopotamus to go about with a neck open half-way down to its waist."

"Ah but I'm not a hippopotamus, you see," said Jullie flippantly, prinking in front of the mirror. "Effie, you've got to teach me smocking. I want to make a smocked jumper in imitation of the kind the Women's Land Army wear, like in the *Daily Mail* pictures we saw. They're tophole."

"You'd never have patience to learn," scoffed Effie.

"Wouldn't I! Oh I'd like to be on the land; it's such a comfortable dress, just knickers and a smock. I'd rather that than any other war work."

"I'm sorry for the land. You wouldn't stand a week of it, infant."

"Hoity toity, grandmother dear!" chanted Jullie dancing round in her nightgown. "Anyway this war is a bore. I don't want to take a roan's place in a stuffy office, as I suppose I'll have to in three months or so, if I pass this infernal exam."

"Jullie, you are *not* to say 'infernal'," commanded Effie sharply, "and if you don't pass the exam, I'll shake the life out of you."

"Why?" asked Jullie blandly.

"Because it's a disgrace us four lolling here at home," declared Effie, fired again. "The sooner you're off, the better. And I've made up my mind to go too one of these days. I have."

"Well if you think you're lolling, I don't," protested Jullie, tumbling into bed. "All the same, this house will fall to pieces the moment you depart."

Five

*They may talk of a comet, or a burning mountain
or some such bagatelle, but to me, a modest woman,
dressed out in all her finery, is the most tremendous
object of the whole creation!*

—SHE STOOPS TO CONQUER

When Nannie chose, she could make herself very agreeable. Her pleasant moods were not so dependable as Effie's, because she was more selfish, but there was more variety in them, for she had studied carefully the art of pleasing in all its branches. She knew well that what is one man's meat is another man's poison; and while Effie was always as natural as she was high-spirited, Nannie modified her voice and expression to suit the occasion, and was a consummate poser. She could be properly deferential, suave and confiding to a patronising lady of position; frank to vulgarity with a member of her own family; modest and much-to-be-approved-of in the eyes of an elderly uncle; or siren-sweet when any likely being in khaki was within beck and call.

On the morning after her talk with Mrs. Gerard, she entered Mr. Traquair's office, prepared to play the familiar and gushing girl with a dear old friend of the family. One hand supported her huge muff beneath her chin, the other was extended in welcome. "It's quite a shame to bother you, Mr. Traquair, but I know you won't mind *me* after all," she began affectionately. Then suddenly, the words trailed into silence and for a brief unmannerly moment Nannie stared.

Mr. Traquair, tall and courtly, with a lawyer's lean, humorous face, was not sitting there at his desk. In his place sat a grave young man on whom Nannie had never set eyes before.

He rose and came slowly forward to meet her. "I'm awfully sorry," he said, "Mr. Traquair is out just now. Can I do anything for you? I am his nephew, David Grant."

It would have taken a good deal to perturb Nannie, and she had recovered by this time. "Thanks," she said with a laugh. "The boy should have told me. It's very nice of you, but I don't know really whether I would be justified in wasting your time on such a frivolous errand."

She was watching him closely as she spoke. He was that rare thing in war time, a young man not in khaki, and a hundred questionings arose in her mind.

"Or perhaps I could take a message for my uncle?" he suggested.

"Well," said Nannie, "it's like this —" She dropped into the nearest chair, with the comfortable manner of one who has the whole morning before her. As a matter of fact, she liked his face; and having noticed that he went lame, and acquitted him in her mind of shirking, she decided to make the most of the interview.

He sat down, too, as though he were rather glad to do so, and waited politely for her to speak. Nannie fancied that he was a little too polite – for a young man; she liked them with more "cheek". He was as courteous as Mr. Traquair himself would have been, and in him it seemed old-fashioned.

"To cut a long story short," she began, altering her manner from a gushing girl to a young lady of assurance, "I came to ask Mr. Traquair if he would help me in a performance we're arranging for a war charity. I've known him, of course, since I was tiny, so I didn't think he would mind *me* bothering him. A family lawyer is something in the same line as a family doctor and parson, isn't he?" She crossed her legs comfortably, and leant back with a challenging smile.

David glanced involuntarily at the clock, then back at Nannie.

"Choice specimen," he reflected. "Painted, too. How she'd make Minnie squirm!"

Aloud he said, "Perhaps I could undertake the rôle," with a suavity of voice and manner which hardly suggested his train of thought.

"Oh but I couldn't think of bothering *you*," protested Nannie. "You see, it would have been an entirely personal favour with Mr. Traquair."

"And why not with me?"

"Well, I don't know you," said she, in a tone which declared as plainly as words, "But I mean to before either of us is much older!"

David was embarrassed, although he admitted his own question had brought it on him. This was the place for him to say something complimentary and charming, but the something would not come. He looked at her, sitting with silk-stockinged legs well apart, skirts up to the knee and chin supported coquettishly on her enormous muff, and he felt the flush rising on his brow. She was just the sort of girl who could play ducks and drakes with his self-possession.

"I'll be very glad to help," he said lamely at length. "My uncle's rather busy anyway. Won't you let me do it instead – as a personal favour, just the same?"

His confusion did not escape Nannie, and her interest was roused; that flush made him very like a boy in spite of his tired mouth and eyes.

"I'd better tell you about myself before you make rash promises," she said gaily. "I'm Nannie Sutherland – though the office boy *did* announce me – and Mr. Traquair will assure you we're quite respectable if you like to ask him. As for the performance, I have the vaguest notions about it. A friend of mine is getting it up, and has gathered a select committee, dumping the post of treasurer on me – Heaven knows why. She told me to get hold of some male and business-like friend, and repair to a committee meeting tomorrow with plenty brilliant ideas, of which I am destitute. So if you have any, they'll be quite as useful as your business capacity."

"Is it to be a play?"

"Well, my friend wants the first part to be an Old Edinburgh pageant, and the second, scenes from Barrie or Stevenson or something like that. I think it's a stale idea, but she has set her mind on it, because she wants something out of the common run."

"An Old Edinburgh pageant! How awfully nice," exclaimed David with enthusiasm.

"Does it appeal to you?" asked Nannie with indifference. "If it does, do enthuse me."

"It would give you plenty scope for dresses," went on David, forgetting his awkwardness. "And there's any number of fine dramatic bits you could work in, from Jeanie Deans to Black Major Weir. You shouldn't leave him out."

"Mercy me! I never heard of him," said Nannie, beginning to suspect that she had made as good a find as Mrs. Gerard.

"He was burnt for witchcraft," David informed her. "Then there's that short play Stevenson wrote founded on him; it's called *Deacon Brodie*, and it might do for you to act, except that it's rather a grim piece. I don't think there's anything of Barrie that would just do."

"You seem to know all about it," said Nannie in high feather. "Look here, Mr. Grant, I must get you put on the committee. Mrs. Gerard has the most aimless set, who can't possibly know anything about Old Edinburgh since they're all English."

"Please don't," he begged her hastily, "I would be no earthly use."

"At least you must come to rehearsals and give us hints," said Nannie in the tone of one who takes no refusal.

David cursed himself for his readiness to help her. Aloud he said, "Really, Miss Sutherland, I know absolutely nothing about acting. I'm only rather keen on things to do with Edinburgh, and I'd be glad to make suggestions, or do anything you needed behind the scenes."

Nannie was much amused by his obvious discomfort, but she did not press the point. "Well, do make some more," she said. "What a pity I haven't a pencil and notebook."

"I have rather a jolly book at home," said David, reflecting. "It's a bit of a family heirloom, with torn yellowed pages, and the leather rubbed white. It's Chambers' *Traditions of Edinburgh*, and I think you would find it useful. If I remember, there's a whole chapter devoted to women's costumes in the eighteenth century. Would you like me to send it?"

"Mr. Grant, you're a perfect gold-mine," cried Nannie rapturously. "But can you trust us with it?"

"I shall be very glad if you find it a help," he answered gravely. He thought he had been complacent enough, and that it was time to choke her off. Would the woman never go? Nannie's conscience certainly told her that she should depart, but she sat on wickedly.

"You're evidently a bookworm," she remarked, trying to draw him further.

"I like reading," he answered cautiously, in a tone which did not suggest that half his bedroom was lined with books.

Nannie sighed. "I'm afraid you'd think me very empty-headed," she said, profoundly satisfied that she had at last turned the conversation in the most interesting direction. "I hardly ever can settle to read a book through."

"Very few people can nowadays," said David.

"But I never could. It's silly; but after all real things are more interesting than fiction. Especially now. All the same, since the war, novels and things have really come more into touch with the things that matter, haven't they?" Her sudden change from flippancy to a pretty earnestness perplexed him like the swift contortions of an acrobat; he said nothing. "That's what they always say, isn't it?" she continued. "After an awful bust-up like this there always *is* a revival of literature and art and all those jolly things. That's one good side of the war, don't you think so?"

"I'm afraid I don't see any good side to this damned business," said David quickly; she was getting unbearable.

She looked at him reproachfully. "I don't think we at home have much to complain of," she said.

David flushed redder than before. "You haven't, and you may thank the Lord for it," he said with nervous bitterness. Would the floor not open and swallow up the creature?

She caught the emphasis on the "you", and saw her mistake. "Ah, you've been to the Front," she cried. "I'm so sorry. How could I say such things? I thought you had never been away because of —"

Fortunately for David, the door opened, and Mr. Traquair himself came in. Nannie sprang to her feet, all smiles and girlishness again. David rose so quickly that he had to catch his breath.

"So sorry I kept you waiting, Miss Sutherland," said Traquair courteously. "My nephew, David Grant… ah, I see you've introduced yourselves. Perhaps I'm intruding, eh?" He laughed. Nannie explained her business.

"But I won't need to bother you after all," she finished, with a gay nod towards David. "I seem to have fallen on my feet with Mr. Grant. I'm only sorry I have wasted so much of his precious time."

She left him in a whirl of merry repartee. David went out into the hall with her.

At the door Nannie turned to him. "And now," she insisted, "as we are properly introduced, you must come down yourself with that book, and stay for dinner! Yes, indeed you must, Mr. Grant. I won't take any excuse. Say Saturday, at seven. Will that suit?"

And so she departed, gleeful, and well content.

The family had a full account of the interview that night.

"My dears," she said, "I never got such a surprise in my life as when I saw a strange man, and a young one at that, there instead of dear old Duncan Traquair. I positively jumped. It was quite fun talking to a civilian again. But I'm afraid I made a mess of it, because I supposed he had been rejected and talked gaily about the bally old war, only to find that he has been discharged wounded."

"You little fool," said Effie scornfully.

"Oh, it was worth it," declared Nannie, "just to see him. He fidgeted for all the world like a bashful kid at school. He was so polite I could hardly breathe."

Effie burst out laughing. "Oh, I wish I'd seen the pair of you," she cried. "So you will," said Nannie calmly, for I've asked him to dinner on Saturday."

"Oh, what an affliction," groaned Marion.

"He'll suit you anyway," remarked Nannie. "You'll look at each other and say yes, and no, and be thoroughly silent and comfortable."

"I hate the way you invite people promiscuously, especially men," snapped Marion.

"*You* don't have to entertain them, at least," said Nannie, with a counter snap.

"No, indeed. Who could get a syllable in edgeways when you and Effie are on the scene?" And Marion for once had the last word.

"He's to bring a book about Edinburgh," said Nannie, changing the subject. "This pageant begins to get quite interesting. He seems to know a heap."

Uncle Alexander suddenly woke up. "Traquair's young nephew," he announced, "has published one or two little tales. Of course I haven't seen them myself, but I believe they were reviewed as unobtrusive but original. Traquair mentioned it himself one day. He did not seem over proud of the fact. I don't think the boy cared as much as his uncle would like about his profession."

This astounding piece of intelligence produced a flutter in the feminine dovecot of the Sutherlands. That Nannie's discovery should prove to be an author on the sly! Marion at once became reconciled to the dinner on Saturday. Jullie scented an autograph. Effie said, "Suppose he should turn out to be 'Taffrail' or 'Boyd Cable' or one of those mysterious anonymous war writers! He ought to know, after being at the Front himself." Billy alone said, "He'll probably be a rotter then!"

Nannie was silent. Attractive vistas had opened out within her imagination. She saw herself amid the glory and glitter of the pageant taking one or two leading parts, supported and assisted at every turn by this original and budding young author, whose enthusiasm and ideas were apparently boundless, whose mufti and limp would make him a conspicuous and heroic figure, and whose very nervousness might be ascribed to an artistic temperament. It was a delightful prospect.

The original and budding author gave William Ross a rather different account of the interview that very afternoon. The two found themselves alone in a third-class smoker on the Castlerig train.

David entered last, flung his hat and stick down on the seat beside him, and taking out his pipe, leant back with evident relief. The Doctor was watching him. "Had a stiff day of it?" he inquired at length.

"Not so very," said David, striking a match. "But I did have half an hour's conversation this morning which left me a mental wreck."

"Who with?" asked the Doctor, beginning to smile his slow smile in anticipation.

"A girl," said David in a tone which caused his friend to burst out in hearty laughter. "A most appalling girl. One of

Uncle's clients. Or rather *her* uncle is. Known him since she was wee, so thought he wouldn't mind unlimited cheek and waste of time. Unfortunately Uncle was out, and I got what was meant for him."

"But what was she like? Pretty?"

"Hum… yes, dashing. And she talked even on."

Ross chuckled with delight.

"Will, you're a beast!" said David. "You would have been every bit as much in a hole yourself."

"I would have had the face to show her the door," said the Doctor.

"But, my dear man, I couldn't. I was there instead of Uncle, and I had to be civil to her. Besides I was rather taken with her project. She came to ask me to help with a war charity matinee they're getting up, and it's to be an Old Edinburgh pageant, or something of the sort. Think what a ripping notion."

"So what happened?"

"In a rash moment I promised to assist. She nearly had me onto the committee, or bound over to act in person… Shut up!"

Will Ross was rocking with laughter.

"Of course I protested till I was red in the face, but she was so busy talking I don't believe she heard. Anyway, I'm to take her some literature on the subject, and I've been inveigled into dining with them on Saturday."

"And after that?"

"After that, she got onto more – er – personal topics, and was excruciating. I simply sat and sweltered. I don't know what she thought of me. She had the worst taste possible. And then, by most blessed luck, Uncle Duncan appeared, and delivered me. All the same I've promised her."

"Were you so taken with her?"

"Taken with her? I dislike her immensely. But I like the pageant idea, and as I say I had to be decent. Oh, let's talk of something nicer. Look at this perfectly delightful old Bible I picked up today, with full-page pictures of Moses and the Flood, and illuminating comments down the sides. It's dated the sixteenth century. And this wee one is a geography primer of about the same date. The map of America is a sight to see, with no West Indies, and a picture of fiends dancing about in the Amazon Valley. I got the two for quite a little."

Ross looked over his friend's shoulder. "You're a quaint one," he said. "Oh, by the way, that farmer's widow at Carlops *is* selling off her stock, and she's got some chicken coops to dispose of. You wanted one, didn't you?"

"No," said David after cogitation. "The old one will last out. Thanks, all the same. Oh, I say, I didn't tell you: The baby incubator's come. You must drop in and see it, Will!"

And so they talked – about "nicer things!"

Six

He is not the man of pleasure who has pleasure; it is the awkward man, whose evening dress does not fit him, whose gloves will not go on, whose compliments will not come off... the faculty of being shy is the first and most delicate of the powers of enjoyment.

—G. K. CHESTERTON

On the following Saturday, David set his teeth, prepared himself for a solid eight hours of polite society, and set off towards his uncle's house in Moray Place like a soldier going into battle.

He was due at the Traquairs' about three o'clock. Alicia was paying one of her frequent visits north, and the children were with her. Isabel expected her fiancé that afternoon who was making the most of a brief leave, and in general there was to be a gathering of the friends and family.

David had not seen Alicia since his return from France; the children he had never seen at all. She was the first to notice him in the crowded drawing-room, and for a few moments they stood together as though they were alone.

The sight of his face shocked her; he seemed to her not to be a boy any longer, and she knew he had suffered that deepness of pain which leaves no man altogether unchanged. But I doubt whether she was more distressed than he was.

He fancied that she had grown taller. It may have been because of her dress of rich, sombre velvet, with heavy lines, beautifully made, and high at the throat, which sat on her with dignity. Her face, under the wide hat, was as young and lovely as ever; she had the same grace, the same grave brow, as when he had adored her with the adoration which only a little, much snubbed, unhappy boy could yield to a fairy princess. But the look in her eyes hurt him. She had married for love, not for money as the story went, and her husband was a brave man, doing more than his duty for their country's sake; so that Alicia, through the days and nights, lived anxiously, and had looked on sorrow as one who must always be prepared for the coming of death. That had made the difference, and David, as they talked, wondered which of the two of them had given the more. And he held his two years of hell very lightly in her presence.

Then she sat down, and the children came threading their way to her through the groups of people, and standing beside her they stared up at David, wondering. They were beautiful children, dressed in white, and the girl had Alicia's brow.

But before they could be introduced, Mrs. Traquair had espied David. "Here you are at last," she said. "Had a chat with Alicia? Yes, the children are growing. Everyone says that. Do you think you would mind handing round? I don't quite like to trouble you, but there aren't many men."

Aunt Margaret had not changed. She seemed as young as Alicia. By art she had kept her looks, and by nature her commanding manner. David professed his willingness to help, and started forth with plates of cookies and scones. His first mishap was to barge into Isabel's fiancé, his second to be barged into by Isabel. Luckily no frocks were ruined, and it served by way of introduction. The fiancé was small and pink; he had but one star on his sleeve, and was making desperate attempts to grow a moustache. Isabel had become almost fat, and the pout was fixed. She wore a mustard-coloured costume, very short in the skirts, and a magnificent engagement ring of sapphires and diamonds, as though she could not proclaim the fact loudly enough. She did not seem at all pleased to see David; and he went back to Alicia, laughing to himself, and fancying that the old days had returned in earnest.

"Tell me all your news," he said.

She considered. "You heard about the old place being turned over for a hospital? It's just ideal for the purpose. The rooms always seemed to me too big before, but they are so splendid now as wards. And the men love the lawns. I really feel that the money we poured into that garden is justified at last."

"And what about…"

"Harry? He's very flourishing, I'm thankful to say. At this present moment I can't tell you where he is, but it doesn't make much difference out there in the mud!" She laughed. "It's a good thing he was always such a fine letter-writer, because I don't think a war is the best place to form the habit; but you've no idea how regularly I hear from him. It makes all the difference. And Len has learned to write in half the time because he is so keen to send a proper epistle to the trenches. Do look at them over there, David! I'm so afraid Len will say something shocking to one of the visitors; he has a startlingly original mind for four. Or else he'll spill his milk. And either way, Mother will be so vexed. Ah, that's nice of Father to give them the little table. Isabel and I used to have that little table when we were allowed into the drawing-room first, you know."

"Where are you staying yourselves, then?"

"In quite a little house, an hour or so out of London, the dearest place possible. You would love it, David. I really think the children prefer it now to Marklake. It's so cosy. You know, I quite thought of the Shieling when we went first. Do you remember, David? What fun we had furnishing it. I'll never forget those little cream curtains with the yellow flowers that Isabel thought so vulgar."

"And the time when I tried to paint the back bedroom!"

"And the apricot jam we made, and Isabel burnt!"

"And the supper you cooked all by yourself, Alicia! I'm afraid we were rather beastly about it."

"I'm sure you weren't. Oh how we did enjoy it! David, don't you feel an old stager now?"

She laughed again, wonderful laughter. Then she said, "Tell me about yourself?"

"There's nothing to tell, said David, smiling. "I'm an awfully uninteresting person really. I would rather listen to you."

So she talked on and told him more about the house, and the children, and all the circle of her interests. He could see that she was regarded as a very great lady now, and knew it; she spoke as mistress, and the manner suited her; and the pride of ownership and the sober gladness of responsibility transformed her in his eyes. The nobler things of the aristocracy of England she had made her own, and she knew well how to be the wife of one of a race who build and rule the empire. But through her speech, there ran a tenderness which she had not known in the past days. The look in her eyes, which David could not forget, explained that.

During the greater part of his call, he did not pay much attention to the other people in the room. There was a handful of young officers laughing inanely at jokes perpetrated by Isabel's fiancé, some elderly ladies in furs, sipping tea, and complaining of the scarcity of sugar, and as many girls, some of them bored, some of them bantering the officers. Save for the khaki the party was such as he had seen often in pre-war days in Duncan Traquair's drawing-room. And even more than in pre-war days, he shrank from the laughter and light talk. It did not seem in tune with things; and the company seemed as remote from the war and as ineffectual as the pictures in that picture-gallery which had disappointed him. Once he had turned from Alicia, and stood among the buzz of talk, the bright lights and the clinking tea-cups, the furs and fine clothes and soft furnishings, those two years of hell seemed to him, as before, of no use. The atmosphere of the room, warmed by a great log fire, stifled him; and taking his leave, he went down into the silent streets, dull and tired.

Nannie Sutherland had fixed the dinner hour at seven, and David arrived at the house in good time. Nannie was waiting for him, the stage carefully set, in the parlour. She would have preferred an ample hall, with a blazing fire, and herself seated on a carved oak chair. But as she lacked these desirable accessories, she had gone to the trouble of dusting and airing the dingy little parlour, which usually reeked of smoke and the last meal. She had pinned red tissue paper round the electric lamp to cast a soft glow, and made up a fire which threatened to set the chimney roaring and roast the company before the kitchen range had finished with the mutton. She had pushed every trace of untidiness under the window seat, and at a quarter to seven took up a post of vantage on the cushion-seat before the hearth, with a grimy novel from the circulating library on her lap; in which position and with the important addition of her best frock, she flattered herself that she looked thoroughly interesting.

Billy, in his original state of grubbiness, opened the door to David, for Jullie was upstairs struggling with her own buttons in the intervals of fastening Marion's, and Effie was at the range, enveloped in her overall, and as crimson as Nannie's artistic lamp-shade. Besides, Nannie had given strict orders that no one was to appear in the parlour until the wheezy clock had started to stake the hour, when they were to enter one by one, gracefully, and not in a bunch, falling over each other, as was the usual bad habit of the Sutherland family.

Nannie received David with delight. "So awfully good of you to come," she said. "I've been telling Mrs. Gerard all about you, and she thinks you're a perfect treasure. She wants to meet you, so I've asked her for Wednesday to tea, if that suits you; only I wanted to have you to myself tonight first, so that we might make some plans before she can shove her oar in!"

David, shaking hands, looked round the solitary room, and hoped in desperation that he would not be left as entirely to Nannie's sole mercies as she seemed to desire.

"Is that the book?" asked Nannie, drawing in the Chesterfield, and motioning to him to sit down beside her.

"This," said David, "is the book." He could see with his mind's eye an interminable string of dinners, teas, committee meetings, and interviews with tedious females, all of which he had brought upon himself by that first unsuspecting remark.

They looked through a few of the pages, Nannie exclaiming gleefully at the quaint woodcuts. Then the clock began to strike, and the family to enter. Five separate introductions would have overwhelmed the boldest of men, and David stood his ground with an effort. First of all, there was Billy whom he had met already, but who, nonetheless offered an unwashed paw, and Uncle Alexander followed him. Uncle Alexander's feeble attempt at discussion of the evening's news was cut short by the entrance of Jullie, sparkling, quite frankly curious, and twice as embarrassing as Nannie. She shook hands in a trying silence, and David sat down beside her and asked her if she had been to any dances, uncertain if he were doing the correct thing or not. Before she could answer, Effie arrived, with cheeks made more blooming by the kitchen fire than Nannie's by rouge, and she grasped the guest's hand, and whirled him into a breathless conversation in which he found himself telling obvious lies about the weather out of sheer nervousness.

Last of all came Marion, slipping in quietly, and standing just within the door. David rose, with resignation, prepared for another strange damsel; then recognised her with a start of glad surprise, and smiled as he gave her his hand. It seemed as though they were old friends. She was wearing a grey dress which did not suit her, and she was untidy; he noticed that even in the first moment. But in spite of it, she seemed to him the one cool, quiet thing in the hot, crowded room, and he gave her a grateful look for it.

Dinner was an anxious meal. Effie was too occupied with the carving – for Uncle Alexander never rose to these occasions – to lead the talk, and she was inclined to fuss about the pudding, which had threatened to be a failure; so that Nannie had the field to herself, and chattered with the very spirit of mischief, while David ate his mutton and tart in a commonplace fashion, thinking of innumerable clever repartees just when it was too late.

Marion was silent – her usual. "I wonder what be thinks of us," she mused. "He looks so manly and nice compared to that feckless uncle of ours. How shiny Billy's jacket is, and oh, why did Nannie lay on the powder extra thick?… he's bound to notice. She's being a little cat; and Effie gets commoner and fussier. Supposing the pastry is burnt, she needn't talk so loud. He must hate it; he's obviously… well, refined is a snobbish word, but anyway he can't be enjoying himself much."

After dinner, matters were rather worse. Effie disappeared into the back regions, and although David confessed to a miserable ignorance of the game, Nannie haled him to the bridge table as her partner against Jullie and Marion. Billy went to do some home lessons, and Uncle Alexander to sleep – audibly, until Jullie flung a cushion at him. Marion yawned, Jullie giggled, Nannie flirted desperately, until her patience failed her, and David scowled and did everything wrong. Then at length the bell rang.

Jullie rushed to the door; there came a noise of steps in the hall, and a peal of giggles, and Effie called, "It's Noël." Nannie hardly waited to make an excuse. She darted out of the parlour, and David and Marion were left alone at the card table, with Uncle Alexander sleeping beside the fire.

David shuffled cards for a nervous moment. Then he caught Marion's eye, and they both burst out laughing. "It was such a killing game," she said by way of apology.

"You may well laugh," said he. "I'm a perfect ass at cards." He wanted her to go on laughing. She had become suddenly lovely when she laughed.

"I hate them myself," said Marion. "I think parlour games are silly."

"Do you prefer music?" asked David. "I like to hear other people, but I can't play myself a bit. My fingers get as hot and sticky as – as melted butter!" She laughed again.

David nodded, with appreciation. "I know the beastly feeling," he said. "I used to try and play my sister's accompaniments, but – one always lands on the wrong note somehow when anyone's listening!"

"It's quite mad for me to say it," she continued, "seeing I am as good at it as at music, but I wish people went in more for conversation nowadays, like, – like they did in the eighteenth century, you know what I mean. Not just the war news and the weather, but interesting things. If by any chance they do discuss decent things, they get so cross and can't agree – like religion. There ought to be rules for conversation just like anything else, and one of them would be, don't lose your temper!"

David clasped his hands round one knee, a favourite comfortable position of his. "To be quite honest," he confessed, "I never can talk about decent things myself; I can't stand having my views picked to pieces by other people. Idiotic, I confess, but it's the fact."

"I'm so used to being picked to pieces that I don't mind now," declared Marion. "That's the advantage of a large family! But it certainly isn't comfortable."

"I had one sister who was a host in herself," said David, laughing. "But I'm afraid even she hasn't developed a thick skin for me."

Even as he spoke the thought crossed his mind: "We seem to be discussing fairly personal things ourselves."

Marion sorted the queens out of the pack and laid them in a row. "That's Nannie's fiancé who came in just now," she said. "He's a lieutenant in the Flying Corps. I hear them taking him into the dining-room to get fed."

David raised his eyebrows. So Nannie was engaged!

"I hope they'll keep him there a while," went on Marion calmly, "and let us talk comfortably in here. I expect Nannie will drop the pageant altogether while he has leave. It's awfully good of you troubling to help her."

"Not a bit. Are any of you to be in it?"

"I don't expect so. Jullie may, but Nannie has a pretty poor opinion of the abilities of her own family. Anyway Effie and I have no time. You see, I'm in Uncle's office all day."

"Do you like it?"

"I loathe it, but what else would I do? You know how deadly dull an office can be."

"Would you like to do war work for a change?"

"Oh I can't be bothered changing. I'm afraid I'm not one of those progressive women. For all the good I would do I don't see the use. And yet there isn't any use in staying here either. There are far too many of us at home as it is."

David looked at her. Her words sounded very like some he had used himself, and did indeed use in his heart every day. The laugh had died out of her eyes, and she sat with her hands folded listlessly. He felt suddenly pity for her, not pity with superiority in it, but the warm, eager pity of one who has been in the same straits himself. He had realised before what marvellous ease of intercourse there was between them, and now he knew that in this talk, such an equal, open talk as he had never had with any girl save Minnie, they had come very close together.

They were silent for a little, and before he could speak, Nannie returned with Noël and the others at her heels.

Marion gave a sigh, and rose to offer a limp hand to the newcomer; and David knew that the pleasure of the night was over.

Noël Wyndham was a tall, loose-limbed young man, not so old as Nannie herself, brown of hair and eyes, with a square chin and an aroused mouth. He sauntered across the room, greeted Marion and Uncle Alexander, and favoured David with a stare.

Nannie made a gushing introduction. "My fiancé, Noël Wyndham, Mr. Grant," she said. "Noël, this is my very kind friend, Mr. Grant, who is giving us such a lot of help with the pageant, you know. I really don't know what I'd do without him. We have been studying the most delightful old book about costumes together. He is really getting me to be quite brainy over it."

She spoke as if they were friends of some years standing, as if not a day passed without a visit from him.

"Very good of you, I'm sure," drawled Noël.

David saw that he was being used by this unconscionable young lady to tease her unfortunate fiancé, and he rebelled.

"Miss Sutherland is far too kind," he protested, meaning the very opposite. "She is magnifying the paltry assistance I offered her."

Nannie laughed merrily, and proceeded to keep them both in misery for ten minutes, much to the amusement of Jullie and Billie in the background. They had risen when Noël came in, and at the end of that time, David, who was not able to stand for long, and who had been losing both breath and patience gradually, could bear it no further, and took a hasty leave of the family, under the pretence of catching the last train to Castlerig, which, as a matter of fact, did not start for another hour.

Seven

Oh self, self, self, are we eternally masking in a domino
that reveals your hideous old face when we could be
most positive we had escaped you?
—DIANA OF THE CROSSWAYS

D avid, as he walked home that night up the Station
Brae, and left behind him the dell and the river and
the sleeping houses, thought much, not of Nannie
or the pageant, but of the girl who had sat with listless hands
and said, "It's no use."

It was as though he had caught sight of himself in a
looking-glass unexpectedly. Her mood was his own; and
her voice, the voice of a girl not five and twenty, sounded
as though there were nothing but grey days before her,
nothing but emptiness at the heart of things. And this
was not the green sickness of seventeen. He had known
that himself, and though it had hurt more than older
folk understood, it had been a romantic thing too, and so
bearable. This was the deadness of spirit which belonged
to men and women who have discovered the dreariness of
the world.

He could not tell about Marion Sutherland, but for himself he knew what it is to do a hard, right thing and find
nothing but barrenness in return, to come within touching
distance of the filthy moral wrong of the world, to find
that systems which he had been brought up to honour
were founded on ignorance and selfishness, to realise the

daily sadness of each separate life in the world, to perceive the veil that is upon the face of all nations.

The war had accentuated all this. It had set a question mark before every established theory, and the easy optimists, and those who were hypocrites without realising it, made matters worse when they talked about the certain victory of right.

After two years of mental numbness and inactivity, books were at first bewildering. And he had looked back through history, and could see nothing but ups and downs, and after every up still another down, with no clear thread of progress.

Friends were of little comfort. As he had said, his very eagerness made him self-conscious in speaking, and they looked at things in different ways from him. He began to see how terribly alone a man must always be in his heart.

There was still work to do, but it seemed thankless.

The purpose had fallen out of life.

And yet, there was a difference between Marion and himself; he did not know her well enough yet to perceive it. She hated life, as a woman may hate the weariful, nagging husband to whom she is tied; he was in love with life, as a man loves his lady in spite of her unresponsive coldness. He was persuaded that there was something finer to be got out of it, and it was a sense of baffled desire which hurt him. For this he blamed his own weakness. He knew that he was hedged in by a barrier which kept him back relentlessly from other men, which he found hard to break through even for a moment. That barrier dated back to Cousin Jessie's rule.

Before that, Minnie and he had both been happy children, full of the delight of living. Then at the beginning of adolescence, after the deaths of their parents, it was permitted to Cousin Jessie to inflict upon them her conception of a godly and wholesome upbringing. Minnie emerged from the process sharper and harder, David diffident and painfully self-conscious. With Minnie's free life in London, and the interest of her chosen profession and the friends she made, the sharpness wore off, and at twenty-eight she was enjoying life, all the more self-reliant because of her old struggles with Cousin Jessie and the fight she had made for independence.

It was otherwise with David. He had grown accustomed to keep his thoughts and ideals very secret because of the inevitable harsh criticism which met them whenever he dared to express them; to judge himself with morbid severity according to the standards of Cousin Jessie's religion; to yield to her wishes in every respect, first of all because she stood to him as a mother or father, and afterwards because she was an elderly, pathetic invalid on her sofa, paralysed and dying. This attitude of mind had become a habit, and long after all reason for it had disappeared, the habit remained. He had cast aside Cousin Jessie's ideas of religion long ago, and he was a man now, alone and independent, with no one's wishes to consult, and no one to censure his behaviour or opinions. But the wall of reserve remained standing, and he loathed it. Those few who came to know him well realised that behind it there was tenderness, the greater because he had been unhappy, and a quality of steadfastness which Jenny called dourness, and Minnie obstinacy, and a quaint imaginative humour which had grown richer by being con-centrated within himself, and having few outlets.

David was not aware of all this. He only knew that for him life was an uncommonly difficult business. It had been the same since that time when he was fifteen, and Minnie had taunted him, and he left her, angry and miserable, to spend his scanty pocket money on cigarettes and a third-rate picture-house, because he felt she was right about the lack in his character, and this seemed to him the best way of making himself a man. It was a boy's escapade, and he laughed at the remembrance.

But it was not for lack of effort that the barrier remained. He had struggled continually to get out of himself, and to live life in a full and worthy fashion, for he had been brought up to be too much of the Puritan to be satisfied with anything less than his best.

Thinking of this, he came to the Shieling. It was a mild night for the end of March. There was a bit of a young horned moon behind a veil of mist, and the sky was patterned over with a network of clouds, the little stars peeping out from the dark spaces between. A great warm wind swept up from over the Pentlands, and David, going up the garden, brushed against a lilac bush; he put out his hand, and first he felt, then dimly he saw the buds on it, formed, and ready to burst, and a thrill went through him at the hope of spring.

A good deal of nonsense has certainly been talked about the artistic temperament, but its real meaning is a simple and wonderful thing; nothing less than the power to understand and love the eternal beauty which is in the world.

Those who have it, know that in the midst of work and sordid days, a beautiful thing is like a long drink of cold sweet water, or the hill winds; or like that magic stuff of which we must suppose immortality is made, which can give to a tired spirit at once the utter relief of rest, and the strength of fresh life.

David knew that. Out in the dusk of the garden, he felt absurdly light-hearted. All things were possible to him; for a few moments. That thrill of spring exhilarated him like wine.

Then it passed, and though he tried to bring it back, he could not.

He went indoors, put out the lamp which Jenny had left burning, and climbed the stair to his own room.

David's room was rather an untidy place. One wall of it was lined with books, and books overflowed from the shelves onto the floor and into every available corner. Book buying was his one extravagance, and he possessed a very catholic collection, from his favourite *Twelfth Night* and *Hamlet* in sumptuous bindings to Wells's latest novel; from such quaint people as George Herbert and Sir Thomas Browne and Elia to the Oxford Books of Verse and Rupert Brooke. Precious first editions, their number limited by the extent of his purse, found themselves in the company of theological works which had belonged to his father, evangelical tales of Cousin Jessie's, legal text-books, and "doubtful" modern fiction; for David was impartial to all save Boswell, whom be placed in an ignominious corner because the great Doctor discredited solitude and lauded conversation to the skies; from which you see that David was still a very young man. Minnie would have burnt half of them cheerfully, especially the modern mystical poets, whom she declared humbugs, and Yeats humbug in chief!

The shelf above David's little brown desk, which he loved in spite of its shabbiness, was sacred to Robert Louis Stevenson – *Kidnapped*, and the rest, *Memories and Portraits*, the poems, the letters, *The Child's Garden*. David did not admire Robert Louis because it is fashionable to do so; he loved him as though they had known each other all their lives. They had so much in common. Mr. Grant had been minister in the old manse where Stevenson's grandfather lived and where the "chief of our aunts" held her sway; and David had dim memories of "the great day nursery, best of all, with pictures pasted on the wall and leaves upon the blind," and of the sunny store-room, and the parlour, and the great yew in the garden near the kirkyard. He, too, knew what Edinburgh looked like in the middle night, when one was a small, sick boy who could not sleep for coughing. He had passed to school and college along the "draughty parallelograms of the New Town," and had gone, not to the Calton cemetery, but at least to the Calton Hill above "to be unhappy". And like Louis, he had sat up on a fold of the Pentlands many a time among the sheep and the curlews, "scribbling bad verses", and wasting a summer's day.

When he was a boy, he had liked to fancy that Louis

was his "pretence-brother" and later, when he was growing up, the brave memory of the man remained with him like a charm against depression and weariness. It was with him strongly that night.

The room was not in complete darkness when he entered it with a lighted candle; the blind was up, and the window was open with a clean smell blowing in from the garden, and the misty moonlight made a bright patch on the floor. He was not sorry when the draught from the window puffed out his candle; he did not relight it, but sat down on the window-seat, his hands clasped round one knee, and looked out upon the garden. He had thrown back his head, leaning it against the shutter; and the light of the moon, striking full on his face, showed it as Jenny had seen it once before in the old difficult days just after Minnie had gone to London and left him with Cousin Jessie, puzzled, angry, rebellious. The fighting spirit was alive in him, and it made him seem what he was in truth, in spite of those two years-young and keen. It was because of that sudden hope which had come to him in the garden, and left him as suddenly, as though he had stretched out his hand to catch a bubble, and it had broken at the touch. He could not bear to lose it. After a while he got up restlessly, shut the window, and lit the candle again. Then he went and stood before the mantelpiece, the candlestick in his hand.

The walls which were not occupied with books were covered with pictures, as thick as "leaves in Vallombrosa" Minnie was wont to say, quoting Milton; some were framed, and the unframed ones were tacked up with drawing-pins. Over the mantelpiece there was a square picture, not very large, of a man's head and shoulders. It was a sombre picture with a very dark background; the only bright things in it were the clean pallor of the man's face, and the red of his ribboned coat. His head was thrown back, and the chin well up; there was pride in the poise of it, and in the lines about his mouth and his aquiline nose; and in the steady brown eyes burnt a defiant flame of loyalty to a lost cause, perhaps, or of a reckless love of life, or, it might be, of devotion to some lady. David did not know who he was; Claverhouse, possibly, or Montrose, a gallant soldier and a gentleman, at least. The picture had always fascinated him.

He held the candle steadily beneath it. "That fellow could fight," he thought, and involuntarily straightened himself.

"Not so lame after all," he muttered. "It's about time I began to live life, not just look on and make pessimistic comments. Oh, my God, to get right out of oneself, to have any amount of energy... and a healthy body... well, health or not I'll do it. I won't be beat. If there was only something to hang on to, something sure... a purpose..."

When he was a boy, he had thought that only fools were sure about things. It had seemed manly to stand in the dark on the lowest stair, to doubt all things, to deal in realism. Twilight had seemed preferable to day then. Perhaps it had been an inevitable stage; but he felt now that to accept that twilight as the final reality was to accept a lie. In that scepticism, that colourless half-life, there was nothing but stagnation. It was possible in such a mood to doubt the existence even of moral right and wrong, to argue all purpose out of things, to live in the growing isolation of selfishness, to come to a despairing standstill.

Such freedom of thought was no freedom; it might help to perfect the machinery of the brain, but it sapped the driving power behind.

His whole soul turned in a passion from that stagnation, crying out for real and sure things, positive things which led somewhere instead of wandering round in a philosophical circle, for faith, for courage, for love, for beauty, for God, and the simple things which modern wisdom has rather discredited. He desired to find that which endures beyond wars, and the generations of men, and is eternally worthwhile, that which is learned with pain, and yet abides when the pain is all past.

Then he realised what it meant – plunging into life all the time, no more shrinking into his shell, giving of himself freely, mixing with people… talking! David had the fortunate grace of being able to laugh at himself. He laughed now.

He also wondered for a moment how the thought of Marion Sutherland had suggested all this… Then he said again, "I'll not be beat."

Eight

I wish I were dead, but I'm no like tae dee.
Oh why do I live to say, wae's me?
— AULD ROBIN GRAY

Noël Wyndham remained till about eleven o'clock at the Sutherlands' house. He found Nannie more tantalising than usual. She could talk of nothing but the pageant, and when he proposed various nights for the theatre and supper, and as many afternoons for tea somewhere, he found she was engaged on them all, as often as not, by her way of it, with David Grant. He gave up trying to entertain her at last, and had an uproarious game of "Pit" with Jullie and Billy, in which Effie joined when she had cleared the table and washed up for the second time.

He was not looking at all happy when he said good night to Nannie. She reached up and spread her hands over his forehead, smoothing it. "Don't scowl, you naughty boy," she commanded.

"Well, I must say you haven't seemed so awfully pleased to see me, Nannie," he protested with a laugh.

"I'm very busy just now," she said.

"Don't tire yourself out with that pageant," he warned with just a shade of sarcasm in his voice.

"Was it jealous then?" cooed Nannie. "Then it didn't ought to be! You don't want me to do nothing for my country, Noël?"

"Heavens no! You're a good little soul, Nannie. I didn't mean to be a wet-blanket, you know."

"Oh hurry up, kiss me, do," said Nannie with a yawn. "I've got a cold, and I can't stand all night in this lobby."

Noël kissed her several times, tenderly. She was a pretty, kissable little thing after all, and one had to put up with any small disagreeables…

"Nan, I like you, do you know?" he said, raising her face to his.

"Just as well. Run away home!" answered his betrothed affectionately, and hurried off into the parlour, with a backward smile.

Effie, discreetly invisible until then, came and saw him to the door. "You won't get anything out of Nannie tonight," she said apologetically. "She's in one of her provoking moods. I say, Noël, we meant to fix up an informal dance for you, just a little hop, you know, ourselves and Beatrice, and say three or four others. Is there any one you'd specially like to ask? I couldn't get Nannie on to the subject at all. All her wits are in the pageant."

"Effie, you're a decent fellow! No there isn't, not specially. Just arrange yourself, and let me know the date. Look here, is it morally impossible to have Nannie to myself for one afternoon? She seems tied up with that – er – pageant, and that – Grant fellow."

Effie laughed quietly. "My dear, Nannie knows him no more than she knows Lloyd George," she replied. "He happens to be helping in this blessed pageant. Couldn't you see the poor chap was as uncomfortable as yourself?"

Noël shook her hand warmly, getting a little red in the dim lobby, "You're a decent fellow," he said again. "Don't think me an awful fool."

"I think you are the most angelically patient man I ever met," laughed Effie, opening the front door. "So long then! Look round tomorrow afternoon. She'll be in, you bet!"

She slammed the door after him, locked it, and put out the lobby light. Then she returned to the parlour. Uncle

Alexander had gone silently to bed; Jullie and Billy were fighting for the bathroom. Marion only remained by the fireplace, and Nannie sat perched on the arm of the sofa, her skirts spread out round her like a crinoline.

"You're a disgusting, vulgar little fool," Marion was saying.

"How much?" inquired Nannie calmly, attending to her nails.

"I was telling Nannie that she's a vulgar little fool. It mayn't do her any good to hear it, but it does me good to get it out," said Marion, flinging the words at her sisters with sudden energy. She sat huddled up on her chair, her round shoulders bent, her elbows resting on her knees, and her dress crumpled up carelessly. The sallowness of her face struck Effie as ghastly, emphasised by the purple, shadowy marks under her eyes. She was very tired, and all on edge. Nannie, with high colour and her hair gradually slipping down her neck in pretty confusion, was equally cross, but did not look it.

"Thanks awfully," she said. "Why this vehemence?"

"You know as well as I do," said Marion.

"Please enlighten me."

"You're a common little flirt. You've done nothing else all evening."

Nannie looked up from her nails. "You're a jealous cat," she retorted. "Just because you couldn't entertain a man yourself for two minutes."

"I believe I managed the feat for twenty," remarked Marion sullenly. "Mr. Grant and I had an extremely nice time by ourselves when you were out of the way."

"How charming!" said Nannie. "I hope you said yes and no at the proper and suitable moments."

"You are a pig."

"And did you do full justice to the weather?"

"I would tell you just exactly what we did say, only you wouldn't believe me," Marion informed her. "Oh, you're awfully clever, Nannie Sutherland, but I'd rather be a dumb, stale, ugly, uninteresting stick than go on with two men the way you've been doing tonight!"

"You were a wee bit nasty to Noël, you know," said Effie, speaking for the first time in the dubious, half-soothing tone of the would-be peacemaker.

"Noël and I understand each other," said Nannie stiffly. "He knows how to take a joke, though you don't. The Sutherland family always was devoid of humour."

Marion's eyes fairly blazed. "Well, if you think it's funny to paint yourself up and make eyes at a man you hardly know with your back turned on your fiancé for an hour at a time, I know *I* don't!" she cried.

Nannie sprang up, all on fire, her face red and ugly with anger. "Marion, you have no right to talk in that disgusting fashion to me, or to anyone else, do you hear?" she almost shouted. "You *are* jealous, so you don't need to talk; and if it's any comfort to know it, you *are* a dumb, stale, ugly stick, and no man in his senses would look at you. You can't dress fit to be seen, and you don't try; you're neither useful nor ornamental, you're just a silly sloppy idiot! There! I can say what I like as well as you!"

And having given as good as she got, Nannie stood panting for a moment, and then banged out of the room, and ran upstairs.

There had been tears in Marion's eyes long before, and now they ran freely down her cheeks. She fumbled for a handkerchief, shaking with sobs the while. "Did you hear her, Effie?" she cried. "Wasn't every word I said true? Isn't she a – a beastly flirt? Why didn't you rub it in when I said it, instead of standing there yawning?"

Effie started, and her hands at her sides clenched tightly. Up till now she had kept her own temper, thinking wisely that it would do more harm than good to take any sides in the affair. Besides, she was half asleep where she stood, and it is not easy to work up an eloquent rage when one is almost nodding with drowsiness. Her sleeves hung unfastened as she had left them in the kitchen, and a tail of hair had unwound itself and stuck rakishly over one ear. Sheer weariness had drained the high colour of the evening from her cheeks. "Well, I do think it's nice of *you* to talk about yawning!" she declared. "If you'd done what I've done this day, Marion Sutherland, you'd be snoring by now. Of course Nannie's a disgraceful flirt, but what else can you expect of her? It's no earthly use to work up a brawl about it. Nannie'll flirt till she's a hundred. And if it worried you so much to watch her, why, for mercy's sake, didn't you come and give me a hand? I had no less than *two* suppers to set and clear away and wash up, and, of course, the fire was half out by the end of Noël's, and there wasn't a drop of hot water. I think you might have offered to dry at least, instead of crouching there half into the fender, you goose! Do you know I've hardly sat down this living day? You knew quite well I had to scrub the kitchen today, because the char couldn't come, and bake for Sunday into the bargain. And then this dinner of Nannie's, and Noël on top of it! And you never offered once to help. You think of nothing and no one but your own useless self, Marion!"

"How dare you say that?" sobbed Marion. "It's not true – it's not fair, Effie! Didn't I offer to pay the books for you this morning, and you wouldn't let me. Said you must do it yourself."

"Well, you forgot everything I told you to ask about last time," said Effie, "so it was less trouble to do it myself."

"And didn't I offer to get the lunch?"

"But you make such a mess, I'd rather…Yes, well, you did offer, Marion, but oh, you know what I mean. You're no earthly good…"

"Yes, I do know what you mean," quavered Marion, springing to her feet. "You don't need to repeat it. I know quite well I'm a burden to everybody, and I wish to Heaven I was dead!"

She rushed out of the room, crying breathlessly, and Effie heard her turn the key in her own door two stairs up.

She gave a big sigh which ended in a yawn. "Well it was true, and perhaps it'll do her good," she told herself. "Marion and Nannie are a pair of… oh well, we're all dead tired, and no wonder we're snappy. It's after twelve. Any one would snarl at this hour. Although why they should be tired beats me. I think Marion was born tired."

And so Effie too went up to bed, turning out all the lights methodically, looking in upon Billy to stop him reading a lurid novelette under the blankets and put out a clean collar where he could not fail to see it in the morning if he tried; winding the eight-day clock on the stair; and finally falling sound asleep as soon as she lay down, to waken next morning as though nothing had happened, on good terms with all the world.

Nannie was a little longer in getting to sleep. To begin with, she sat shivering until the bath was filled, and then discovered that she had let the water run cold, and a bath was out of the question.

Marion, on the other hand, did not try to sleep, nor even to undress. She lay face downwards on the top of her bed, crying as though her heart would break, crying noisily like a child, with big gulping sobs, and a wail in her voice. Half the family would be asleep, she knew, and it was improbable that the others would hear her, with her face muffled in pillows. She cried on and on till she was almost sick, stopping every now and then for breath, and then breaking out again, kicking on the bed with her slippered feet, knotting her soaking handkerchief into a tight ball. She might have been a child of five sent to bed in disgrace and a temper instead of a grown-up girl of twenty-four with a bank-account and a latch-key of her own. She knew it was horribly undignified, but she cared not a scrap.

Marion had often cried quietly in her bedroom at nights.

Sometimes during the day in a crowded room the tears would well up in her eyes so that she could not trust herself to speak. She had been ashamed and irritated at that. But tonight she felt as though crying were a glorious relief, as though the loudest screaming would hardly suffice her. She could not stand life for a moment longer. "Oh I wish I was dead... I wish I was dead," she sobbed into the pillows.

Now Marion, in spite of all her faults, was no fool. She did at that moment hate Nannie and Effie intensely, but she would never have cried in this abandonment of misery because of momentary spite. She cried for an infinitely better reason, because she knew that what they said was true from beginning to end.

She knew that she was that tragic product of modern times, a woman who has lost her womanliness, and possesses nothing to put in its place. When she was a child, she had been healthy and happy enough; a little slack, perhaps, a little irritable. But people said, "Oh she's growing so fast, poor dear, she can't help being tired."

She liked to invent queer games of her own, and sit about in odd corners, or behind the bushes in their old country garden, talking away to herself. She was quite pleased when her mother gave her scraps to make a doll's dress, or the cook let her into the kitchen to bake a real cake "all her own self". But she played with the doll for exactly two days, and then the petticoat had two holes cut in it to make a highwayman's mask, and the white frock was torn up to bandage some imaginary hero's wounds; and as she ran away in the middle of the cooking, and left the cake to burn and flour all over the floor, cook said, "Never again!"

She came, too, at an odd gap in the family, Nannie and Pat had each other, and afterwards there were Effie and Jullie, and Billy the baby, whom every one spoilt.

Nannie was so much prettier that people petted her, and Pat and Effie were so much more good-natured that they were always asked to do things; and so Marion slid into the background. At school, too, she was supposed to be the clever one. Nannie and Effie were often taken away to go somewhere with their mother, but Mrs. Sutherland said, "Dear Marion mustn't be disturbed in her studies. I want her to have the best chance. She does so splendidly." So while the others were disporting themselves in the country, or their best frocks, Marion remained at home in an inky blouse, preparing for interminable examinations which she certainly always passed. She did not mind herself; indeed, she was rather proud of being so clever, as it was the only thing she had to be proud of. But she was sorry afterwards.

She stayed at school fully a year longer than any of the others; then their parents died, and money became scarce, and instead of a university career, Marion found herself obliged to learn typing, and help Uncle Alexander in the office. It seemed to her that she had left all her brains and all her energy behind her, along with her algebra book and Latin grammar. Whatever had happened to them, they were little enough use to her now.

In spite of all her learning, the others seemed to have put their girlhood to better use. Even Effie had outstripped her, had grown up before her. She and Nannie were women, fit to be the lovers and wives and mothers of men, able to carry with them the colour and variety and spirit which a womanly woman brings wherever she goes. They were far from perfect. With all her heart Marion despised Effie's shallowness and loud laughter and want of imagination, and Nannie's affected manners and flirtatiousness. But compared with them, she herself seemed a half-grown, lanky schoolgirl, with no manner and no conversation.

She had not even the consolation of the woman who poses as mannish. She had no love of games and outdoor occupations, no flamboyant independence, no rights to defend. She hated making arrangements and talking to strangers and

Nine

No rumour reaches her at all,
Beyond her safe encompassing wall,
Of a mad world that slays and slays;
She sees a little one that plays
And sleeps at even-fall.

—KATHARINE TYNAN

When Mrs. Gerard "took up" anything, she certainly threw herself into it wholeheartedly. It was as well for her poor husband that he was serving his country somewhere in England, for he might have found his home reminiscent of spring-cleaning, while preparations for the pageant were in progress.

He would have found, one afternoon in early April, a dressmaker established in his own bedroom, clicking away at a sewing-machine as though her life depended on it, surrounded by meshes of cotton thread, snippets of cloth, piles of cheap, brilliant-coloured sateen, and the contents of Mrs. Gerard's last year's wardrobe to be made over for theatrical purposes. He would have found an untidy maiden, in an artistic pinafore, encamped upon the bathroom floor, cutting stencil patterns, and oil paints freely circulating in the bath itself, where Peter, unknown to all, had spilt them some moments before.

He would have found the sanctity of his study invaded by a fat, small woman in a sealskin coat, who was Mrs. Woodward, the artist, drilling a bored young lady and a nervous young man in the mazes of an obscure country dance, which had been revived for the occasion as "perfectly ducky and so uncommon, besides being quite in keeping with the eighteenth century". He would have found a sumptuous tea spread in the dining-room for the benefit of the army of performers, helpers, sewers, and stencillers; three little people, including his son, closeted in the pantry eating up the cuttings from sandwiches, and licking the papers which had been peeled from the bottom of the cakes; and, finally, a grand rehearsal in progress in the drawing-room.

The room had been cleared, as though for a dance. Chairs were ranged along the wall, more chairs stacked by the door, the piano pushed into a corner, and all the more valuable ornaments removed out of danger's way. Even with these precautions, the thirty odd people who were trying to make room for themselves within the four walls seemed to find breathing a decided effort. Mrs. Gerard's house was not of the largest size, being situated in one of those narrow Edinburgh streets whose area stairs seem to rush precipitately into the basement windows, and whose front doors throw breathless visitors headlong into the dining-room.

In the midst of this unhappy throng, a space had been cleared by way of stage. Upon it stood a girl in a very short and scanty coat frock, her hands engulfed in a muff of huge proportions, and one eye barely visible beneath her fashionable hat, balancing herself upon one leg, and protesting at intervals, whenever she remembered the words, that she "lo'ed her Jamie weel," and would follow him to the world's end if necessity and her mother drove her to it. To her entered a young married lady, panting, and trying to get her tongue round the Doric, but in vain. After some stuttering, and a good deal of prompting from the maid of the coat frock, she uttered in one breath: "You wuthless limmah, run and bring the cattle into the shed!"

Mrs. Gerard, who had been surveying the pair critically

from a vantage point behind the piano (representing a spectator in the back gallery who requires every word to be shouted at him), danced forward at this in excitement.

"The kye, dear Daisy, the kye… into the byre!" she entreated; she called it "byah" herself.

"Sorry," panted Mrs. Jones meekly. "I never will remember."

"But it isn't time for the kye yet, anyway," objected Mrs. Gerard, very flushed. "This is the time when you… er… seize the broom… I mean the besom… no, no, it isn't that either, Mr. Grant!"

She turned in desperation towards the window seat. David Grant sat there, the prompter's book on his knees. He had sacrificed a Saturday afternoon in the interests of the pageant and Mrs. Gerard, and by this time was wishing them both far enough. The only good point about the proceedings was that they gave him an opportunity of putting his new resolutions into practice. But like most of us when the time comes, he could cheerfully have dispensed with it.

He looked up with a desperate smile. "Eh, yes, the kye do appear," he stated, sticking to truth and the book at the risk of offending Mrs. Gerard.

"Well, there's something not quite right, I'm certain," said Mrs. Gerard huffily. She had been on her feet since ten that morning, so one had to excuse her moments of irritation.

"Perhaps if Mrs.… er… were to roll her 'r's a wee bit more," suggested David, offending the other lady in her turn, "it would sound better."

He would not have dared to offer such frank criticism at the beginning of the afternoon; but by four o'clock he had a crick at the back of his neck trying to choke down his laughter, cramp in both legs by being squeezed into one immovable position by two fat ladies, and incipient rheumatism in both shoulders because of the open window above him through which the March winds were sweeping briskly, and in the circumstances he was no longer disposed to stand on ceremony.

"That's it, roll your 'r's, Daisy dear," said Mrs. Gerard encouragingly.

"Limmurrrrr," remarked the maid of the coat frock. "That way, you know."

"What is a limmer?" gasped Mrs. Daisy Jones, feeling sat upon.

"It's a... I mean... she's a... well, it's rather a vulgar expression, isn't it, Mr. Grant?" replied Mrs. Gerard, turning upon him, for the thousandth time that afternoon. David cursed himself for being Scotch.

"Oh, not so bad," he said. "Just like wench or jade, maybe."

"I thought jade was a horse," said Mrs. Jones aside to the maid of the coat frock.

At this moment, a bell clanged. "Oh, tea," cried Mrs. Gerard, looking hastily at her wristlet watch. There was a rustle of relief throughout the room. Mrs. Gerard surveyed the crowd sternly, as they were about to depart. "The procession isn't wanted," she observed, "nor the Four Maries, nor the Rob Roy people, nor Sir Walter Scott. They had better go down. Sara, darling, will you pour out, and perhaps Nannie will help you. Daisy, my dear, and Miss Rankeillor, and you, of course, Miss Buckmaster, you won't mind finishing this mother scene, will you? We've been interrupted so often." She fixed an awful eye on David, who was escaping to the dining-room under the pretence of handing round cakes.

"Mr. Grant, you surely won't desert me," she commanded. "I know from experience that it's impossible to prompt and stage manage at the same time."

David sighed, and sat down again on the window seat. There was more room to breathe now that twenty of the thirty had made their exodus.

Mrs. Gerard sighed too. She was thinking of tea and rich cream in it, but she turned sternly to business.

"Come now," she said, clapping her hands. "The mother...

Daisy, my dear! And roll your 'r's. We'll begin after the kye, please."

Mrs. Jones clasped her hands, and assumed the expression of a victim on the dentist's doorstep.

"Wuthless limmah," she began.

"Oh Daisy!" interrupted Mrs. Gerard, a world of reproach in her voice. "Show her how, Mr. Grant, please!"

David turned rather red, and addressed the maid of the coat frock in his best accent, which did credit to Jenny's training. The other ladies giggled in delight, and Mrs. Jones clasped her hands with new determination.

"Oh, but you mustn't," exclaimed Mrs. Gerard, before she had spoken a word. "You *must* seize that besom… I'm sure the br… besom comes in here, Mr. Grant. Do look at the stage directions. Eh? Well, never mind, I insist on it coming in. Take the besom, and threaten her, Daisy, threaten her! This way!" Mrs. Gerard charged down on Jamie's lover like a herd of wild cattle, but she had the misfortune to trip over the tassels of the hearthrug, which ruined the effect.

For a solid hour they drilled poor Mrs. Jones, until she began to show some glimmerings of a Scots accent and a violent temper. By that time, everyone was very hot and thirsty, and the host below was clamouring for immediate attention. Indeed, the Four Maries announced that they had all pressing engagements, and that they didn't see the use of their being present when the Queen herself was laid up. So they were suffered to depart, and David brought cups of cold tea to the artists in the drawing-room; after which the procession was called up, and the rehearsal went on without a break. It was mainly a matter of posing and effect; but everyone was required to be on the spot; and Mrs. Woodward was summoned from her dancing class, and the artistic young lady from her stencils to suggest and criticise and arrange the grouping. When the gases were lit the room became hot to suffocation, and everybody seemed to lose their tempers and their purses, and trod on other people's toes in revenge. David stood at one side, for he was needed no longer as prompter, wondering how soon he might attempt to escape. Then as the procession broke up finally, and a council was called to discuss dresses, Nannie came over to him.

"Are you going?" she asked. "I wish I could, I'm sure, but I've got to stay for another half-hour and see about the costumes for Queen Mary's court. Will you do me a favour? There are my sister-in-law Beatrice's two kiddies who were lent for the group upon strict condition that I brought them home in time for bed, and it's now half-past six. Do you think you could take them round? Oh, thanks ever so. Awfully sweet of you."

She disappeared again, to disentangle the children from little Peter Gerard, who was offering half his bed to them if only they would stay the night, and then came back, leading one by each hand.

"Here they are," she announced. "Alison and Babs, this is kind Mr. Grant who is going to take you home. That's right. For mercy's sake don't kiss me, Babs, you're all jam. Run along. Night, Mr. Grant. See you on Tuesday."

David found himself left standing in the Gerards' hall with the two children.

He looked down at them thoughtfully. The girl might have been nine or ten. She had on a bright red, warm coat, and a big black bonnet, something like the coal-scuttle her great-grandmother probably wore. Underneath the red coat the hem of her kilted green velvet dress stuck out stiffly all round, and underneath the bonnet her short dark hair curled. Her sturdy legs were in black stockings, and she carried a pair of black worsted gloves carefully in one hand. Her clothes were as gay as the holly on a Christmas card, but her round face, with the big, black eyes and gypsy colouring, was solemn. The little boy was four. He wore a grey woolly cap, a bluish-grey serge coat, and long grey gaiters over his socks and bare knees. He had sandy hair, and soft, blinking, grey eyes, which opened very wide when he was surprised or excited; and he looked a dear little rabbity person. Indeed, Babs was a contraction for rabbit, being preferred by common consent to Bunny, although he had been christened Patrick after his father.

"What quaint and delightful bairns!" thought David. "But what on earth am I to say to them?"

Alison solved the problem for him. She fixed her eyes on him, and sighed. "We are so sticky," she said. "You see, we had grown-up tea without plates – only we didn't spill – and then remains in the pantry with Peter. And no one told us where the bathroom is. And tomato sandwiches are so sticky – well, not sticky exactly, but sloshywoshy all over you. The fact is, I don't like to put on my gloves."

"Oh, I think we can mend that," said David gravely. "I believe the bathroom is along that passage. Shall I… do you wash your – er – own hands?"

"I do," said Alison proudly, "and Babs thinks he can. But the fact is, Nana always holds his sleeves back."

"Perhaps I could do it as well as Nana," suggested David, leading the way.

"Nana's had such a lot of practice," said Alison doubtfully.

In spite of her suspicions, David proved equal to the task, and when the two pairs of hands were thoroughly clean, their owners set out with him towards their home.

They walked one on each side of him, and Alison took his arm confidingly, although Babs could only reach his hand. They also thought it their duty to entertain him. Alison began the conversation with a profound remark. "Mrs. Gerard is very rich."

"Indeed," said David politely, being rather staggered.

"Yes, she's rich. When I was a little wee girl I used to think she was poor, 'cause Peter never wore stockings. But I know she's rich now. She had sandwiches, you know."

This was convincing proof, so David agreed heartily.

"Sandwiches," said Babs, speaking for the first time, with a sudden rush, "is just *lov*ully, just the crusts with bits of fishes between, fishes called anchovies, all pink, with nasty juice inside them that they squirt at other fish they don't like, that people makes into sauce. Anchovies is *lov*ully."

"He's mixed it all up," said Alison scornfully. "He had part of that read to him out of the *Green Nature Book*, the bit about the nasty juice, and Peter told us the rest just now. I don't like anchovies. I like tomato far better."

"Being out at night is *lov*ully," announced Babs. It was exactly a quarter to seven, and still twilight, but the lamps were lit. "Mr. Grant, who lights the lamps?"

"The lamplighter," said David. "Haven't you seen him often going round?"

"And who pays the lamplighter?" went on Babs. David hesitated, wondering how he could unfold the complicated system of municipal rates and taxes to an infant mind. Fortunately Babs passed on to something else without a pause. "Where does the gas come from? Who made it?"

"God, of course," struck in Alison.

David coughed instead of laughing. He had not thought of such a simple answer. "It comes in pipes," he explained, "from the gasworks."

"No, but how?" insisted Babs. "How in pipes? Does it come on wheels? Or does God send it?"

David avoided theology, and then lost himself in the mazes of natural science. He realised that he had never clearly grasped how gas does come himself. "Children do certainly enlighten you on the subject of your own ignorance," he thought.

"Tell us a story," demanded Babs.

"No, don't," said Alison. "We're nearly home, and it would spoil it to stop in the middle."

"Do you like stories?" asked David.

"I love them," said Alison. "The fact is, I can write stories myself!"

"Will you let me read some? I would love to."

"Course I will. The fact is, we have a magazine, Babs and me, and sometimes Mummie and Nana, and Auntie Marion once; and Daddie's our special correspondent at the Front. Will you join? Do join, please. We are very anxious to increase the circumstration." Alison stumbled a little over the big word, and then resumed editorial dignity. "We publish it every month, if I have time, that is. The fact is, I do lessons now, and I haven't very much. And then the Family write for it."

"The Family?" said David. "You mean all the Sutherlands?"

"No, our own family. We each have one, only Babs is rather silly 'cause he's too wee to do it properly. A make-up family, you know. And we put in all the nice people we read about in books as relations. My family is orphans, and they live with a cruel aunt. Meg and Jo and the girls in *Little Women* are their cousins, and Ivanhoe is their big brother away at the war. Sir William Wallace is a distant relation, and Moses and Aaron are their uncles. Mummie didn't want us to have Moses and Aaron 'cause they're in the Bible. Only they make such nice uncles, and we have them always in Sunday School, and it would be dull having them so much if we couldn't pretend about them."

"What a very interesting family!" remarked David. "What about Babs's?"

"Oh, Babs just has two balls that he calls Lipton and Fluffy. Mother made Fluffy out of scraps of wool. And there's his racket that he calls Mary, after Nana. I think it's silly. Only when you're wee, I suppose you must have something you can really feel to play with."

"And there's Sheepie-darling!" added Babs.

"That's our doggie," explained Alison. "He is a beautiful and pedigreed spaniel, and his proper name is Prince, only we never call him that. He's so woolly we call him the Sheep."

"Mr. Grant," said Babs suddenly. "Why are all sheep mothers?"

David broke out into a cough. But before the conversation could proceed, Alison pointed out the door of her home to him, and the three went up the common stair. Pat and Beatrice Sutherland had a top flat in a street of small, pleasant houses which looked out upon gardens. Beatrice herself opened the door to them. "It's Nana's night out," said Alison in a loud whisper. Nana was not merely nurse but maid of all work to the family, and devoted to them all. She had been with Beatrice's family for years, and had proved herself a treasure to her young lady when she married. There was a rumour that one of these days Nana intended to get married herself; indeed, it was an intention of some years' standing, but she had solemnly refused to go before the first baby, and then afterwards she couldn't bear to leave until Miss Ailie had got her teeth; and it wasn't to be thought of that having seen the first baby safely into the world she should desert the second, and no decent woman worth her salt would leave the mistress till Master Babs was into breeks. And so it went on. Whether Nana expected a third baby or not, no one knew. But Beatrice was only too glad to postpone the evil hour of her departure.

When their mother had shaken hands with David, she knelt down on the threshold, and the children ran to her and hugged her. Then she picked up Babs, and asked David if he wouldn't come in.

"You have been so kind in bringing them home," she said. "I don't know about trains, but I expect they have made you miss one. Why not wait till the next, and have some supper?"

David said he couldn't think of troubling her, and that it was quite all right about trains – which it wasn't, and made a few other nervous excuses. She would have none of it. "You mustn't think of us as being strangers," she declared, to put him at his ease. "You are quite a friend of the family now, Mr. Grant!"

David laughed. "Do you know," he said, "I think those family friends are one of the greatest nuisances invented? They are always in the way, or turn up when they're not wanted. I mustn't really earn such a bad character, Mrs. Sutherland."

"Oh, what nonsense," she cried gaily; and so without quite knowing how it happened, David found himself in the little drawing-room, with Beatrice Sutherland poking the fire into a blaze, and the children highly excited at the prospect of being allowed to stay up for supper.

David always remembered the Sutherlands' flat as a beautiful place, with a warm glow of firelight about it.

They had supper of coffee and eggs, with home-baked scones and oatcakes, and plenty of milk for the children; the big milk jug had a green parrot perched on it, whose tail did duty as handle, and Babs had a plate of his own with the story of the Three Bears depicted upon it in bright colours. The clean cloth, and bright silver made a wonderfully pretty picture in the light of the shaded electric lamp. David had forgotten that meals could be so delightful.

After supper, Beatrice looked at the two, and said "Bed!" And they looked at her, and Alison said, "Oh, Mummie!" and Babs said, "Stories!"

Their mother laughed. "I am not the mistress of this household," she said to David. "They always insist on stories, only tonight I thought they would be tired out. Do you mind? It won't take long. Perhaps you would like one of Pat's cigarettes to pass the time?"

She held out the box to him, and David sat down by the window to watch and listen. Beatrice pulled in a chair, and Alison set herself in a bunch on one arm, while Babs wormed his way onto his mother's lap between her breast and the book. It was the story of *Thomas the Rhymer* that she read to them, in a pleasant, even voice, pitched rather low;

the story of True Thomas who went to Fairyland for seven years, though it seemed one night to him, and saw the Fairy Queen, and came back to earth, having looked on strange things, with the gift of prophecy and the power to tell no lie. As she read, the light of the spring twilight faded into green, and the stars came out. David's cigarette made one spark of brightness in the gloaming, and the shadows of the three by the fire loomed huge against the opposite wall. He watched them, a little cold over by the window, and fancied that a spell had fallen about them, a kindly firelight spell wherein they sat secure from harm, and very happy.

Then the story finished, and Alison asked complainingly: "Is that the very end? But what did really happen to Thomas when he disappeared?" And Babs demanded with a child's terrifying suddenness and irrelevancy, "Mummie, what's cheese made of?"

The spell broke; Beatrice rose, and stretched out her arms, laughing, "You have had too much supper, Bunny boy, I'm afraid," she said. "Come, away you go, or you'll miss the boat to Dreamland!"

And she swept them out of the room, when they had both said good night, as politely as drowsiness would permit. The last thing that David heard was Babs's voice, heavy with yawns: "Is there really a boat, Mummie? What's it made of?"

He laughed softly to himself.

Beatrice was back in a moment. "I set them to wash their faces, which they can do perfectly well when they please," she said. "I'm afraid you will think I have neglected you."

David crossed to the door. "I think I have been very much in your way," he said. "It has been so good of you to let me stay, Mrs. Sutherland. I'm sure I have enjoyed the story as much as either of them."

"*Thomas* is one of my old favourites," said Beatrice. "But if you knew the business I have to keep myself in fresh ones! There's one good thing, I can always fall back on the *Arabian*

Nights which they adore – the too gruesome bits left out, of course."

David looked at her as she spoke. She was wearing a dark brown dress of some soft silky material which matched the brown of her hair and eyes. There was a steady, bright gladness about her, a confidence in herself which gave her dignity. She seemed well content with her life, well fitted for her work, a strong radiant woman; and yet there was that shadow in her eyes which had been in Alicia's, and David honoured her the more because of it. She gave him her hand, and he thanked her again; and then went down the stair into the streets.

Ten

What shall Cordelia do?
Love, and be silent.

—KING LEAR

The pageant was a distinct success. David hired one of the large Edinburgh halls, and saw that the thing was well advertised. He gave himself endless worry about the tickets and arrangement of seats, and spent two precious afternoons at the dress rehearsals. Finally, he agreed to act as prompter on the day itself; and altogether Mrs. Gerard, who by this time was thoroughly sick of the affair which she had undertaken so gaily, and had resolved that such an event should never happen again, confided to Nannie with truth that she "didn't know what they should ever have done if it hadn't been for that obliging Mr. Grant".

She never guessed that the obliging Mr. Grant was sicker of the business than she herself, and that he considered it excellent discipline for his character.

Nannie's triumph was not quite so brilliant as she had hoped; nevertheless she had her share of the glory. She was not cast for Mary of Scots, and spent a good deal of breath at mealtimes telling her family what a plain person had been selected for that rôle, how wooden her acting was, and how her voice sounded like a cockney costermonger's wife. Nannie herself received the rather minor part of Flora Macdonald; still, she made the most of it, and had a touching passage with the Prince which was quite impromptu, and designed to display her fair neck and languishing glances with better effect; but which, as it was entirely unplanned and unexpected, considerably flurried Mrs. Gerard and David in the wings, and upset the Prince himself more than anyone else on the stage. Her cup was filled to overflowing, however, at the end of the performance. There was a call for the originators and managers of the piece, and loud applause from the audience. Mrs. Gerard preened herself hastily, and dabbed some powder on her hot cheeks.

"Mr. Grant, you must lead me on," she insisted in a loud undertone. David shook his head, and turned redder, if that were possible, than he already was. The calls were repeated. "Someone said there were charming flowers," continued Mrs. Gerard, extending her hand with a stagey air. David saw there was no hope, and no time to waste; so he took the tips of her fingers gingerly, as he was evidently expected to do. "And Nannie, of course," cried Mrs. Gerard excitedly. "Come on, dear. You've been as much at the bottom of this as me. Take his other hand. Now!"

David had never appeared on a public platform before in his life. Dazzled with the lights, he groped his way before the curtain, a lady on each arm, feeling as if he were in the crisis of an appalling nightmare, and must wake up at any moment.

The audience applauded vehemently. Cheers were heard from an admirer at the very back of the gallery. Then someone handed up an expensive bouquet, which David had the presence of mind to catch and pass to Mrs. Gerard with a bow. And someone else – it was Noël – handed up an enormous box of chocolates, tied with a flaunting bow, which he presented to Nannie.

Mrs. Gerard bowed and smiled and fluttered like the Queen – or a jack-in-the-box. Nannie stared into space, with would-be dignity, and what she hoped was a superior smile. David saw nothing but a glare, and felt the biggest fool in the United Kingdom. Then in a moment, they were behind the curtain again, and Mrs. Gerard refreshed herself with eau-de-Cologne, and Nannie requested David graciously to see if her cab had come, apparently oblivious to the thousand other duties which he had to perform. She was going to get the most out of this hour.

So far, her wishes were certainly fulfilled. He escorted her to the door of the hall, called a policeman to see to the cab, and held up an umbrella over her uncovered hair, for it was pouring rain. That was all very well, and plenty of people looked at her waiting there, and she saw smiles, and heard them speak her name – and doubtless his too; and probably they thought how handsome he was, and how sad it was that such a young man should be so lame; and they would assuredly tell each other his story – or invent it, which came to the same thing. They might even cast the glamour of a V.C. over him, and the reflected glory would be hers. As a matter of fact, Nannie's hair was on the point of coming down, and she looked like an actress who had seen better days, having only partially washed off her make-up; and David's hair was wet on his forehead and trickling cold drops down his burning cheeks. So it is to be doubted whether the pretty picture which she conjured up for herself had the slightest correspondence to truth. Even if it had, the romance was soon dispelled.

David caught sight of Marion and Jullie, who were wet and draggled, and searching for their distinguished sister. With hardly a word of excuse – thus Nannie, communing with her outraged feelings – he thrust the umbrella into her already full hands, and returning to the vestibule for another, he hastened with it to meet the pair. Nannie stood like a statue, her evening cloak trailing in the mud, as she afterwards discovered, although she could hardly blame David for that, wondering if anyone had ever been so insulted. She called to him, but he was so occupied in piloting these children through the crowd, and holding the umbrella over their shabby hats, which mattered nothing to anybody, that he did not hear her. He actually had the cheek to place them in the cab first when it did arrive, and never thought of apologising for his misconduct when they parted.

Nannie did not care to remember how prettily Marion had smiled while she was sharing David's umbrella. She contented herself with calling him boorish and rude, and hugging Noël's box of chocolates. For the past month, she had deluded herself into believing that David had fallen before her charms, that his wholehearted zeal anent the pageant was on her account, that his nervousness hid deeper and more interesting feelings. And now in one moment, being very tired and excited, she had arrived by the most approved logical method at the conclusion that he cared no more about her than about Marion, forsooth, which as it happened was true. And the little affair which she had planned so carefully fell to pieces, and left her in a very bad temper.

She sat in aggrieved silence all the way home, while Jullie talked like a mechanical doll wound up, only with more vivacity.

"It really wasn't bad," she said condescendingly. "The play was pretty putrid, but the dresses were top-hole. The conceit of you coming before the curtain, Nan! You've done nothing but dance around after Mr. Grant, while he did the work. He must be glad it's all over. He's a decent sort, if he wasn't so reserved. You do look an owl with that paint all over you! Wasn't it a rag, Noël getting these chocs! They're fearfully dear I know. He told us he was going to beforehand. I put him up to the kind I like best – almonds, you know, and hard toffees that you can suck."

"You brat," said Nannie. "I hate almonds, and anything hard."

"Well, you can hand them over to me, which was what I intended," laughed Jullie.

Nannie swallowed this in silence. She gathered up the hem of her pale blue cloak, and tried to wipe the mud off with her frill of a handkerchief. "Just look at this," she broke out at length, as the cab drew up at their own door. "It'll never come out. I can't possibly afford to send it to be cleaned. It was the coolest thing I ever saw, David Grant running off that way and leaving me in all the mud and rain, when he knew I had on things to spoil."

"You don't need to snap our heads off," remarked Jullie, as they went into the house.

"Well, why didn't you bring your own umbrellas?" demanded Nannie.

"Oh, it wasn't for that…" began Marion in explanation.

"Oh, it wasn't?" cried Nannie, turning in the dark little hall with a gesture which would have suited Flora Macdonald. "The superior attraction, I suppose! I see. Yes, I remember you said you got on together so well that night when I was out of the way. Who's carrying on now? Don't you talk to me again about flirting. And before all the people, too!"

The tears darted suddenly to Marion's eyes. "How dare you say such a thing," she burst out. "You are an unfair little cat, Nannie! I was going to have said, he came to show us to your cab, but you never let anyone else get a single word in except yourself! As if I would dream of carrying on the way you do! And Mr. Grant's far too nice to think of such a thing."

"Ah, it's coming out now," teased Nannie. "You looked as if you thought he was very nice when you were under his umbrella."

"Oh, shut up! You simply won't understand a single thing I say. Or rather you don't want to understand. You try not to," cried Marion, with a sob in her voice. "I don't see how you have the face to talk that way after making yourself a public disgrace for the last three weeks!"

She fled up the stairs before them all, and Nannie let her pass with an angry shrug of her shoulders.

It was a good thing for Marion in her frequent times of violent grief, and more continuous fits of depression, that she had a room to herself. She had declined to share one with any of the others, and the others cordially refused to have her as roommate; so the arrangement suited both parties. It was a dark room, looking out to the back, and the carpet, curtains, and paper were of a nondescript washed out appearance. It had one advantage, a gas fire, which Marion lit when she was feeling cheerful, sitting down beside it on the worn hearthrug. When she was unhappy, on the other hand, she perched herself on a large hassock in the window recess, her chin touching the sill, and her brow pressed against the pane, and looked down upon the damp squares of back green, which ran in a monotonous row behind the houses. When she was utterly miserable, she would lie face downwards on her bed.

On this occasion, she sought her bed; but she did not cry. She was too startled to cry. For Nannie's taunts had laid bare in her heart a feeling of which she had barely been conscious herself, and she realised now that she had liked David Grant very much.

He had been such a comfortable person to get on with, for one thing; he did not talk too much, and her own family possessed tongues of exceptional length. And he was not in khaki; and Marion was sick of khaki. She knew that was a very dreadful and unpatriotic thing to say, but she couldn't help it. She knew of no valid reason why khaki should cover a multitude of sins – or inanities; and the officers who composed the circle of Nannie and Effie's acquaintance had caused her to conceive the greatest repugnance for the entire British army.

But there was something more than a negative reason, something in himself which she knew had attracted her.

For want of a better way of expressing that something, she told herself it was because he was such a thorough gentleman. But she did not mean that she liked him because, for instance, he always opened the door for her, or because his trousers were immaculately creased – as a matter of fact, they were not.

Marion was a very critical person at all times, and especially with men. Being perfectly assured in her mind that no man, in the capacity of a lover at least, would ever dream of paying her the slightest attention, and relieved by Nannie and Effie of the responsibility of being pleasant, she could sit quietly in her own corner, and pass the severest of judgments at her pleasure; and most of the men who came to the Sutherlands' house and smiled patronisingly at the dumb little girl with the white face as they would have smiled at a child, would have been thoroughly astonished if they had known that the said little girl was weighing them in her balance the while, and finding them wanting.

She divided them into classes, and labelled each appropriately when she had taken his measure. A very limited section she dubbed Bounders, without hesitation; the Selfish Lumps and the Silly Asses were equally numerous; they were the commonest in her collection, but she extended a like scorn to the Nice Boys, and to the Dear Old Things – friends of Uncle Alexander, for the most part. The Bounders were too objectionable, and the Dear Old Things too harmless for consideration; the Selfish Lumps were the sort that sat solid in their comfortable chairs and let you pass them tea, hardly tearing themselves away from Nannie's conversation to thank you; the Silly Asses went to the other extreme and were positively effusive, attempting either to be funny, or to be sentimental, which was worse; and the Nice Boys were foolish beyond expression.

Her brother Pat alone was an exception, and him she considered a good sort in every way. Now had come David Grant to be classified, and Marion started, half uneasily, to find that without realising it she had set him apart in a class entirely by himself.

In a sense, he had no manners at all, being nervous; in another sense, he had the nicest manners of any man she knew. It was because he possessed that rare thing, reverence for other people and for himself.

A frequent boast of today is that free camaraderie between man and girl, old and young; a bright breezy manner is made a virtue, and men and women like to hustle along with a good deal of advertisement. And then they wonder that their lives are shallow and little, and empty of originality. They would do well to have more quiet spaces for thought in their spirits, more leisure in the things of love and friendship, more graciousness and less haste.

There is a look which you often see in a shy person's eyes, a look which warms your heart, entreating you to make him your friend, promising you that there are many fair things in his heart which you shall discover little by little and delight in, if you do but deal courteously with him as he with you. And you may be sure that in such a friendship there will be no rough familiarity, but a strong and kind reverence.

This Marion had seen in David's eyes, and it was this which attracted her. She trusted him, and thought how wonderfully pleasant it would be if they should come to know each other better.

Of falling in love she had not so much as dreamed. She had seen Nannie fall in love several times within the year, and Effie rather less often. Marion was in bitter rebellion against all the things they delighted in and talked about; dance partners, tennis partners, officers, presents, kisses, other people's weddings and quarrels. The very idea of associating such vulgar rubbish with herself and David Grant made her blood boil furiously hot all through her body.

Now Nannie had associated them, and her friendship, the one interesting friendship she had made, was spoilt for good.

The thoughts which had so pleased her before sickened her now. "Perhaps it looked like that," she kept on saying, "perhaps other people thought the same as Nannie." She could never look him in the face again.

There is nothing more bitter than to have the sweetness of a friendship turned sour by a few interfering words, or the jests of thoughtless outsiders. The harm is done in a few moments, and yet things can never be the same again. Or so it seemed to Marion. She sat silently on the edge of her bed, growing angrier and angrier with Nannie, and sorer and sorer of heart. "She has enough fun... she might have left me that little bit of enjoyment without getting jealous," she thought. "It's not fair. Nothing is fair." Her anger roused all the spirit in her, so that she clenched her hands, and cried, "I have a right to be friends with anyone I like. They can say what they please."

For a little while she felt bold enough to face it out, and give Nannie a lesson. Then that strange weakness in the heart of her conquered, and the dreariness and bareness of her life crept up about her like a sullen sea. And she covered her face with her hands, and wished herself dead. It was her favourite wish.

Eleven

D avid was at his second cup of sugarless tea some mornings later when Jenny brought in his letters and the paper. She always scrutinised carefully the writing on the envelopes before she opened the dining-room door, although she never read the postcards. Today there was a strange handwriting which puzzled her – a lady's, bold and pretty.

He glanced through the paper first, frowned over some bad news – British repulses on the Western Front, more treachery in Russia, heavy shipping losses for the week; then threw it down, and turned to his correspondence. Most of his business letters went to the office, but there was one with typed direction and formal air, one receipted account, an advertisement for garden seeds, and the lady's communication which perplexed David as much as it had Jenny.

He tore it open, and found that the mysterious writer was Effie Sutherland. The letter matched the writing and the writer; it was breezy and hearty, one that she might have written to her brother, and it took David's breath away for a moment.

"We shall be so glad," Effie had written, "if you can come down on Saturday evening at eight for a little dance; just ourselves, you know, and quite informal. So sorry to give such short notice, but we had to keep Mr. Wyndham's arrangements in view, and he wasn't sure till the last moment whether he would be able to stay so long. Perhaps you won't care to dance, but in any case, I dare say we could make four for bridge, and there's always the supper which I'm afraid will be meagre, and strictly in accordance with war economy. Anyway we will be delighted to see you." She misspelt a few words, and signed herself always his very sincerely.

David leant back in his chair and pondered this invitation. Of course, he wouldn't go; to begin with, he could not dance. Cousin Jessie had included such entertainment, along with the theatre, under her anathema, and he had almost forgotten the few steps his cousins had ever taught him. As for sitting out with some second edition of Nannie, and talking to her in solid lumps, the bare idea turned him cold. It was quite impossible that he should go. He would get Ross to invite him down for the evening, and then plead another engagement – perfectly simple. He wondered very much, all the same, why they had asked him.

"Is Nannie at the back of it?" he mused. "Hardly, since her ladyship is pleased to be huffy with me nowadays since that ghastly pageant." He found himself wondering whether "she" danced; Marion was already "she" in his mind. He half regretted that he was not going; he would like to have seen her. He began to picture what she would wear; it was an age untold since he had seen women in evening gowns, and a "party frock" had always had a sort of mystical fascination for him, as a thing belonging to another world than his. Cousin Jessie had never the money to spend on such unnecessary and trivial things, and Minnie hated frills. He remembered Alicia in a certain lavender frock; the skirts had swished softly when she passed…

Suddenly his resolution rose up and reproached him. "You fool, man," it said, "running away from a few girls!"

David folded Effie's letter, and smiled grimly to himself. "I'll go," he decided. "I'll make my social debut, and do it in style."

Jenny regarded the whole affair with disapproval. She came into the hall on Saturday evening as he was getting into his overcoat, and held up hands of dismay.

"Lovanendie, Mr. Davie! What for did ye grease yer bonnie hair?" she groaned. "Ye're no yersel ava' in thae braws. Ye're ower sleek."

David, however, was reassured by her remarks, which he took as a sign that the efforts spent over his toilet had not been in vain. Nevertheless, he arrived at the Sutherlands' in fear and trembling a little after the appointed hour, and he was still tugging viciously at his very new and tight gloves as he entered the drawing-room. He was convinced that he was later than anyone else; that his tie was crooked, that his hair had reverted to its habitual untidiness, that his evening clothes, which he had not worn for two years, were hanging on him in disreputable looseness.

It in no way lessened his discomfort to receive a frigid stare from Nannie, and the tips of her fingers by way of a handshake. It occurred to him that there might be something radically wrong with his get-up and he glanced nervously round at the other men, which did not help him much as they were all in khaki. But when he found himself in Marion's company and received an even colder glance, and an unspeakably limp hand in greeting, his nerves were completely upset, and he looked quickly down at his feet wondering for a dreadful moment if he had forgotten to take off his overshoes.

He did not know that he was the most unwelcome of guests.

Effie had arranged the whole affair herself, and in simple good-heartedness had sent invitations to a select few whom she considered established friends of the family. When it transpired that she had asked David Grant there was a small explosion.

"You've spoilt the whole thing," said Nannie crossly. "He's a rude beast, and I have no desire to pursue his acquaintance. And when the whole idea of the dance was for Noël, to go and ask him! I know Noël hates him ever since I teased him so that night. Effie Sutherland, you are a great fool!"

Effie turned beet-red, and became much confused. She had meant no harm at all, but she saw that Nannie's frame of mind was entirely changed. "You're a little turncoat," she said vexatiously. "You couldn't hear enough of David Grant the other day. What's gone and upset you? You must just make the best of it now, for he is asked."

Nannie tossed her head. "I'll do just what I like about it," she said defiantly, and added to herself, "Seeing he must come he shall jolly well be paid out, and it won't be difficult to do, either." And she laughed.

Marion said nothing, but bit her lip. For an entirely different reason she was angry with Effie for asking David. She never wished him to come near the house again. She could think of nothing but Nannie's hateful words and her spoilt friendship.

"Why didn't you consult us before you wrote?" she asked at length, and Nannie took up the tale. "Yes, why on earth didn't you?" she echoed.

At that, Effie lost her temper. "Well, if that isn't the limit," she cried. "After me nagging and worrying at you two for the past week to take some interest in the dance, and discuss arrangements properly. And you wouldn't. Marion said it was silly rot and she hadn't time, and Nannie, of course, hadn't a moment. And you said, do it yourself, and don't worry us. I suppose you'd like to cook the supper yourselves, too, and polish the drawing-room floor, and turn the rest of the place upside down to have it decent, and lug chairs from every part of the house till your backs were fit to break. And you'd rather I didn't interfere at all. Wouldn't you?"

So she had marched out of the room, and left them.

It was she alone, very high of colour and hot, her long gloves crumpled already and her ankles twisting every moment as she rushed about in perilously high-heeled shoes, who gave David a bright smile, and a hasty but gay greeting which restored his disordered reason for the time. He stood just within the door, surveying the field of battle, as it were, and wondering where his society manner had disappeared to.

On a man naturally reserved and shy, the mere sight of a number of people has a paralysing effect; tortoise-like, he withdraws into himself, and his ordinary human instincts for conversation and laughter are dried up at their sources. David experienced this peculiar sense of atrophy – for by no means the first time in his life. He remained where he was for a few moments, feeling that the Sutherlands' insignificant drawing-room had become unaccountably large. At the other end of the room, he spied Beatrice in a wine-coloured dress, surrounded by a laughing group. Noël Wyndham was lounging against the mantelpiece, chaffing Jullie, while Billy unobserved in a corner was experimenting in a series of slides on the polish of the floor.

As to the dresses, disillusionment came to David with increasing self-possession; and he realised with regret that girls could be very commonplace, and that vulgar women were never so vulgar as in evening frocks. It was a pitiful thing to realise, when all through the mud and ugliness of war the remembrance of Alicia in her lavender silk had been to him a symbol of home and graciousness.

Marion, he noticed, was in plain white; but it was refreshing to look at her in the midst of that crowd of bright colours ill-assorted with the wearers' complexions, of cheap fur trimmings, and gaudy sequins. David's musings were interrupted by the sound of the piano, and the appearance of Jullie before him. She wore a large pink bow on the top of her head, and exhibited a length of pink silk stocking beneath her short skirts. Her eyes danced invitingly.

"Foxtrot, Mr. Grant?" she inquired. It was obviously his part to ask the question, but all things are forgiven unto the flapper.

"Awfully sorry," he replied, thinking how abominably overdressed she was for sixteen.

"Never mind, you'll soon pick it up." Jullie extended her arms with the air of one who takes no excuse, and David, cursing his fate, had perforce to submit. "This way," she said encouragingly, like a mother over her baby's first steps. "No, the other foot… now, one two, one two… oh heavens, you're all out of time… listen to the music. Now watch Noël; see how he swings her round? That's what you've got to do to me. Go on."

David, with an envious scowl at Lieutenant Wyndham, obeyed. The result was not happy. "Confoundedly sorry," he gasped to two outraged couples.

"Never mind them," said his Amazon callously. "Come on… backwards, now. There's heaps more steps I want to show you. Topping one the girl does in *Waggle Waggle!* Seen it? First-class show. No? Well, have you seen *The Powder Monkey*? No? I say, *do* you ever go to the theatre… ahhh… that really was *their* fault this time, but how you squeezed my foot!"

They brought up near the door with a final wild pirouette.

"Thanks muchly," said Jullie condescendingly.

"Mine was the pleasure. Don't mention it. Dances are so simple and informal nowadays… can do pretty much what you like without being thought a fool," replied David with rather breathless irony.

"Oh, of course," she agreed, failing so obviously to see the sarcasm that David could hardly help laughing; she was just a kid after all in spite of her airs, and a jolly kid, too. Nannie, passing just then, fancied that he was enjoying himself; and she frowned because he was not being paid out as she had intended.

David turned towards the stairs, and offered his arm.

Jullie waved him aside. "Oh, don't bother getting me an ice," she said. "There's only enough for two each, and I want to save up till after the reels. Go and have some fizz yourself, though. I must grab that boy there… he promised to do the Boston…" So she left him.

It is fairly certain, considering the dress she was wearing, that Nannie did not of set purpose request Billy, at the supper table, to sweep a plate of wartime trifle and a flower vase into her lap, as he leant across to seize the dish of oranges. But in spite of the confusion, she remained fully alive to her opportunities.

Noël had taken her down to supper, and was standing at her side talking to Marion's partner; on her other side stood David, supplying Effie with lemonade. When the catastrophe happened, Nannie pushed back her chair and drew in her skirts, saying nothing. David noticed it first; and immediately he went down on his knees beside her, picking up the sticky spoon and fork, and collecting the oozy fragments of trifle into the plate. Then he caught a napkin from the table, and began to mop up the jam and cream and custard which were trickling down Nannie's pale blue charmeuse with ruinous effect.

But she gave him no time to repair the damage. Rising to her feet quickly, she pulled her dress from under his very hands, and half turning her back on him, she called impatiently: "Here, Noël, help me, for goodness' sake! See what a mess that disgusting kid has made. Do bring a serviette." It was the snub direct, a piece of deliberate rudeness, and she could not have done it if many people had been watching. But Nannie took care to manage the whole business so swiftly that only two others noticed what happened.

David got to his feet flushing angrily. He knew very well that she had done it on purpose, and though he cared as little for Nannie's insults as for her attentions, he felt the rebuff almost like a slap on the face. By this time Nannie had gathered a crowd of assistants round her, and the excitement was great. No one noticed him, except Effie, who was one of those other two who saw. She was furious with Nannie, but the thing which seemed to her of most urgency was the mess which she would have to clear up. She darted into the pantry, and came running back with a dish-cloth and a piece of rag; and while the others fussed over Nannie's frock, she cleared away the debris, and swept together the fragments of the vase.

It was then that David realised that a move had been made towards the door while he still stood there stupidly, and that people were looking at him. He grew a shade redder, and made haste to follow his partner. Suddenly he saw that Marion had noticed it all too. She was standing apart near the door, her hands at her sides, her eyes upon him. They met his for one minute, and he felt at once that he had surprised that look, and that she would never have dared to give it if she had thought he was observing her. It was a look not of curiosity nor amusement, but of understanding more complete and tender than anyone had given him in his life; and it thrilled him as the hope of spring had thrilled him in his Castlerig garden.

Supper was followed by a reel, which David danced with Effie; and when it was over, she sent him downstairs to search for her fan, which she declared she had dropped in the confusion of Nannie's accident. Meeting with no success in the dining-room, David stumbled heedlessly into the little back parlour, imagining it to be empty; and so it was that he came face to face with Marion again.

She was sitting by the hearth where the remaining embers of a fire were dying out; her white frock had become very crushed, and there was an ugly, irregular tear down the front breadth. It could not have been in a more obvious place. When David came in, she smoothed down the torn edges and sprang up. "Oh, I didn't know…" she began awkwardly, "I didn't think anyone was coming in here."

She was evidently upset. David smiled his quick smile, "My fault," he said. "Look here… can I do anything for you. Miss Sutherland?"

She glanced at the tear. "Such a nuisance," she said wearily, "I did it on a nail in the pantry when I was helping Effie clear up that mess."

"Oh, hard lines!" David bent and examined it. "What about pins?" he suggested with manlike vagueness.

She shook her head. "It would show too awfully. It's the very front."

"I see; that's a bore." He tried clumsily to fit the torn edges together, and the muslin felt wonderfully soft to his touch. As he did so, their two heads came very close; then, he felt Marion draw herself away, and he too stepped back. She looked pitifully tired; evidently she was not enjoying herself, and he fancied that she had been crying.

"Can't I get you something?" he said persuasively. "Lemonade…?"

"It would make me sick," she said shortly.

"Well, coffee, then."

"No, please. I don't want it."

David saw that for some reason or other she was trying to treat him stiffly; perhaps it was because of that look of hers which he had surprised. But she was plainly longing for something hot and comforting.

"Black or white?" he asked, smiling.

She yielded. "White… please," she said, and sat down again by the fire.

He returned shortly from the dining-room, with a cup of steaming coffee in one hand, and a plate of cakes in the other. She took the coffee and drank it eagerly.

David stood before the fire, watching her. "I'm afraid you're tired," he said gently. "You've been dancing too much."

"No I haven't," she contradicted. "Only about half the time. I… hate dancing." What she wanted to say was, "Please go away and leave me alone." Nannie's taunt about flirting rang in her ears, and she kept glancing nervously towards the door. "If any of them were to barge in just now," she kept thinking, "I'd never hear the end of it. Oh, why will people always think you want to be sloppy? Nannie's just spoilt things for me…"

David, having no idea of what was passing in her mind, racked his brains for the reason behind her coldness. But oddly enough, he did not feel repelled; rather his determination was roused. Two women were not going to make a fool of him in one evening. At all costs he must get her to smile, to look again as she had looked in the dining-room. What had happened to her? Had he said or done anything?

"You haven't had a cake," he said, offering her the plate. "I'd recommend that white sugary one. Won't you? Or the jam sandwich? I never can make up my mind which to take. When we were kids, I remember my sister and I always used to halve our cakes so that each could taste a bit of the other's. It wasn't such a bad scheme, but not exactly popular with our elderly aunts when they had us out to tea. There was one trying occasion when Min – my sister – shouted at me across a crowded drawing-room 'Sneak! You've sucked all the cream out of my bit as well as your own!'"

Marion hardly smiled, but she took the sugary cake.

"Had you just the one sister?" she asked after a moment.

David took heart of grace. "Actually said something on her own initiative," he marvelled; "we're coming on." Aloud he answered, "Yes, we were twins, and that was all the family.

Nice and compact! I think you score with a larger number."

"I don't," said Marion with decision. "I always wanted to be an only." She had finished the coffee, and seemed to be forgetting her diffidence.

"It's becoming interesting," thought David. But her next speech was like a douche of cold water; she had heard steps outside.

"I think we'd better go back to the drawing-room," she said, getting up quickly.

"If you think so," said David regretfully, opening the door for her. "May I have the next? It'll probably be something I can't dance, but never mind."

She did not respond to his smile. "I told you I hated dancing," she said almost crossly. "Besides, I can't come in again tonight with this." She crumpled the torn breadth of her frock with nervous fingers. "I meant… you go back, Mr. Grant." She was on tenterhooks to get away, but after all, it was too late.

As they came out of the parlour, Nannie and her latest partner sailed across the hall towards the dining-room. The situation was obvious; David held the empty coffee cup and the depleted plate of cakes as incriminating evidence. He had no idea of the significance of it all, but he saw Nannie raise her eyebrows with amusement and her partner turn his head, and Marion by his side flush crimson, and he guessed at something, and lied compassionately, trusting that Nannie could not see that the cup *was* empty.

"Wonder where my partner has removed herself to," he remarked in a distinct tone to Marion. "I was sure I left her in there. This coffee will be cold." The door closed behind Nannie and her cavalier. Marion looked at David and he coloured as she did; they were conspirators together.

Then: "*That* wouldn't take her in," murmured Marion bitterly, and fled upstairs. And David felt snubbed for the second time that evening.

He went home a confirmed misogynist. "What a fool I am," he taunted himself. "I'd better stick to solitude. Social successes are born, not made, evidently. I wonder what I looked like grovelling about among the custard… touching picture of a Young Man in Search of the Fuller Life!"

He laughed in spite of himself. Yet Marion was not a laughing matter. What had happened to her? Was she ashamed to be seen with him, he wondered? Quite clearly she loathed him; he went over his besetting vices and tried to decide which was responsible.

And yet, that look of hers… no, he was doing her injustice. She had had sympathy for him. In that moment, at least, she understood.

What wonderful eyes she had when she looked like that; there was a calm in them that was not in Effie's, and they shone like the lamps in the home of a man's soul. If she would only always look like that he knew that people would call her beautiful. He saw them again in the dark of the country night, as he walked up the brae. He came to the gate and stood awhile beside it, his hand on the bars. It was a windy night, with hardly any stars out, but he felt it very pleasant to stand alone there among the sleeping garden trees.

He thought still of Marion; and as he thought, he grew angry with her – angry, for her own sake. It seemed to him a shame that she should be content to let people think her listless and commonplace when there was beauty hidden in her all the time. Of course, her family were to blame; but had no one found it out before? Had no one seen what was in her heart? Perhaps she had let no one see.

He felt like a man who has made a great discovery, and wishes the glory of this hitherto secret and undreamt-of thing to be revealed to all the world. It hurt him to think that she was missing the admiration and the reverence which was due to her real, hidden self. It was as though he had found the woman he loved masquerading in a beggar's rags.

The woman he loved? After all, he had nothing to do with Marion Sutherland, and she had nothing to do with him. Or had she? David did not stop to define his feelings; at that moment they would not allow of definition. He went into the silent house, and shut the door behind him.

Twelve

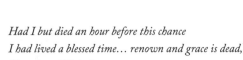

Had I but died an hour before this chance
I had lived a blessed time… renown and grace is dead,
The wine of life is drawn.

—MACBETH

E ffie had completed her winter's course at Atholl
Crescent by the end of March; and so far, she had not
seen her way to take it up again. Nannie had been so
engaged with the pageant that she was not to be depended
upon at any time, Jullie was working extra hard in preparation
for her examination, Marion was at her usual, and it seemed
impossible to get a suitable maid. Effie had haunted registries,
and wasted her substance in advertisements; and as a result,
they had been blessed for one weekend with a cook who
disappeared early on Monday morning taking a good part of
the family rations with her, and a general servant who stayed
on sufferance from the Monday to the following Friday, and
then produced an inconvenient mother in the clutches of
pneumonia, and left forthwith. After that, Effie decided to
take the whole responsibility herself, and she did not feel
equal to strenuous days of cooking and laundry training in
addition.

So Atholl Crescent was dropped, never, as it happened, to
be resumed; and Effie devoted her time to making the family
machinery run rather more smoothly than it had done for
many months.

Then there came a day when Effie decided to take an

afternoon off. She said so at the breakfast table, because Uncle Alexander happened to announce to Marion that he wouldn't need her in the office after one o'clock. He shook his head very solemnly, and said business was drying up, and soon would reach the invisible stage.

"Oh!" said Effie suddenly, setting down her cup.

"Burnt your tongue?" inquired Jullie.

"Shall I slap your back?" suggested Billy hopefully.

"Just shut up, and oblige yours truly," said Effie quickly, but not crossly. "No, I was thinking… Marion, are you wanting to do anything special?"

Marion shook her head.

"Well, I did want to go out to Craigleith, to see that poor chap in hospital," said Effie. "Bob Trotter, you know, that Daisy wrote me about. He isn't walking yet, so I wouldn't stay long. But I might manage to look in and see him if I ran off immediately after lunch, and got the one-fifteen. Then I would be back for half-past four tea. It'll be a bit of a jaunt, and I think I deserve it." Effie was not troubled with false modesty. "I haven't seen a shop window except the butcher's for a good fortnight, let alone a railway."

"All right," said Marion. "I don't mind."

"I'll be out anyway," remarked Nannie, looking up from her large correspondence. "Mrs. Gerard's organised a joy-ride for some wounded men, and she's been lucky enough to get the loan of a friend's motor, that is a doctor and has simply heaps of petrol in his garage, and she wants me to come and help things along."

"Oh you lucky dog!" said Jullie enviously.

"Well, I'll fly round and get most things done before lunch," continued Effie. "I'll make an Uncle Tom, and he can simmer all afternoon, if you'll just keep an eye on him, Marion; and the meat's in the casserole, and has just to be heated up for night."

"All right," said Marion again.

True to her word, Effie "flew round", but she possessed only the usual number of hands, and her time was limited.

"You'll need to wash up," she said to Marion. "I've simply got to fly. What a pity I didn't manage the baking."

"I'll bake," said Marion, rather unexpectedly.

"Will you?" said Effie, staring at her. "Can you now? You'll be awfully out of the way of it?"

"It'll be practice for me," said Marion, in a tone which surprised Effie. "I can't go wrong with *Tried Favourites* to refer to, so long as you've marked which bag is soda and which cream of tartar distinctly."

"Very well," said Effie, much relieved. "Take the pound of flour in the crock. Make white scones, drop scones, and oatcakes if you've time. I thought of a plain gingerbread, but maybe you won't feel equal to that. Anyway, there's a bit of lunch cake in the press."

Marion looked defiance at her. "I feel quite equal to a gingerbread," she retorted. "I never understood that there was anything so immensely difficult about baking for people of ordinary intelligence."

Effie hurried off, quite uncrushed by this sarcasm, caught up her best white gloves and bag, and ran for the train. She marvelled at Marion's changed mood as she went, but felt no further disturbance.

Marion watched her go from the dining-room window, then turned to clear the lunch table. She made an auspicious beginning by letting the dishful of remains of shepherd's pie slide to the floor, the spoon and fork clattering out of it on their own account, and gravy and potato strewing the carpet. Then she mopped up the mess with the nearest towel, which happened to be a china cloth. And at that moment Nannie called her to come and fasten some ungetatable buttons, and after that, Jullie engaged her in a frantic search for a shorthand book which must be found before she left at two, or there would be the dickens to pay – Jullie's own expression.

When all these disturbances were overpast, Marion stood alone in the silent house and rubbed her eyes. She looked at the sticky, crumby lunch table, and thought it could wait a while. So she went upstairs, and got a novel of Henry James's, which she had begun to read, and lay down on her bed. "I'll read till half-past," she told herself, and read till three minutes after. Then she looked at her watch crossly. "Oh I must finish the chapter," she decided, and did not hear the hall clock strike three.

By the time the chapter was finished, she was drowsy, stretched herself on her tired back, and drew up the quilt cosily. She had slept badly the night before, and forty winks would not make the slightest difference to anybody. If she wakened sharp at half-past three, and ran down to the kitchen, she would have a good hour, and the cake could go on first.

So she turned her head, and made a little hollow in the pillows for it, and with a deep breath of relief, she fell fast asleep.

Effie enjoyed playing the ministering angel, and the convalescent Bob Trotter gave her a warm welcome; surprisingly warm, indeed. She had not remembered that they were such good friends in the old days. Bob was an engineer in civil life, and he had been a prosaic, rather heavy young man, who could talk little but shop. Effie was wont to find his technicalities dull, for like many boys interested in machinery he could think of no better way to entertain a girl than by describing to her with infinite patience the working of an engine or the internal mechanism of a motor car. Effie had openly preferred the society of her more frivolous men friends; and she had a good selection to choose from.

But the war had changed Bob. He was a man now, bigger than ever, it seemed, and with a look of health about him in spite of his wound. He had acquired a little human experience, and a broad, pleasant grin, and he did not talk shop at all. Instead he talked about a photograph which Effie never remembered giving him, and said how much she had altered.

She came away in a pensive frame of mind, which was rare for her.

Coming from her train, at the West End of Princes Street, she caught sight of David Grant. He was clearly going to catch his, from the office, and Dr. Ross was with him. Effie had to wait for some traffic to pass, and she had an opportunity of watching the two. She had been pondering over men in general, and Bob Trotter in particular, and as she waited she compared him in her mind to David. They were very different; this man was slight, tall, with a little stoop acquired by bending over books much, and accentuated by his present lameness, and he had the look of one who thinks, and is sensitive towards life. The scholarly type did not appeal to Effie, and she had been half-puzzled, half-amused with David, but she realised now that he had somehow changed since they had met first. The expression of indifference and weariness was leaving him; and she had to admit that there was as much strength, though of another kind, in his face as in Bob's, and far more charm. She decided that she approved of him; and when Effie approved of anyone, she did it in no half-hearted fashion.

At the corner, David recognised her, and stopped, raising his hat, while the doctor passed on. Effie greeted him smiling. "Homeward bound?" she said. "What a lovely day!"

"Isn't it?" he answered. "Miss Effie, I must apologise. I ought to have called after the other night. I've been meaning to come down. I hope Miss Sutherland's dress wasn't absolutely spoilt?"

"Not a bit," Effie assured him. "Nannie makes a fuss about everything." As she spoke, her mind was made up. She felt that her family owed him a little friendliness after Nannie's slight; besides, she was in a specially generous mood at the moment.

"Come and make your call now," she suggested. "I'm sure you could spare time, and get a later train. I wouldn't make bold to ask you to take pot luck with us in these days of rations, but I know for a certainty that Marion was to bake this afternoon, and she would be highly honoured if you condescended to taste her handiwork."

Effie had no notion how the wind sat; it was simply part of her nature to open her whole heart to guests, and take them into the domestic situation whether it was pleasant or unpleasant, as though they were members of the family. But her words settled the matter. David thanked her, and, calling to Ross not to wait for him, he turned back with Effie.

"Of course," she laughed, "you must be prepared. Marion isn't an experienced hand, though if she goes by my recipes she shouldn't be far out. You see, we're always specially open to visitors on baking day, a little less the next, less still the day after, and so on, tailing down to the end of the week when there's only a heel of the loaf left in the bread-crock and Billy and Jullie kick up a row, and make it an excuse to have sardines for their tea. Anyone with a healthy appetite is a trial to a housekeeper nowadays."

So they made good company for each other on the way down; and when they entered the house, David was very much at his ease and in a state of pleasant anticipation, and Effie felt a glorious relief that someone else and not she would set the cloth and boil the kettle for once in a way.

Effie had a latchkey, and she let herself in, and David followed, and shut the door. The house was very quiet; there was not even the friendly crackle of a fire to be heard. Effie paused uncertainly at the foot of the stairs. Marion must be upstairs tidying herself, or else down in the kitchen. She did not call, but turned to David.

"Won't you come into the dining-room?" she said, "while I hunt out Marion and the tea." Then she threw open the dining-room door, and stood absolutely still on the threshold.

The table was as she had left it, with crumbs on the soiled cloth, greasy plates and dirty forks and spoons, and half-empty tumblers of water; the pie dish was deposited on the floor where Marion had left it, and a crumpled dirty cloth beside it. The windows were tightly closed, and a smell of heavy cooking still hung in the air; and the fire was dead out, with only ashes in the grate.

Effie fairly gasped, and her usual high colour left her, as it always did when she grew angry.

She said not a word to David, but turned and ran down the kitchen stair, pulling off her gloves as she ran.

On the kitchen table stood the flour, and the baking board quite unused; there was a pile of unwashed dishes in the sink, and the fire in the range was at its last dull ember. She had left it for Marion to make up when she went to catch the train.

It was plain that nothing had been baked, and there was neither tea, nor teapot, nor kettle set out in readiness.

Effie stood with twitching fingers and quivering lip in a white heat of sheer temper. "It's too bad!" she cried in her heart. "It's just like her. She's forgotten all about it. No, she couldn't have forgotten. How could she with the very table before her nose to be cleared? She's done it out of spite. The beast! Just the one afternoon I go away! This is all she cares!"

She ran back up the stair, two steps at a time. David was standing in the hall where she had left him, his hat in his hand, perplexed. She went again to the foot of the second stair, and called: "Marion… Marion! Where are you? Come here this instant!"

Up in her room, Marion had wakened only two minutes before Effie called. For a moment she was blissfully comfortable among the pillows, and then knowledge came to her, and she glanced at her watch, and turned sick and wretched. What had she done? Then came Effie's call, and Marion forced back the tears and staggered to her feet sleepy and headachy, furious with herself, and accordingly with

Effie, but determined to brazen it out. It was not the first of their rows occasioned by her carelessness and forgetfulness.

She went to the stair, and descended slowly, her lips forming a hard sulky line. Then at the turning, she caught sight of the hall clearly, and stood still. She had come straight from her bed thinking that Effie was alone; her hair was rumpled over her forehead, and half uncoiling down her neck; her clothes were all untidy, her eyes dazed with sleep; and as she stood, a deep flush of unbearable shame crept over her face.

There was Effie, all in her best, pretty and vivid, with a gay blue hat and some primroses twisted into her buttonhole; her two hands clasped her gloves, and her eyes were fierce, almost like an animal's.

And there was David Grant, drawing back as though he had intruded where he had no right to be…

Marion had no power to move, either backwards or forwards. She stood at the turn of the stair, her eyes cast down, and wished herself dead.

Then Effie spoke.

"Where have you been? What have you been doing? Why haven't you got the tea? Why didn't you bake, and clear the lunch, and wash up? And why did you let the dining-room fire out, and the kitchen range out, when you knew I would be back by half-past four, and the others shortly after, and when I've brought Mr. Grant? How could you dream of doing such a thing? You are the most selfish, thoughtless, heedless creature I ever knew. You never by any chance do anything right. You are always giving other people trouble, when other people slave day after day to make you comfortable. And just the few things I asked you to do… just the one short afternoon I happen to go out! It isn't fair, it's perfectly mean and horrible of you. And just now, too, when everything's so difficult, and we have all so much to put up with. I was ashamed when I saw these men in hospital, and thought of all they had gone through because of us at home... because of you. You aren't worth it. And if I stay here pampering you and Nannie a day longer, I shan't be worth it either. But I won't stay. I made up my mind long ago. You can do your own work now for a bit, and see how you like living in a house without fires and thick with dust and all the dishes unwashed and nothing done that ought to be! As soon as the Red Cross will take me, I'm going, and you can sink or swim after that for all I care. Do you hear, Marion Sutherland?"

Effie poured out the words as they came into her head, never stopping to think. She had no need. They were the embodiment of her daily thoughts of all the past winter, and it only needed some big, sudden accident to force them out. She was hurt beyond measure, when she thought of all she had done herself, and the return which had been made to her. She regretted that she had stayed at home so long. And regret and reproach and shame and anger mingled together in the cruel sentences she cast at Marion, careless of the fact that they were not alone. She seemed entirely to forget that David was in the house, behind her. She lost control of herself for that one rare occasion, and said her say to the end without a pause.

When she finished, there was silence. Marion dared not lift her eyes; the tears were gathering in them fast, and she knew she must let herself go in a moment. She only prayed that David would take his departure before she shamed herself any further. Effie began to realise the situation, and what she had said. She did not wish a word of it back, but she regretted her second unwilling listener, and had the grace to blush as she turned to him.

As for David, he had been mystified at first, but now all his other feelings were merged into a burning indignation. Effie might be in the right of it, but suddenly he hated her, with her capable manner and pretty clothes. The shame of Marion's humiliation made him hot; he had suffered such shame often and knew how it hurt a man past bearing. It was intolerable, that a girl should be made to endure it, Marion certainly was wrong; but she had been insulted, she stood there shrinking and blushing, and – she was the woman he loved. His indignation had discovered that fact for him. He rushed to her defence, searching in his mind for a way to spare her further shame.

"Look here," he said bluntly, "Miss Marion was tired, and I'm glad she took the rest. It doesn't matter a bit for me, in fact it's given me a splendid opportunity of wiping out my debts. I owe you heaps of teas by this time, you know, and it's my turn to be host. Won't you be my guests at Jenners or somewhere?" He glanced hastily at his watch. "We've still time before it gets crowded."

Effie drew a breath, and Marion raised her head; somehow the tension of the moment relaxed. A man may be, and often is, clumsy and matter of fact, but even in these very qualities there is something sane and steadying when he assists at a quarrel between women with its heated emotions.

Effie answered for them both, while Marion's hands, now that her mind was comparatively disengaged, went instinctively to her untidy hair. "I'm so sorry, it's awfully good of you, Mr. Grant, and we would both have loved to come. But you see, my uncle will be in shortly, and then the kids, and I'll need to stay and get things going before they appear. But do wait, if you'll excuse a regular picnic meal. I'll have a kettle boiling in no time."

Effie gave this invitation in all good faith, but she almost sighed with relief when he refused. "I wouldn't dream of bothering you," he said, and gave her his hand; but when he turned to say good-bye, Marion was gone.

She had run to her room, feeling that the very worst had happened to her. Of course, she cried, but it brought her no relief, only more of a headache. She had been disgraced before him, shown up at her poorest, with not a scrap of self-respect left her; and if any trace of their friendship had survived Nannie's scorn, it had withered absolutely beneath Effie's anger... Effie's just anger.

For, of course, it was her own fault; it was a mad, terribly careless thing to do, worse than anything she had ever done before. But she could have borne it if he had not known. He must have seen by now that she was untidy, ugly, uninteresting; and all her obvious faults must be well known to him as they were to other people. But somehow she had longed in her heart that he should think some good of her. From the first he had treated her as no one else did, in such a way as to give her faith in herself, not continually expecting her to make mistakes. But she supposed wearily that that could not last. That was only because he did not know her; now he knew her, and probably wished... why, of course, he must wish to know nothing more of her. Those excuses he had made out of formal politeness.

He would avoid her now, and since Nannie had quarrelled with him from pique, he would stop coming to the house, and there would be an end of all their acquaintanceship. And she was certain that life would never be the same again if he were to go out of it, once having entered.

Marion felt vaguely that it was just because people expected her to make mistakes that she made them. She had got into a rut. It would not be so if she could start again.

She grew wretched as she thought of her ideal, of the fair and tender thing she longed to make of her life. It was always present with her alongside of the actual pitiful failure. She did not wish any longer to be clever, as she used to wish, feeling that it was all she was good for, with a forlorn sort of pride in the remembrance of her school successes. She only wished now to be a gracious woman – a harder thing.

"Something like Beatrice," she thought. "Beatrice! And I go and let the fire out and forget to wash the dishes."

Thirteen

I would give you violets…
—Hamlet

David went home in a turmoil of thought; he had felt stirrings of this for days past, but now all pretence with himself was swept away by Marion's helplessness and her need of a defender. His heart had responded to that need, and the fact that he loved her could be a secret no longer. The face of every girl he passed in the street reminded him of it with a shock of wonderful, sweet surprise.

He had always liked his world romantic, a place of dragons, and haunted castles, and high quests; now in truth he had come upon the princess in distress, and his adventure had found an end. But his new intimacy with romance brought him a better knowledge of its fabric. The gold and silver threads were shot with sober colours. His princess in distress was a diffident and unhappy woman, who made mistakes and suffered shame in a sordid fashion. David felt that his quest, so far from ending, had only begun. Was his love more than pity? He knew it was, with a passionate certainty, but they must make no mistake at the very outset. And what would she have to say to him? He felt it behoved him rather to ask, "Am I worthy of her?" than "Is she worthy of me?" For with a chivalry which might disgust some modern girls who base all their claims on the principle of impartial fairness and on pure desert without regard to sex, he held that a woman, whatever her own faults, and simply because she is a woman, deserves only the best in the character of her lover.

David thought it out that evening, walking in his garden. Perhaps his ideas about women were old fashioned; at least, they had the advantage of being reverent. He had two conceptions of what a woman should be; they were based on the two women he had known best, Alicia and Minnie. She might be a gracious and lovely creature, not familiar, but with a certain reserve, and set above the commonplace and soiled lives of men like an inspiration; or she might be a brave comrade, sharing work, and suffering with a man, and not afraid to dirty her hands with the least attractive of his concerns. It seemed to him that the ideal woman for any man to love must be a combination of both types, with enough beauty and mystery to inspire him continually, and enough courage and humour to stand by him in the unromantic passages of their common life.

Yet here he was seemingly, acting in the face of all his theories. Where was the inspiration of beauty in Marion, and where the faculty for helpful friendship?

He put the questions aside impatiently.

"Logic's beside the point," he cried in his heart. "I want her, and God knows that's all that matters. I know there's beauty and goodness in her, but it's been squashed out of sight by the life she leads with that precious family of hers. She's been starved… the things I could give her —"

He stopped, for he had come to the end of the garden where it met the orchard, and this was his favourite place. Above, the great stretch of sky arched, grey and tender like a brooding bird's wing; on the one hand, his view was bounded by the hills, peewit-haunted, and lonely with the voices of sheep; and on the other hand, by the last of the sunset. "I could give her this," he thought. "I'd give all I possess to take away that defiant loneliness out of her eyes."

He glanced down, and there at his feet were the first of

the violets. An idea occurred to him and he bent and picked them carefully, rooting up a handful of the damp moss round about, and adding some leaves. He felt that he had to do something for her there and then; something that would take the soreness out of that day's memories.

He smiled as he carried them into the house.

"I'll bet she doesn't often get flowers," he said, "let alone Castlerig violets."

Jenny wondered what he wanted a small cardboard box for the next morning, but he never told her the reason. He posted the parcel on his way to the train.

*

Although Effie had spoken in haste to Marion, and in the heat of anger, she had meant what she said. She was not going to stay at home any longer; she had been uneasy about it for months, and this was an opportunity to carry out her desire.

She told the family the next day at tea. Of course, when Jullie came in from her class, and Billy from school, and Uncle Alexander from the office on the previous afternoon, they had found Effie, girt about with an overall, trying to do everything at once, and that called for an explanation of some sort. Effie gave one, secretly a little ashamed, but quite frankly; and Marion's red eyes and white face when at last she appeared some hours later supplemented the story. But none of them knew of Effie's decision, until she had "slept on it," and thought it over with a remarkable amount of caution.

"Yes, I'm going," Effie said, when she had poured out six cups of tea, and replenished the teapot. "I gave in my name to the Red Cross people today. I'm a qualified cook – I have my certificate, and I told them I wanted to go to some hospital."

"But, my dear Effie," said Uncle Alexander a little

breathlessly, "I think you shouldn't be so hasty. Remember, we have no servant, and we have all been depending upon your excellent housekeeping…"

"Yes, and I'm not going to be a general without wages any longer," retorted Effie, with heat. "It is trying to be taken for granted by one's family."

"Effie, you're a freak," said Nannie, very crossly; the prospect was not pleasing for herself.

"*Do* you want us to die off in batches?" asked Jullie. "I wouldn't eat Nannie's cooking if you paid me, and we all know that though Marion's spirit is willing, her flesh is weak."

"Don't you worry, young woman," said Effie decidedly. "I'm going to get you settled before I leave. There was a thing in the papers today that would suit you fine, and you'll just be advised by me, and put up your hair, and behave like a Christian and go and bag it." Jullie had passed her examination a week ago. She was rather squashed by this summary disposal of her interesting self, but considered the idea, and found it not unreasonable.

Nannie crumbled cake angrily; she was working herself up into a temper. "You're trying to be funny, Effie," she remarked. "Do talk sense."

"You may as well face facts," Effie assured her. "Perhaps it would pay for you to spend a little time inside a registry this week."

Marion said nothing; she had hardly opened her mouth during the whole day. Now she sat and sipped her tea, which she had allowed to grow cold.

Uncle Alexander rose, and slipped away. Billy took another cookie; he was too busy to enter the discussion. Effie rose also, and began to remove dirty cups.

Then Nannie turned on Marion. "It's all thanks to you, this," she said viciously. "If you hadn't been such an unmitigated fool, she'd never have thought of it. Well you can jolly well do the work."

"Oh *you* don't need to talk about fools," flashed Marion.

"You pair of silly infants," said Effie from the sideboard. "I made my own plans without bothering my head about either of you."

"Well, you're the nastiest cat out," cried Nannie, "to run off and leave us. I do think home comes first, even in war time. And you don't need to say I've been doing nothing for the war, because I have. You're just tired of us. Marion, you're a goat to have put it into her head."

Marion pushed back her chair, and went out of the room. All the spirit had left her, and she did not feel fit to engage Nannie in one of their old battles of words. She left them still bickering, Effie scolding Billy for eating too much, and Nannie launching another tirade against everyone. Marion shut the door behind her, and felt weary and sick.

On the hall table were some letters and a packet. Post had just come in. Marion looked them over without much curiosity, then caught sight of her name on the parcel, and stood still, amazed. She received a letter once in the proverbial blue moon, let alone a parcel.

The writing was strange to her – nice straight writing – a man's. Curiosity eager as a child's seized her. "Whoever he is, he's spelt my name with an 'on', not 'an' like most silly people," she thought, catching up the wonderful packet, and hurrying away to her room before anyone else should come out of the dining-room.

She sat down on the hassock in the window, and cut the string with her little embroidery scissors. Beneath the lid was a bit of paper – just wrapping paper with no writing on it, and then damp moss; she raised it, and peeped. The dark, cool violets lay among their leaves, still wet from the water where David had kept them all night, smelling wonderfully sweet, of the clean garden, and the earth and grass, and the country in April. "Oh…!" Marion cried out with pleasure, and buried her face among them. For the moment, she thought only of the flowers; they were cold against her hot cheeks, and the beauty of them satisfied her heart.

Then the fact that some one had thought of her surprised her again; it was the first time in her life that anyone had sent her flowers, the first time, she would have told you bitterly, that anyone had taken the trouble to do her a kindness. Who was it cared? Who would have done so gracious a thing? They were country violets, too, not shop ones tied up stiffly; and they were packed carefully among moss. It was beautiful… a warmth came into her heart, and sudden shame. Kneeling by the window, she bent her head low over the box, and gathered the flowers up into her hands. Then a thought came to her, and the colour ran rosy over her face.

Could it have been him? What had made him do it? After yesterday, did he still think her fit for flowers. "Oh…!" breathed Marion very low. "If only it's him, if only he really cares, I don't mind a bit about anything else, about any of the others. I never… never thought he cared as much as this."

She knelt there by the window for some time, the violets on her lap. Somehow the raw place which Effie's words had made in her heart was healing. He cared for her, and he wanted her; beauty and tenderness had come into her life at last.

For a little while, she was very happy; then she rose to put the violets into a shallow green ware bowl upon her dressing-table; and a thought came to her.

"They'll see them and wonder… ask who sent them, maybe. That little fool Jullie won't let me hear the end of it. And Nannie… oh I couldn't stand it! I can't keep them."

She gathered the violets together in a gust of anger, and crushed them into the box again. She tried to think of someone to whom she might give them. "Anyway," she decided, "I'd rather fling them out on the back green than have a horrible, vulgar fuss made."

Even as she said it, she paused. "Talk about fools, well, I'm a fool! I said I didn't mind anything else, and neither I do – if he cares." She smiled, and there was something like pride in her smile; then she put the flowers back into their bowl.

*

About the middle of the following week, Effie came in from the hasty outing she had snatched as soon as tea was over, and before it was time to make the pudding for dinner. She found Jullie in their room, playing with a new packet of hairpins.

Effie's cheeks were flushed with walking, and there was a satisfied sparkle in her eyes as she laid down some parcels on the bed, and flung off her scarf.

"Well, it's settled," she announced.

Jullie looked round. "What is?" she asked, combing her hair vigorously, and dragging teeth from the old comb in her attempts.

"I'm going to cook at Craigleith," said Effie. "This day week they want me. So that's a load off my mind, anyway, and joy for Nannie and the rest of you."

"Don't worry," said Jullie, hairpins in her mouth. "I'm going to have my dinner out, so I'll probably escape with my life. Green Café for me!"

"Dinners every day mount up, infant," Effie warned her. "And then the rations."

"Hmm. I can defy the world with thirty bob a week," said Jullie with infinite superiority, stabbing a long comb through the unshapely knob on the back of her head.

"Glad to hear it," said Effie calmly.

"Now!" Jullie pranced across the room, and drew up before the wardrobe mirror, "Some swank, *n'est-ce-pas?*"

"Do you suppose you've done your hair?" inquired Effie crushingly. "There's one piece like a hen's comb wagging on the top, and another dangling down behind your ear, and you've dropped five hairpins. Come here!"

Jullie obeyed; flung herself into the nearest chair, on the top of a pile of clean clothes, and submitted herself to the hands of the experienced elder sister. "Work your will," she commanded, closing her eyes, and opened them again, five minutes later, to fly into raptures over a "quite French coiffure."

A week later, Effie left home, very cosy in a new navy serge coat, with her belongings stowed away in an equally new suitcase.

"Keep your hair on – literally!" she said to Jullie. "I'll see Bob Trotter probably, Nannie; send love? Ta ta Billy-boy. Coming, Uncle – the train won't run away."

Last of all, her eyes met Marion's. "For mercy's sake keep the flues clean and the range right," was all she said, in a matter of fact voice.

But to Marion, standing behind the others, at the foot of the stair, it seemed that she had flung out a challenge.

When Billy slammed the front door, and the others returned to their early and interrupted tea, Marion went down to the kitchen, put coal on the already blazing fire, and looked round nervously.

"Fish-pie for supper, bacon for breakfast, two pints morning milk, half a crown to the char," she repeated like a lesson, then faltered, "or was it a quart morning milk, and – oh, mercy, she didn't say how much suet for the dumpling tomorrow, and we're out of firelighters and I can't light a fire for love or money, and do you fry bacon in fat or just itself? Oh I know nothing whatsoever about it. I can't do it. How shall I manage?"

She sat down forlornly on the table, where Effie used to sit. It might seem funny to the others, but Marion felt utterly hopeless. All this great house depended for the time on her, all the fires, all the meals; and if she failed, there was no one else to step in and set her mistakes right again. For a moment she longed passionately to hear Effie's brisk step, and flow of reproaches, and to see her whisking dishes and dusters about with the energy which used to get on her nerves. "She was such a comfortable person to have," moaned Marion, "she could say what she liked to me if only she was here."

Then Jullie appeared at the top of the kitchen stairs, her hair hanging gracefully over her ears instead of coiling round her head, and an empty jug in her hand.

"Any more milk going?" she called.

Marion got to her feet, and ran feverishly to the larder, then to the scullery, and finally to the pantry. But she recollected Effie's counsel in time, and went up to Jullie with a determined expression.

"You've had all you can get," she said firmly. "The rest's for supper. And I must say, you are an extravagant set!"

"Thanks awfully," said Jullie, but she walked meekly back to the dining-room, and Marion followed her, quaking in spirit, yet mistress of the house.

Fourteen

Shall not loveliness be loved for ever?
—Euripides

It was a Sunday afternoon, and David found himself in Edinburgh with two hours of idleness before him, and nothing to do. Beatrice Sutherland had asked him to tea at her flat; but although his engagement was not till four, the wartime train service between Castlerig and the city was inconvenient and meagre, and he had perforce to take a train which arrived shortly after two.

He did think of calling at his uncle's, but dismissed the idea.

"It would be profanation of this glorious day to spend it in Aunt Margaret's airless drawing-room," he decided. "She'll probably be snoozing just now, too, along with the spaniel; Isabel will be smoking with some bounders on the front lawn, and the uncle will be pretending to read the *Spectator* in front of the study fire. Oh, I can see them all. No thanks!"

For a moment, the Sutherlands occurred to him. "I don't think so," he thought, "I'd be certain to run into Nannie or someone undesirable." He let it rest at that, although it was not the real reason.

He took his way in a leisurely fashion along the street from the station, and so came to the West End. Half Edinburgh, in holiday mood, was streaming up and down Princes Street, arm in arm; and David watched the faces he passed curiously, and marvelled that people always looked so uninteresting in their best clothes. There were all sorts and conditions; tired women with babies trailing at their skirts, good-natured, commonplace little fathers pushing perambulators, girls clinging to soldiers, half-grown boys smoking cigarette ends, flappers in rows, their arms linked together. They drifted along, a few with cheerful countenances, the greater number vacuous of expression.

David was in a meditative mood that afternoon; he had been reading in Plato's *Republic* in the morning, out in his garden, of the lovers and defenders of the ideal state, and how it may best be contrived that they should become worthy and perfect men. It had been necessary for him since he had come home from the war to think things out again; and he had gone back to the oldest books of all, for he had learned that there is never a thought so wildly revolutionary, but it has been written down centuries before, and that Plato and Job and the author of *Ecclesiastes* are as modern as the newest Socialist theory and the latest sorrow brought by the casualty lists.

The passion for right behind the smooth Greek dialogues had seemed to him of wonderful refreshment, and he had been lifted into a clear atmosphere above perplexity and doubt. But among this crowd, it all grew far away and vain and intangible.

At a street corner, as he passed, there was an open-air meeting; an old man with an accordion in his hands had attracted a ring of boys and soldiers. He was blind, and he stared fixedly upwards, his voice quavering in prayer. Beside him, to guide him, stood his daughter, a neatly dressed, simple girl with blue eyes and a blue ribbon on her straw hat. She looked nervous, but gazed steadily before her. David felt sorry for her. At the opposite corner, there was a knot of people gathered around two figures, and a woman's voice, shrill, outworn, rose wailing into the air.

David walked on. What had it all to do with Plato and fine

thoughts? Thinkers long ago had made Utopias for them-selves and the world; and the world had no place for their Utopias. And still starving women sang in the streets for bread, and feeble old men faltered ineffectual words to save sinners who did not wish to be saved.

The bells rang out in the warm afternoon; afternoon services are rare nowadays, but there are still a few. David thought he would go to church; it would just fill in the time, and he did not feel attracted by the street. He turned off from the noise of traffic to a church set low in its old churchyard, forgotten of the busy streets about it. There was no difficulty in finding a seat, for the place was not half full.

It was a handsome city church, the walls a warm red, the pews comfortable, much colour and carving about the part which Englishmen would call the chancel, and which had been decorated as nearly after the Episcopalian fashion as was possible in a Scots church. Every window was stained with beautiful and dim figures; the choir sat in oaken stalls, and the organ played solemn music. All this David appreci-ated; he loved an ornate service as well as a simple one, for there is beauty in both. And he liked to hear them chant the prose psalms, which is not a common thing in Scotland, but becoming more common. The metrical psalms were often nothing more than the barest metre; the noble sentences sounding to a minor chant through the great space of the church were a cry from the heart: "I had fainted unless I had believed to see the goodness of the Lord in the land of the living…Wait on the Lord, be of good courage, and he shall strengthen thine heart… Wait, I say, on the Lord."

David listened with bent head; it was not prose, it was poetry, and poetry made the rough places plain.

With the beginning of the sermon, his attention wandered…

Before the war, he used to go once to church of a Sunday pretty regularly, more because he loved the old Castlerig church dearly than for any other reason; but he was not a church member.

He could remember yet like an extraordinarily vivid dream the time when Cousin Jessie had spoken first to Minnie and himself, aged fifteen, about joining the church. They had been walking home from prayer meeting on a week-night, and he had felt ashamed of carrying a Bible through the streets and wondered what people thought of him. The glaring yellow lamps and jingly piano, and stuffy atmosphere of the church hall were woven into his memories of the night; and he remembered how on that walk home his poor, conscientious heart, which Cousin Jessie had tormented and teased in her efforts to make him good, had been puzzled and overwrought with the fears and wonderings of a child.

Minnie had been openly defiant; she wasn't going to tie herself down to any one religion so early in the day, and she knew her own mind, and didn't care twopence although she seemed to Cousin Jessie to be talking blasphemy. But he had shrunk from any decision, and tried to put it off, wondering all the time if he were not very wicked to hesitate so. On the whole, his memories of that time were not pleasant.

Then Minnie discovered the existence of Higher Criticism, and began to read Bernard Shaw and Wells, and she emerged from her course of modernity a confirmed agnostic at the age of eighteen.

And he had gone on wondering and saying little; trying desperately to believe in a far-off Right which was God, to bring his own hopes and desires into line with orthodox Christianity as interpreted by Cousin Jessie, to read a meaning from religion into the little painful happenings of everyday life. Like Minnie, he had made discoveries. He had discovered beauty, and the deep, compelling wonder of the out of doors world; he had discovered the power of worthy tradition, and at the same time the necessity for every man to go on an adventure after truth for himself; he had discovered the bitterness in the make of things, and that because of it the symbol of the Cross was inevitable. Yet he had gradually come to believe that Minnie was right with her agnosticism.

The war had not so much changed his outlook on things as intensified his feelings about them.

It had brought him pain in a great mass amounting to agony; but he had known pain before, although spread out in small portions over many commonplace days. It had shown him what a narrow and artificial thing the religion of many devout people is, but he had known that to his cost since he was a child. It made him wonder that Christianity should shut out so many brave hearts who would subscribe to no creed; but he had wondered so long ago. Thus when he returned, he thought of life in exactly the same way; but he felt far more strongly the hopelessness and the perplexity that is in it.

The war had not solved his problems; it had shown the need of something greater which should be able to solve them.

He looked round on the congregation, scattered among empty pews. There was a sprinkling of poor folk at the back, one or two children and young girls, a solitary boy, half a dozen elderly men, and two soldiers yawning behind their hands and staring about restlessly as though they had come into the wrong place by mistake and wondered very much how they could get out again. But the greater part of it was women – elderly ladies in toques.

David wondered why it was that congregations usually were composed of elderly ladies in toques. Women had as good a right to be religious as anyone else; but it sometimes seemed as if Christianity had been specially invented for the benefit of these said elderly ladies. He thought of the drifting crowds outside; and he wondered whether the churches had really become things as aloof and unheeded in the life of the nation as that quiet place was aloof from the sunny street. People were saying so. Perhaps it was all right. From many points of view religion seemed an unnatural thing which wrought men up to an emotional pitch and introduced artificial fears and hopes into their lives, a thing which tended to fussiness, which people were putting away today as they put away early Victorian furniture so that they might lead a simpler existence. Was it so?

He himself knew the keen delight of sweeping aside the dust and cobwebs of hampering creeds and restrictions; it was very good to be free. He knew too that exultation in this present world which comes to a man sometimes and makes him feel that ordinary human efforts and loves and desires are saner and finer than any supernatural aspiration.

But if it was so, why did these women come every Sunday to worship? The thing must satisfy, however vaguely, some need within themselves. It seemed to David that there was the heart of religion. It was not an external thing to be slipped on like a gaudy, ill-fitting coat. It was a living part of a man, growing out of his very soul; not a thing to stint life of colour and growth, not a thing to snub the faulty human desires, but rather to bring them to perfection.

So he tried to believe; he knew for certain that it was impossible to live life without some great unifying power in his heart like an inspiration. The difficulty was to find that power. That was the mischief. The Church should have offered it, but she did not speak with authority; if she did, that half-empty building would have attracted more of the wanderers in the streets. If it were actually true that some hundreds of years ago, God, the Being whose existence had in all ages been the supreme mystery, had lived and died in a human body, and risen again, leaving a definite message of love for suffering and perplexed men and women, why in Heaven's name were the churches not crowded every Sunday because of the wonder and the hope of the thing; why were Spiritualists and Socialists, men of select faiths of their own and men of no faith at all, still groping after that central power and meaning in life, while ordinary people went their own way heavy and uncheered, communing with sorrow and passing to death?

So wondered David as he knelt during the long prayer which followed the sermon. Then he rose as the service ended, and went out slowly, feeling sorry that he had come, and very bitter. And there in the churchyard, the spring evening met him, so that he forgot his bitterness.

The tombs of generations lay tranquilly in that quiet place in the midst of the city, the stones old and discoloured, recumbent between grassy paths; and there were green hawthorns and gardens all about. Above rose the streets and the houses apart by themselves, very grey; and the sky was clear, and the air cool, and the blackbirds called and warbled. A poem of Masefield's came swiftly to his mind in fragments; the first verse:

> *The kings go by with jewelled crowns,*
> *Their horses gleam, their banners shake, their*
>   *spears are many…*
> *The way they take*
> *Leaves but a ruin in the break,*
> *And in the furrow that the ploughmen make*
> *A stampless penny: a tale, a dream.*

The second verse:

> *The merchants reckon up their gold,*
> *Their letters come, their ships arrive, their*
>   *freights are glories…*
> *A tale, a dream.*

The third, with the same refrain:

The priests are singing in their stalls,
Their singing lifts, their incense burns, their
    praying clamours,
Yet God is as the sparrow falls…
A tale, a dream.

And the last glorious cry:

O Beauty – let me know again
The green earth cold, the April rain,
The quiet waters figuring sky,
The one star risen.
So shall I pass into the feast…
Escape from prison.

And David, too, within himself, cried, "O Beauty!" For it seemed to him the one sure thing abiding amid all the perplexity of the world and his own heart. It did not change; wars might come and pass, but it endured. There was something, after all, which did endure.

Here, surely, was the great steadying power for which he had sought; men might argue away religion, but they could not deny Beauty. It was there, every morning and every evening, serene and encompassing, and the marvel and healing of it was continually new.

Fifteen

Where in half-darkness... How the heart remembers!
We talked of beauty and those fiery things
To which the divine, desirous spirit clings.

—F. BRETT YOUNG

David went straight from the church to Beatrice Sutherland's flat, fearing lest he should be late; but he found that he was the first to arrive.

"Do you mind going into the nursery before tea for a minute or two?" she asked him, half-apologetically. "I faithfully promised the children that you would come and see them, and not spend all your time in silly, grown-up talk! You know, you have quite won their hearts, Mr. Grant."

David laughed. "I don't know how I did it, then," he protested. "I never thought I was any use with kids at all, Mrs. Sutherland."

"There are some people," said Beatrice, "who pride themselves on their manner with children, and the children simply hate them. Perhaps it was because you treated them just as gravely and sensibly as if they were grown-ups. Kids do loathe being laughed at, and I think they know when you talk down to them."

"And what games may I play with them, without corrupting their morals?" asked David.

"Oh I think they know very well what's suitable for Sunday," said their mother. "They'll tell you all their usual games without waiting to be asked." She smiled, and opened the nursery door.

Alison and Babs sprang up from the hearthrug, where they were occupied with a giant Noah's Ark, and fairly threw themselves upon David. In less time than it takes to tell, they had him seated between them on the rug; although he did not know it, he had mutilated a sheep and deprived the mother dove of one wing as he sat down, but Alison kept him in ignorance for fear of hurting his feelings, and laid the cripples away behind a cushion.

"Well, what shall we do?" asked David, by way of an opening.

"No's Ark," said Babs at once.

"Och no," said Alison. "We've been playing with the Ark for hours. We had it in the bathroom, and had a really proper flood, and we got so wet that Nana was cross, and made us change, and the stripes have all come off the mother and daddy hyena."

"What else do you do on Sundays?"

"There's Bible characters. Like this, you see. Supposing it's my turn to choose, then I choose. And you say, is it a man? And I say yes. And you say, was he good, and was he old, and had he a wife and three sons, Ham, Shem, and Jeffrey, and two of all the animals, and did he make a nark? And I say yes. And so you see, it would be Noah," finished Alison, taking up that worthy's wooden effigy, and tenderly washing his face with her pocket handkerchief.

"Only you mustn't take Jesus," warned Babs.

"No, nor Satan," added Alison. "And you can ask, 'Was he in the Old or the New', and 'Was he before the Flood, or before the Judges, or before the Kings, or one of the Kings, or after the Captivity?' That always helps!"

David was fairly staggered at this display of biblical knowledge, but Cousin Jessie had not brought him up for nothing, and he entered into the game with right good will.

It went brilliantly for some time, and then faded away into an altercation as to whether Esau could properly be called a good man, and lived before the Flood. David saw tears approaching, so he made haste to ask what other games they played.

"Well," said Alison, "if we were in the drawing-room, there's hymns… Mummy plays a hymn, and you've to guess which it is. And there's saying texts all round beginning with A and B and C. The fact is…"

"Tell a story," broke in Babs. David had been preparing himself for this event during the last ten minutes, so he did not have to keep them waiting. First he told them about Perseus and the Gorgon, then after much urging, he gave them *The Water Babies*, boiled down; and finally when Alison settled herself on his knee and Babs was thoroughly absorbed in the works of his watch, he finished up with the story of the Fourth Wise Man, which was a favourite of his because it was so beautiful.

After that, Nana appeared with their feeders, and the Sheep came rushing in at her heels.

"No," said Babs loudly. "Nother one!"

"The fact is, I'm not hungry, Nana," added Alison.

David gently abstracted his watch, and Babs, feeling Nana's inexorable hands and the feeder strings about his neck, began to wail. David, to distract his attention, caught up the silky dog, who put out a fragment of pink tongue, and rolled beseeching eyes towards the nursery tea-table. "The Sheep wants his tea, anyway," said David, and quoted George Macdonald:

"Oh little dog, who blest you
With such white toothy-pegs?
And who was it that dressed you
In such a lot of legs?"

Alison laughed delightedly, and Babs was so interested in the poetry that he submitted to the feeder; whereupon David escaped to the drawing-room.

He found that another guest had arrived, a girl who was a teacher, and one of Beatrice's best friends. Shortly after, a cousin of Beatrice's came in, a man who wore glasses, and looked old to be in the King's uniform, and he was followed by a young war widow who lived on the same stair as the Sutherlands. They were all solitary people who would have sat down to tea alone or among strangers that afternoon, if Beatrice had not invited them. As a matter of fact, the teacher took her Sunday teas more often than not at the Sutherlands' house, and the cousin had *carte blanche* with regard to the flat while he was quartered in Edinburgh.

When they had been seated for a time, and were drinking their tea, the door opened again, and Marion stood on the threshold.

"May I come in?" she asked. "So sorry I'm late!"

David started at the sound of her voice; it was the first time that they had come together since the episode of the violets. How would she treat him? What could he say to her? The pleasant drawing-room suddenly became for him a place of wildly thrilling romance. When she came in, he had been helping Beatrice with the tea kettle, and Marion did not notice him, bent over the fire, for a few moments. He had time to look at her steadily before she realised his presence, and he was conscious of staring. Back to his mind came that picture in the Sutherlands' shabby hall – the girl on the stairs, untidy, flushing, shamed; and he set it side by side with this. What had happened to her? She was different; she was not Marion at all. Then his heart leapt at the truth. She was the real Marion, and the masquerading was over and done with.

She had put a new ribbon on her old hat, a pretty ribbon of purple and silver interwoven; there was colour in her cheeks with her haste, and her furs had been thrown back carelessly on either shoulder. Now as she stood there, in an attitude of hesitation, smiling to Beatrice, she was without doubt beautiful. What had he said about Beauty in the churchyard? Oh, that was all cold and impersonal compared with her... his eyes travelled from her face downwards, and suddenly everything within him seemed to give a great bound. She was wearing his violets! There were just a few of them, and not very fresh now; it was obvious that she had stuck them into the lapel of her jacket perhaps the day before and forgotten to take them out – she certainly had not dressed with the idea of meeting him. But the knowledge that she cared, that she had gone about with them fastened to her dress, glad to look down and see them there, glad to be constantly reminded of their significance, stirred in him an unreasoning joy like the singing of a thousand birds.

Marion had guessed aright who the sender of the violets was; the very postmark left her in no doubt. Castlerig could only mean one thing. And with the realisation of this, self-respect had sprung alive in her. If he believed in her, she might surely believe in herself. A candle had been lit in her twilight of self-contempt and loneliness; a secret, delicious lightness came into her heart, and it seemed not only worthwhile, but absolutely necessary to make herself look nice. The new ribbon was the flag of her joy which she dared not yet express in words.

The change in her was patent to all. Beatrice saw it too, more soberly than David the lover. She knew that Marion was still a little dowdy, still rather tired; but the difference was more wonderful than these things. "My dear, do come in," she cried. "How nice of you to run round! There's a vacant chair somewhere, I imagine."

Marion came in, and it was then that she saw David. He had stood up, and was looking at her over the head of the little widow. This time it was she who surprised the look and her eyes fell immediately. More colour came into her face, so that she looked lovelier than before; but she shrunk back into herself, and moved and spoke with her usual embarrassment.

David brought her a cup and plate, and she thanked him shyly, and answered Beatrice's inquiries about the family in some confusion.

Then as gloaming fell, they all gathered nearer the fire comfortably, and the talk became general, and she relapsed into silence.

The war widow, a marvellously bright little creature, opened the conversation by remarking on the success of the recent war savings week in town; and then the teacher asked what everybody thought about the lottery prizes as a stimulus to saving, and the cousin said it was stuff and nonsense. "The people whose patriotism needs that sort of inducement have a pretty poor sort of patriotism," he said bluntly; he was a plain man, and prided himself upon it.

"Do you think patriotism has sent men into the Army?" asked the teacher. Her name was Miss Armstrong, and she was a slim, young girl with keen eyes.

"Their motives are fairly mixed," stated the cousin, "but on the whole, they do care about doing their bit, I must say."

"I'm glad," said Miss Armstrong. "Sometimes, judging from the home people, I wonder whether we know anything at all about patriotism now."

"Perhaps not in the sentimental sense," said the cousin. "People pay their taxes, and let the war go on in spite of rations, and they think they're doing pretty well by their country."

"You couldn't be sentimental over the present government," said Miss Armstrong tartly.

David drew his chair closer. Up till now, the talk had been a duet between the cousin and Miss Armstrong. "The government's not the country, though," he said, looking across at Miss Armstrong.

"You mean, we oughtn't to criticise," she asked.

"No, I mean more than that," he answered. "I mean our notions about patriotism need rubbing up altogether. I wish we could look at things like the Greeks did. Wasn't it Pericles told them they had got to be lovers of Athens? It was a ripping way of putting it. I mean it wasn't a hard and fast bargain with the State. We'll pay the taxes, and you'll protect our rights and give us free education and a decent water supply and that sort of thing, and we'll rub along with as little bother as possible. They cared so about their State, tried to make her just the very best."

In the heat of the moment, with whole paragraphs of the *Republic* dancing through his brain, David had accomplished a very marvellous feat; he had forgotten himself entirely, and was speaking from his heart, with a smile on his lips.

Beatrice nodded sympathetically. "Yes, it was fine," she said.

"Sounds all right," said the cousin drily, "but you won't get the average selfish ratepayer raised to such heights."

"More shame to him," said David, warming up.

"Yes, Mr. Grant's right," said Miss Armstrong, with kindling eyes. "It's just the old story – materialism, and no vision, and so forth."

"That's it," said David. "It's not devilish wickedness with us as it is with Germany. It's that we're spiritually stuck. And that's quite as bad."

"But people are thinking a lot about spiritual sort of things," struck in the war widow, a little timidly; Miss Armstrong and David were so very keen, and the cousin was so very ready to squash one. He pounced on her at once. "Sentiment," he said. "It's always the way in a war."

"What do you think about spiritualism?" asked Miss Armstrong of the company at large, and especially David. "I have been reading Sir Oliver Lodge's *Raymond*. It's a most extraordinary book."

"Pack of nonsense," said the cousin without hesitation.

"I don't know," said David thoughtfully. "There are a lot of queer things in the subconscious part of one's mind; but still…"

The widow interrupted him to relate a psychological experience of her sister's which was absolutely genuine and not on any account to be doubted. And then Miss Armstrong led the talk to psychological novels, and had a passage of arms with the cousin; and that led to literature in general, and particularly the question of style versus subject matter. Miss Armstrong and the cousin forgot their previous difference, and supported each other cordially on the side of matter which they considered of first importance. Their arguments were unanswerable, and they settled the whole matter nicely; literature according to them was to be a noble thing, but of puritanical dullness.

Then David, with all the day's experience behind him, leant forward in the firelight and flung a challenge at them.

"You've left out Beauty!" he said.

There was silence for a moment, till Marion, to the infinite surprise of them all, spoke up from her corner. "I don't see how people can leave it out," she began. "It's the one thing… it makes such a difference… at least to me… I mean…" Her sentence ended in disorder, and she grew red. She had spoken on an impulse; all the while she had watched him in admiration, she had been proud of him as though he belonged to her indeed. Then he had spoken her very thought, and it seemed imperative to back him up; she was glad she had done it, even though she had made a fool of herself as usual. David looked over towards her with quick sympathy; the fact that she had agreed with him was sweet beyond words.

Then when Beatrice engaged the cousin on the subject of his probable departure from Edinburgh, and Miss Armstrong and the widow dropped their voices over some purely feminine affair, he made an effort to draw her into such another pleasant talk as they had had together that first time he dined at the Sutherlands'. But matters had gone too far now. The violets had to be reckoned with.

Marion looked fixedly at the fire, and was monosyllabic to the last degree.

David tried manfully to be playful. "I hope Miss Sutherland's dress recovered from the custard that night?" he asked, thinking what an absurd question it was when Effie had already reassured him on the point.

"I really don't know," said Marion, inspecting her gloves.

David coughed, and felt repulsed. "Does Mr. Wyndham have long leave?" he ventured next.

"Yes – I mean, I don't think so," she informed him.

This was even worse. He tried a third tack, getting away from personalities. "Have you seen the new Barrie playlet?" he asked her. "It's a charming thing; heroine an old char-woman, you know. Shows the good stuff in very unpromising people, and – er – that sort of thing…" His voice trailed away as he saw her stifle a yawn. "What am I blethering platitudes for?" he wondered. "She's bored stiff. Why the deuce can't we be sane and comfortable? Have I put my foot in it?" He began to grow self-conscious; he would have felt worse if he had known that Beatrice was watching them.

She did not catch what they were saying to each other, or she might have laughed; as it was they seemed to her a very young and awkward pair, and for the first time the reason dawned on her, although, womanlike, she had observed little things before without thinking out their meaning definitely. It was not far to seek on David's side.

"He puts his heart into his eyes," she thought. "Marion's a little stupid. No, that's not fair. She knows; that's what's changed her so. If she could only *keep* changed… poor soul. Oh, I hope they're not making a mess of it, which is just what they probably are doing."

She was relieved when the other people went away. The

cousin rose first, declaring that he ought to hurry, and that he had been lazing by the fire too long. Then the little widow felt that she had made a perfect visitation, and Miss Armstrong was like-minded. So they departed. David's train did not leave for an hour yet, besides he did not feel moved to go.

When Beatrice came back from speeding her guests, Marion looked up. "Heard from Pat?" she asked. "We haven't, and we were wondering, because of that push beginning yesterday."

"I know." Beatrice sat down in the big armchair, dropping her society manner, and looking suddenly weary. "I had a letter last night. Would you like to take it round? It's just a line to say he's in high spirits and everything is in first-rate order for the advance. The men are so keen to get out of the trenches and do a little fighting, he says."

"It's ghastly," said Marion with a sigh.

Beatrice got up from the chair, then seemed to forget why she had risen, and hesitated. At last she said, "I'll go and say good night to the kiddies, and get the letter for you," and she went out of the room.

A realisation that he might have been out there on the eve of battle instead of alone with the woman he loved, and of the value of such an opportunity, made David speak after a space of silence.

He turned to Marion.

"You – liked the violets?" he asked.

"I – oh they were beautiful," she said very low.

Then Beatrice came back, and the sentence he was beginning died away, and the two coloured. Beatrice could not help seeing; she had recovered her composure and her gaiety – perhaps because of Alison's good night hug and Babs's wet kiss – and she was very tender as she handed the letter to Marion. "That ought to cheer the Uncle up," she said. "I thank Heaven continually that Pat was born an optimist."

It was then that David took his leave. His farewell to

Marion was constrained, but Beatrice relaxed the strain with her laughter, and insisted on going to the door with him.

When she came back to the parlour, she invited Marion to stay for supper.

"Can I?" said Marion gratefully, "I'd like to. There's a rowdy crowd at home as usual, and I don't specially want to go."

They had a cosy meal together, although Marion merely played with a bit of toast; she seemed preoccupied with something.

Beatrice pressed good things on her, with persuasion: "Now, May, do take a decent fat scone, and won't you have some of this bramble jelly? It's perfectly scrumptious – a relic of our summer holiday; the kiddies gathered the brambles, and we brought them home in biscuit boxes. You know, Sandyknowes is a glorious place for brambles and all sorts of berries. The rowans there are the biggest I've ever seen. And I wish you could see the colours in autumn; the little roads by the shore are white with dust of broken shells, and they're bordered with haws and hips and bracken of the richest reds and golds." She talked on, hoping that Marion would forget, and eat something without knowing it. But the indirect treatment failed, and when pressed directly, Marion shook her head.

"I'll have another cup, though," she said. "I love my tea. I could do with nothing else, I believe. It's lucky for the others these days of rations, because they can have all my sugar and butter and things."

Beatrice looked at her, but said nothing. She never knew when it was safe to speak her mind to Marion; she remembered times when Marion had grown irritable because people were hiding their real opinion from her, and other times when that real opinion, too frankly expressed, brought quick tears to her eyes.

Beatrice's meditation was interrupted by an unexpected question. "Bea," asked Marion abruptly, "how do you do your hair that way? It looks so nice."

Beatrice laughed. "Oh, I just tuck it up with two tortoise-shell pins. But you couldn't – you have such a lot of hair, it wouldn't tuck away nicely."

"I can never get it decent," sighed Marion.

"You should go to a hairdresser's, and see how they'd do it for you."

"Can't afford it. Besides, I wouldn't be able to do it myself as well. There's never time. I'm so tired I always sleep in, and then have to jump in a beastly scurry."

They rose from supper, and then Beatrice determined to speak her mind. "But it isn't fair," she said. "You don't do yourself justice, May, when you really are so – pretty." She waited trembling for the effect of her words; she was prepared for tears of despondency, or at least a sulky contradiction. Neither came. Marion stood where she was, very straight, one hand on the back of her chair, the other raised to her hat, fingering the soft ribbon; the colour came into her face, but she held her chin high with a hint of shy obstinacy in her attitude.

"Do you think I am pretty?" she asked.

"I do," said Beatrice.

"D'you mean it?" challenged Marion, adding petulantly, "Oh, I know perfectly well that most people don't, and I know the reason. I'm not quite such a fool." She caught her skirts and held them out round her. "Look at this – and it's my best. Disreputable, shabby rag, and a horrid colour, and it droops terribly at the back. I don't know why I bought it."

"You didn't care then," said Beatrice softly.

Marion looked at her quickly, blushing. "I know I didn't. No one living in our house could. It was partly reaction against Nannie and Effie, and… I got sick of their continual clothes, clothes… yes, and I was… envious too. They do look nice. So I pretended I didn't care. Well, and I don't. If there isn't anything nice about a girl except clothes…"

Beatrice came close to her, and played with the withered

violets. "Dear heart," she said, "everyone isn't so shallow as to stick at clothes. I don't think… David Grant did!"

Marion crimsoned, and caught Beatrice's hands. "How did you know?" she said with a little gasp.

Beatrice kissed her. "You dear!" she laughed.

They were both between crying and laughing for a few minutes.

"And yet…" began Marion, smiling. "I'm ashamed of myself just because he cares. I hope it's not silly. Only… Bea, I get my quarter's pay this week. Let's go shopping!"

They planned it together, sitting by the fire for a long time; and then they fell silent.

"Bea," said Marion rising, "I have been happy tonight. I don't know when I was so happy. I do believe there's a sort of spell about this flat. I'm as afraid of going home as of waking up from a lovely dream. I know it'll all vanish." She felt as David had felt before. There *was* a spell, the spell that a gracious woman inevitably casts, so that wherever she happens to be is home.

"It won't vanish," said Beatrice steadily.

"You can say so, but you always seem to be happy," said Marion with bitterness.

"I'm not," Beatrice answered her quickly. "There's Pat."

"Yes," said Marion, "but it's different. If he was to be killed, you wouldn't feel you had really lost him, because… because… you are both so splendid. It's when you're unhappy inside yourself, just because of yourself, and all about yourself that it's so awful."

Beatrice was baffled by that, for she knew it was terribly true. After Marion had gone, she went to her desk to write her Sunday-night letter to Pat, but instead of writing, she sat for a long time, her chin on her hands, thinking.

"What will happen?" she wondered. "Oh, I'd like to play fairy-godmother to Marion, to take her and give her a good rest cure and feed her up on the things she doesn't like, and make her walk and golf, and show her how to do her hair… well, I just will. I'm twenty years too young for the job, and an interfering cat, doubtless, but I will… he's such a nice fellow. I thought he was dreadfully worn out when I saw him first, but he looked so keen tonight when they were talking. I like a man with ideals; anyone can see he's brainy and sensitive and all that. And Marion's brainy too – at least she used to be. Anyway, she's the pale, nervy sort, whether it means brains or not. I suppose she can't take things quite like ordinary people… "

She looked up. Above, in the very centre of the ledge of her desk, there was a photo of Pat in a brown frame; he was laughing, and he looked very reliable and kind. She stretched out her hands to him, scarcely realising that she did so. It seemed that he was very near.

"We were just ordinary people, Patrick," she said, "but we were happy. Oh, Pat… Pat!"

Sixteen

In one short hour since you died,
The book of grief
Lies read from end to end, and nothing more
Can add a word unto the printed score.
—LADY SYBIL GRANT

The Tea-Cup Lady was calling on the Sutherlands. It is true that Nannie had printed on her cards "First and Second Fridays", but since the war, no one cared to devote any one afternoon in particular to the dull polite routine of calls, and the at-home day had been regarded as a relic.

That was part of the unreasonableness of the Tea-Cup Lady.

The other part was, that it happened to be a cold sleety afternoon, more like November than April, when well-behaved old ladies are expected to keep to the fireside.

Marion was in a very old, ink-stained dress, ironing handkerchiefs, when she called, and Nannie was in bed; on bed, rather, under the quilt, in her petticoat, reading a novel and nursing a headache.

It was left for Jullie to open the door and entertain the visitor, in what time Nannie slipped into a pale primrose silk jumper, and dabbed powder on her nose, and Marion heated scones, and infused tea in the heavy Queen Anne teapot. No one asked afterwards what Jullie said to the Tea-Cup Lady, or what the Tea-Cup Lady said to Jullie. It did not even bear guessing.

They called her the Tea-Cup Lady because she was old and fragile; "an old, colourless, brittle tea-cup that breaks when you look at it," Jullie had said, "the kind you see through, fearfully fine china, and correspondingly finicky." And it was rather a good description of Mrs. Johnstone. Her complexion was just the washed out, putty colour of certain cups; she was continually in a flutter, rather deaf, and apt to take one up wrongly in a conversation. That very descriptive word, "nebby", fitted her excellently.

When Nannie sailed into the drawing-room, a deathlike silence was being preserved between Mrs. Johnstone and Jullie. But the old lady sprang to her feet at once, and fluttered to meet her hostess.

"How are you, dear child? Yes, such a dreadful day for April. I've just been scolding this childie here; *look* at her skirts! So short… sure to catch cold. I don't approve at all of the short skirts girls wear nowadays; so ungraceful… I like something pretty… pretty lines, you know."

Nannie kissed her cheek, and sat down, with a discreet pose, which served to hide the scantiness of her own garments.

"I don't know how you dared to come out," she said.

"Oh, I don't coddle," said the Tea-Cup Lady briskly, her small eyes very bright. "I don't approve at all of coddling. I go out in all weathers."

"I'm not so brave as you, I'm afraid," laughed Nannie. "I've been lying down this afternoon, trying to keep warm, and that's why I've kept you waiting so long. Please excuse…"

"Oh, you mustn't, my dear child, at your age," cried Mrs. Johnstone shrilly. "You'll get soft – just you see… Ah, what a nice photograph! Who is that *nice* boy?" She broke off, as was her habit, and began to dance about the room, stopping in front of Noël's portrait.

Nannie stifled a yawn, "My fiancé," she explained. "Noël Wyndham. In the Flying Corps."

"Now, how thoughtless of him," squeaked the Tea-Cup Lady. "I always say that married and engaged men ought to take care of themselves… oughtn't to *dream* of the Flying Corps. How cruel… how reckless of the young man… how *anxious* you must be!"

"Oh, Noël's lucky," said Nannie lightly. "He's been through several tight places before this."

"Do you believe in luck? *I* don't. I don't approve of talking about luck," declared Mrs. Johnstone. "It's not nice… it's not religious. And these mascots, too. Oh, there are such a terrible lot of abuses corrupting our young people. Look at the crystal gazers…"

She left the crystal gazers suspended, as it were, in mid-air, and caught up a slim green book which was lying on the table. It was the one modest production which David Grant had published; in the early days of their intimacy Nannie had bought a copy, hoping much, and it had been left lying about.

"Another novel?" demanded Mrs. Johnstone.

"Not exactly," said Nannie. "It's a silly book, awfully boring. I only read the first chapter, I don't know what it's meant to be about."

"I've been reading such a *nice* book lately," said the Tea-Cup Lady. "I must say I like nice books. I don't approve of authors who write about nasty things."

"I haven't much time for reading," said Nannie indifferently. "I do like Ethel Dell, though…"

"Oh, my dear child, not *the* Ethel Dell?" asked Mrs. Johnstone in an agonised tone. "So… so, well, I just don't think she's *nice*. Girls can't be too careful… ah, ah! Anne dear, I didn't think it of you, I didn't!"

Nannie almost jumped at the sudden change of subject, wondering of what terrible transgression she was now guilty.

"Heels!" squeaked the Tea-Cup Lady, pointing an accusing finger. "You'll break your ankles with these high heels!

When I was a girl, nice low comfortable dancing sandals… not that we danced much, of course. Mamma liked it, but Papa being the minister, we had to set an example… ah, I knew a girl once… Oh, Marion, my dear child! You're not looking well. What have you been doing…? Toasted muffins? Dare I? They look tempting, still, they may be heavy… I was at a really *nice* tea the other day, quite the nicest I've been at since the war. The things were so nicely set out… Did you bake the scones yourself, childie? Ah, you must let my Eliza show you how to make real old girdle scones… are they good? Oh, just the least bit doughy. I know! I expect that's what's affected your complexion, childie. You ought only to eat Veda bread, and get up at six for a cold bath."

She talked incessantly all through tea-time, fluttered from end to end of the room, knocked over vases, made crumbs, and finally left, having rubbed everyone up the wrong way.

By that time Uncle Alexander came in, and mildly desired tea.

"This is cold, my dear," he ventured, sipping it.

"I'm not going downstairs again," said Marion snappily.

"You shouldn't be so late," added Nannie.

"I had business," said Uncle Alexander. "I am sorry to inconvenience you, but I could not help it."

"What about my allowance?" asked Nannie.

"My dear, can you wait till…"

"No I can't," snapped Nannie. "I can't wait at all. I've a milliner's account as old as the hills, and I need heaps of things for the summer. You've put me off twice already."

"I am very sorry," said her uncle humbly, and added without much tact, but desirous of getting it over, "I'm afraid I can only manage eight pounds, my dear, this time. Business, you know… the war…"

"And you expect *me* to be decent on eight pounds?" cried Nannie, balancing herself on tiptoe on the fender, and swinging to and fro petulantly.

"We have all to make sacrifices," suggested Uncle Alexander mildly, "and you are always properly dressed, I'm sure."

"Oh, I'm sick of this sacrifice talk," burst out Nannie. "It's deny this, deny that; no butter, no puddings, no clothes, no fun. I'm jolly well fed up."

"What sacrifices have *you* made?" demanded Marion suddenly. "Think of our…"

"Brave soldiers," finished Nannie with a sneer. "I assure you our brave soldiers don't like to come home and find us in rags and long faces."

"But if it's between a little shabbiness and defeat," said Marion sharply, "surely there's no question. I'm sure if you were to ask Noël his opinion on the subject…"

"Noël can go to pot," broke in Nannie rudely, "and you too. And if you can't afford to keep me, Uncle Alexander, please say as much, and I'll hurry and get married and be off your hands."

"I am very sorry, my dear," said her uncle again, and went out of the room looking small and old.

"You mean cat!" flashed Marion, putting the tea-things together. "How could you say that to him? Look at all he does for us, and him so worried and bothered…"

"Oh, you're getting a bit too moral," scoffed Nannie.

"You meant to hurt his feelings," insisted Marion.

"Well, if I did," retorted Nannie, picking up a magazine. "He doesn't really mind much. He's too old and sleepy…"

Marion slammed the door in the middle of her speech, and disappeared, carrying the tea-tray.

Nannie had the drawing-room to herself at last. She went and sat on the fender stool before the fire, and gave herself up to unpleasant thoughts. She was really a little startled at the manner in which she had spoken to Uncle Alexander; she had not meant to be quite so rude. But everything had gone wrong that afternoon; first there had been her headache, then Mrs. Johnstone had come, and irritated them all, and the weather alone was enough to put anyone into a fit of the sulks. She went and drummed on the pane with her fingers; the sleet danced down on the roofs, and was whirled across the bleak street by gusts of wind. It was growing steadily darker.

Nannie turned impatiently from the window. She saw David Grant's book lying on the table, and catching it up, she thrust it away out of sight under the window seat behind some other papers. Then she sat down again on the fender stool. Marion's question was dinning itself in her ears, and unconsciously, in self-defence, she began to run over the list of her wartime activities. She had gone to a canteen once a week before Christmas, and cleaned sphagnum moss every Thursday in January and February; then came the pageant – that had ousted everything else for the time, and she had settled to nothing since then. There were also one or two flag days to be taken into account, with the colds resulting from standing about under Edinburgh skies in white silk stockings and the accompanying finery. Her time had certainly been occupied.

Nannie shifted her position restlessly, and drew nearer the fire, her slim body shivering under the thin silk jumper. Outside, the rain pelted down in straight sheets. There was a curious thing in the sky; on the horizon, a long black line of cloud was creeping up, swallowing the leaden light of the afternoon like a sinister creature with wide jaws. Nannie watched, fascinated; half the city was under the pall in a few minutes, and the light that remained seemed as ghastly as the darkness which was pursuing it.

She remembered a sky something like that when they were small children; Pat and Effie had stood awestruck at the window, and she had run and cried, and the housemaid had told the nurse that it looked like the end of the world.

Nannie jumped up quickly; she could not bear the

depression of the empty room, and that nightmare sky for another moment. She ran to the door; the rest of the house seemed equally silent. Marion must be in the kitchen in the basement. The hall clock ticked with monotonous thuds; the weights creaked as they creak at night when one lies awake alone. On the glass cupola, the steady rain battered.

Nannie turned back into the room. "Well, I'm a donkey," she said aloud, "to mind a storm of sleet!" She walked over to the piano, picked out a new song which needed practising, and ran over some trills and opening chords which sounded a jingly defiance to the patter of the rain.

Nannie could only read the music with difficulty in the growing darkness. She stopped after a moment to search for the matches, and light the candles by the piano, thinking it absurd as she did so. The front door bell rang with a sudden jangle; but it did not startle Nannie, who had seen the postman coming down the street. She bent over the keys and played on.

After a bar or two, the door of the drawing-room was opened, and Marion came in with letters in her hand. "One for you," she remarked, and observing the postmark of an English town, added, "News of Noël, eh?"

"*Probablement*," said Nannie lightly, whirling round on the piano stool and catching the letter. "Let's hope for another leave." She tore the envelope open; and Marion threw herself down in the largest armchair to examine her own correspondence. There was a note from Effie full of hints and underlinings and chance meetings with Bob Trotter, and a pencilled scribble from Pat in the trenches. Marion leant over to the fire, and screwed up her eyes, trying to decipher his hasty writing. Then she became aware of a silence in the room. Nannie usually read her letters with a running commentary. Marion looked up abruptly.

Nannie sat upright by the piano in the strange light, half storm-shadow, half candle-flare, like a thing cut out of ivory.

The candles threw a yellow brightness on her powdered face, pencilling out lines of black under her eyes, about her nostrils, and her pretty chin, making the colour of her skin one with the colour of her pale gold hair twisted high round a comb, and the silken stuff of her frock. Her two hands, the rings sparkling, held the letter before her; she was as motionless as death.

"Nannie… what… what's the matter?" said Marion stiffly and jerkily.

Nannie raised her eyes.

"Noël's killed," she said, in a level tone. "Noël's killed. It's from his mother. Read it."

Marion sprang across the room and took the letter from her. She read it with an odd feeling – a letter from a mother to her son's lover, unknown and unseen by her. It was bravely written. Marion was half glad that his mother had not seen the girl she wrote to, and then reproached herself for such gladness. Tears rose in her eyes; her voice choked. She handed the letter back to Nannie, saying nothing, and Nannie said nothing either. Mechanically, Marion blew out the ghastly candles, spotted the piano with grease, then tried to scrape it off. The sky outside cleared slowly; watery light broke through.

Then Nannie laid her hands on the edge of the piano, and her head on her hands, and cried loudly and wildly till she was half hysterical.

Marion stood by, paralysed. She felt she ought to put her arms about Nannie and comfort her, yet she could not. And Nannie cried on.

The clock struck six. Marion's mind began to work again. Notwithstanding the sorrow of death, there were things which must be done.

"Don't cry, Nannie," she faltered. "You'll be ill. Come and sit in a comfortable chair by the fire, and rest. I'm dreadfully sorry. But you mustn't cry yourself sick. I'll bring you some water. Wait."

She ran to the nearest bedroom, and returned with a glass. Nannie raised her head; the tears had made pitiful lines down the powder on her cheeks, and her eyes were all red. She gulped down the water, spilling some on her dress; then ran to the door, still crying, and sought her own room.

Marion stared after her, perplexed. Then she went downstairs to the kitchen, put on the potatoes and the soup for dinner, and returned to the parlour. Uncle Alexander was there at his desk. Marion stood a long time, fidgeting with her hands. She wanted to tell him, but could not. She hated to speak about such things. Then Jullie came in, and it could not be hid.

"What's the matter?" she demanded, her eyes big and wondering. "Nannie's locked herself in, and is howling fit to burst. Do tell me?"

"Noël's killed," said Marion. "It happened two days ago. His mother, of course, had an official telegram, and has written Nannie at once. An awfully decent letter… poor soul."

"Good heavens!" said Jullie, with a kind of awed gasp. "I didn't think Nan would have cared so much."

"Oh, you mustn't say things like that," reproved Marion, who had thought the very same. "Run and set the table, please, Jullie."

She herself went up to Nannie's door. She knocked; there was no answer. She tried the handle. "Please, Nannie," she called; then, "Nannie, you *must* let me in."

She waited some moments, then called again. At length the door opened, and she came upon Nannie getting back into bed.

"Can I do anything?" she asked. "Are you ill?"

"I'm so sick," answered Nannie, huddled among the bedclothes. "I don't want supper. Let me alone, and say good night."

"You must eat something," protested Marion. "Bovril or… or hot milk."

"No, nothing. Do go away," Nannie spoke in a fretful moan, and turned her head towards the wall.

"Want a hot bottle?" asked Marion awkwardly. It did not come natural to her to be a nurse or a comforter.

"Nothing," moaned Nannie again, and Marion left her, feeling a heavy weight of foreboding settling upon her heart. If there was to be any illness, any trouble, any mourning, she was not fit to deal with it. Effie could have done it, Beatrice could have done it. Marion felt very helpless.

Nannie fell asleep in about an hour after Marion left her, and dozed restlessly till it was past twelve o'clock. Then she woke, conscious that she had gone to bed without washing, or brushing out her hair, very hot, sick, and wretched, with the dull sense that something had gone wrong which could never be put right again.

She buried her face in the pillow, and tried to sleep, but the harder she tried, the wider awake she grew. Then her mind began to move again, and she remembered what that "something" was.

She longed to cry, but could not; she moved uneasily, trying to find a cool spot in the bed, and wondering what time it was. Then the clock struck one, and she groaned aloud at the thought of a long night yet to be endured. She did not desire morning; all the mornings that might ever come seemed as though they would bring vacant days, with a want in them. But she wished for light, coolness, comfort; and she could not lie there alone with her own thoughts so long.

Whatever she had thought of other men, she had loved Noël; selfishly perhaps, because he was good to her, and amusing, and handsome. But he had become part of her life, and remained in all her thoughts.

Her mind turned backwards, seizing on inconsequent trifles, playing with the pictures of past things. Now it was the first time she had danced with him, and then that pantomime he had taken them to last Christmas, where Jullie and

Billy sniggered, and made personal jokes, till she could have slapped them.

And there was a game of tennis, and one morning at church, and clearer than all, the picnic on the Braid Hills. She had worn a fine voile frock, of a patterned grey, like shimmering spiders' webs, and shoes to match, and he had scolded her for coming out in that rag.

She remembered that dress; it was a pretty thing, and had run away with half her quarter's allowance. Where was it now? Yes, surely, in the little attic, in the large black trunk. She would get it out, and see... only Effie at the lunch had spilt milk down the front hem. That was a nuisance, but then she would have to wear mourning, she imagined dully.

Such half thoughts drifted through her mind, and with them always the ache of loss – nagging and weary.

In this, her sorrow, she considered herself only. Of course, in a vague way, she felt it was hard on his mother and home people, and knew she would have to write a proper and sympathetic letter. But they hardly mattered. And she did not think of Noël as existing at all now. It couldn't be. She knew what they said in church, but some people had exploded all that. Nannie had never given immortality an hour's consecutive thought; she had heard that there were such things as critics who said the Bible was just an old document, possessing no authority, and Nannie, who considered the Bible deadly dull, was quite glad. But she had taken all her theories second hand.

That grey dress... his hand had been on her arm, and his head bent close to hers, and they had thrown plums to each other over the picnic table-cloth till one fell in a cup of tea, and splashed her. And they had laughed together. It couldn't be; all the theories in the world, one way or another, could make no difference. He had been beside her, warm, living, full of laughter; and he was dead now, shattered by a shell, his splendid body broken hideously, he himself vanished, gone out like the flame of a candle blown by the wind. There was no more Noël. She shut her eyes in the dark, and pressed them against the pillow to hide what would come before them.

That grey dress... she felt the warm air flapping through its thinness against her neck and arms.

"Mourning... black... I hate black," she whispered to herself.

But after all, did it matter? What would her life be after this? What would she do with herself all day?

She had a curiously restricted circle of interests, after all. She had never pretended to be intellectual; she fancied Omar Khayyam on lazy summer afternoons, but, as a rule, *Nash's Magazine*, or the *Tatler* served her very well. She was not the modern young woman who prides herself on being something of an art critic, has read all the Russian novelists – in translation – and can discuss sociology or international relations at a moment's notice. She was modern in nothing, save, perhaps, her hatred of sewing. Town life did not afford much opportunity for games, although she played a little tennis when the spirit moved her. Gardening was a bore, cooking was a bore, children were a bore. Dancing was not a bore; but war time was a sober time. And clothes, the all-absorbing, were decidedly not a bore; anything from a pair of stockings to a Sunday hat bewitched Nannie from afar. But her allowance was steadily shrivelling along with Uncle Alexander's business.

And men were not a bore; they were partly included under the head of dancing, partly under clothes, inasmuch as they were there to admire. But in spite of all her fooling, men had come more and more to mean just Noël. And there was no more Noël; and Nannie felt then as though there never could be anyone else.

She twisted about, feverishly hot. Jullie must have the grey dress; she would tear it up sooner than wear it again.

"And he seemed such a part of everything," she moaned. "Oh why… how could he just *stop* being?"

Death had never concerned her. All her days she had walked in brightness. She was the pretty one of the family, and they had spoilt her. Pat was the only one who had attempted to treat her sensibly. The others gave in, and formed the habit of doing her dirty work for her, that she might not soil her hands. Nannie had accepted it all calmly, and enjoyed life.

Now that brightness was slipping away, she felt very lost. She had formed no atmosphere for herself; there was no background to her life. She had not made in her heart ideals, working them out in vexation and strife. She had lived lightly from day to day, depending on outward things. And this was ended.

For the first time, Nannie realised that there was a law of change in the world, and that all which endured was the house of her spirit which she had built for herself. She found it a barren house.

She heard two o'clock, and three, and then four. Sometimes she began to sleep, then woke with a start. The heaviness, almost amounting to sickness, which comes to those who lie long awake, weighed her down. As a matter of fact, she had taken cold the morning before, in the damp; an illness was working in her body as well as distress in her mind.

Marion found her in the morning, flushed and hot, unable to take breakfast, or to rise. Nannie held out for a while, but at last she agreed to have the doctor. By night, she was feverish with influenza, and Marion's foreboding was fulfilled.

Seventeen

Life that is mean to the mean of heart
And only brave to the brave.
— G. K. CHESTERTON

Two o'clock of the afternoon in a house where there is sickness is the dreariest of times.

When Marion had cleared away the lunch dishes, and made Nannie lie down with the blind drawn, she went and flung herself on the sofa in the parlour, and allowed herself the luxury of feeling tired. There was nothing more that could be done just then, and if there had been, Marion felt she could not have done it; there was the limpness down her back, and the hot dizziness in her head that always came when she was overtired. She felt she could not go on.

The town was quiet outside; Edinburgh is extraordinarily quiet after midday. She could hear dully the clang of a slow tramcar climbing up the hill, and sparrows chirped on the backgreen. The emptiness of the house haunted her.

Actually, Nannie was a great deal better. She rose for an hour before lunch, and again for tea and the evening. The fever had entirely left her, but there was still something wrong. She would break into tears on the slightest provocation; she was fretful, could settle to do nothing, and hated to be left alone. She had hardly energy to do her hair, and would sit in the big chair in the parlour, untidy and dismal, all her lively spirit gone, a very crumpled, limp creature compared with what she had been.

So Marion was worried still; and still could get no servant. When Jullie obtained a post in Glasgow, and went to live with cousins there, it certainly made less work; but the strain was not really lessened.

Beatrice had been a godsend; she lent Nannie books, and every now and then brought round a small basket of good things very precious in war time. "A wee bit of butter," she would say. "I am very wicked evading the Food Controller, but it came straight from a Border farm, and it's for *you*, Marion, my child, and not for our dear invalid upstairs only. Now promise to eat it and grow fat! And here's a pot of red currant jelly I unearthed quite by accident. Do take it from me, and save me from paying the penalty of a food-hoarder. And these white puddings are the real thing – oatmeal, and mysterious parts of a sheep, seasoned just right! Billy will like them, and your uncle. They came from the same farm as the butter. I always do pity English people for not knowing white puddings."

Marion thought of Beatrice as she lay half-dreaming on the sofa. There were times when she envied her, because she went through life such a calm, lovely creature, always with nice things to say which she really meant, and ready hands and laughter, and just the right sort of clothes at the right time. But Marion loved her more than she envied.

"I'll go round," she murmured, "just in five minutes. I must snooze a bit. I'll go round after forty winks, and have a grouse with Bea, and take the air. Nannie's sound asleep, and no one comes near this mausoleum till tea-time anyway."

Marion's arithmetic was elastic; and the forty winks doubled themselves. When she opened her eyes, it was three o'clock; and she ran for her hat, and went out quietly, taking her latch-key with her.

The walk did her good; Beatrice's flat was in a pleasant wide road, running up from busy streets round by gardens to the Castle. On the opposite side of the road was a gravelled walk, with trees; and behind their mist of buds rose the Castle rock, with the wild wallflower yellow on its ledges. There was pale sunlight over the gardens, and a little wind abroad. Marion felt cooler.

"It's a curiously open space in the midst of the city," she thought, "just like Bea. She's a sort of open space in the middle of one's muddled, stupid life – oh, such a sweet space."

She rang the bell, and went up the stone stair at her leisure. Beatrice herself opened the door. She wore a big coat of a rich plum purple, with a wide collar of chinchilla fur, and a small hat caught with a veil; the coat was open, and Marion could see the heavy filigree of an Indian silver belt clasping her gown at the waist. She wondered for the hundredth time how Beatrice managed to look so nice on no large income; then noticed that her face seemed as white as her white, firm throat, all with a clear, even pallor; but she blamed the bright coat for the effect.

"Come in!" said Beatrice, kissing her, and taking her hands. "I'm so glad you appeared, old thing. I was wanting you." Marion followed her into the parlour and sat down; there was a bright fire burning, a doll of Alison's on the hearthrug, and an opened telegram on the table. Marion did not notice the telegram; she was never observant, and today was preoccupied.

"I'm afraid I've only come to be comforted," she said with a laugh. "I felt everything so deadly dreary that I had to get half-an-hour with you to buck me up. Nannie annoys me, Bea. There's nothing wrong with her, and there's everything wrong. I liked it better when she was outright ill – though I didn't think so then. I believe she needs a change. And uncle's so mopy. He seems to see the workhouse looming in our family background. And, do you know, I fairly miss Jullie, though it's less to cook. She was such a mad child. Oh, and Billy went and upset a bottle of hair lotion over the new bedroom carpet. I shouldn't say the new, but at least the newest carpet in the house. And I was so annoyed. I jolly well lost my temper at him. He was trying to be knutty, he said, and I could well believe he would have been if his head had got that sticky stuff over it. It's raised all the pile of the carpet into bristling lumps!"

She leant back breathless; laughing. "Oh, it's all such little things, but it does me good to get it out to someone as angelic as you. I'm better already, only... Nannie's not a 'little thing'."

"No," said Beatrice, "Nannie's not a little thing. I'm so... sorry." She had picked up Alison's doll, and set it on her lap, and began mechanically to tidy its clothes. It was a rag creation, with the uncanny eyes and faultlessly level profile common to rags; and it wore a discarded pink flannel night-gown of Alison's, and Alison's best hair ribbon. Alison called it Doddles; there had been a twin by the name of Diddles, now deceased.

Beatrice took off the hair ribbon, and wound it about her long fingers, smoothing out the creases. She said nothing, and Marion was puzzled.

"I am a bore," she said remorsefully. "I'm keeping you from getting out too. Come away this minute. Why didn't you mention frankly that I was in the way?"

Beatrice looked up straight at Marion. Her eyes were filled with tears. "I'm going to London," she said, "by the night train... at once. Darling May, Pat's there. He's been... wounded. He needs me. I was coming round to tell you."

Marion gave a queer little gasp. Her hand went out to the table to steady herself; then she saw the telegram, and would have opened it, but Beatrice caught it up, and held it, clasping her hands behind her back. It said, "Dying."

"Oh Bea," Marion faltered. "Why didn't you tell me at once instead of letting me ramble on?"

"I don't know, I couldn't, somehow," Beatrice answered her, with a nervous laugh which was nearly a sob.

"When did you hear? What's the matter?" asked Marion.

"Half an hour ago," said Beatrice, her voice steadying. "We'd just finished dinner when the thing came." She crinkled the telegram between her fingers. "It doesn't say exactly what's wrong, just wounded... and it's serious... and I've to go."

"And... and what about everything?" gasped Marion confusedly, "packing, and clothes, and things, I mean? Can I do anything for you?"

Beatrice caught her hands. "May, there's only one thing, and... and I hate to ask it," she said quickly. "Nana's getting out my case from the boxroom, and I'll tumble in all my little things in ten minutes. It's not that... it's the children."

"Yes, of course, the children," echoed Marion blankly. She had forgotten them.

Beatrice paused. "Could you... could you possibly take them, May darling? It's simply heaping trouble upon your poor self, I know, but you would have Nana too, of course, and she's a perfect saint. She'll do anything for you – light the fires, and do the range, and clean. You'll not need to slave half so much with her. It'll be a sort of compensation... if only you could take my children. And it mayn't... be for long." She broke off.

"Of course," breathed Marion very low. "Of course I'll take them. Don't you worry, Bea, I'd... do anything for you." She put her arm round Beatrice's shoulder, and they drew close together.

"You dear," said Beatrice. "But don't be rash. Have you room for them? I *could* send them to their grannie's in Fife, but..."

"But you won't," finished Marion. "You won't dream of it. They can have Effie and Jullie's room. It's been so depressing to see it empty after the row they used to make. It'll be a first-class nursery. And there's the wee room upstairs for Nana. When will they be ready? Supper time?"

"Might they?" said Beatrice. "If I could bring them round

for hot milk and bed just before I run off to the train that would be best. Marion, you are good."

"No, I'm not… I'm not," cried Marion. "I should have said it myself without being asked. Tell me more about Pat. Was this quite unexpected? What was the last news you had? Which hospital is he in?"

She led Beatrice to the sofa, and they sat down together still holding hands. They talked for about twenty minutes; then Marion rose, and said she must run home to give Nannie her tea, and look out clean sheets for the beds.

When Marion was gone, Beatrice went to tell the children. They clung about her. "Take us too," said Alison. "We wouldn't be a bover," entreated Babs. "I'spect we could go on the rack, Mummy!" Then the door bell rang again.

It was David Grant. Nana opened the door, and put out her head. "Ye canna…" she began; then, "Bide a meenute."

And David heard her open the parlour door, and call out: "That's the laddie Grant, but ye'll no see him, Mem?" Beatrice's answer was indistinct, but in a moment Nana was back, ushering him into the hall.

Beatrice came to meet him, a smile on her lips; as with Marion, she had no words to tell her news. And even as Marion, David began to speak, realising nothing.

"Am I interrupting you?" he said. "I shan't keep you a minute, Mrs. Sutherland. I just brought along that book you were wanting for the children." He drew out *Puck of Pook's Hill* in a small, beautiful red leather edition. "I know they'll like it," he said. "Minnie and I got it and the other one, *Rewards and Fairies*, long after we grew up, and we were perfectly fascinated. I remember the first evening we got them, she sat down on the one side of the fire and I on the other, and I'm sure we read till twelve o'clock. Some people swear by his Indian things, of course, but I don't know when Kipling is more charming than when he's bringing bits of old Sussex or Kent to life again just for kids."

He laid the slender little book down on the table.

"Thank you very much," said Beatrice. "I don't know, though, if you ought to leave it, Mr. Grant. It might get lost if... when I'm away. I go to London tonight. My husband has been wounded... dangerously." The last word slipped from her dry lips as though it hurt her to speak it.

The colour went out of David's face. "Oh... I'm sorry," he said in a low voice.

"I just heard this afternoon," explained Beatrice, "by wire. I am going by the ten o'clock train. The children go to my sister-in-law – Marion's house. She is very kind, and promised to take charge of them till... I come back."

"But you have some hope?" asked David slowly.

"Oh..." she drew a breath. "I don't know. I can't tell. The wire doesn't give me any. I hope I shall see him; that's all," She held out the bit of paper to him, and he read the scrawled words, and then looked back into her face.

"Dying."

He had not thought it possible that death could have touched this home. It had always seemed to him a charmed place, like an enclosed garden or a fairy ring; it was a piece of romance and delight, a beautiful thing in the world. Outside, there might be sorrow; to him, or to Marion, or to Nannie Sutherland, sudden pain, and days of dreariness might come. But... not here. Often when he was discouraged, the mere thought of Beatrice's home, and Alison and Babs, had been a proof to show him that there was still happiness under the sun.

He looked about the room; he remembered when the firelight was warm, and he had sat by the window and heard stories as eagerly as the children; he remembered the sweetness of that spring twilight, and the gay supper table, with the green parrot jug, and Babs's insatiable questions; he remembered too when Marion had stood at the door, one Sunday afternoon, flushed and lovely, and how, later, they two had been alone there for a few moments. It was a kind room, full of memories. Then he looked at Beatrice, straight and young, her chin raised; she was not thinking of him, she was not looking at the familiar things, but with all her soul and every muscle in her body she was defying that hopeless word. And David's heart was wrung. He tried to think of something kind to say to her. "If there's anything at all I could do for the children while you're away, please ask Miss Sutherland to tell me," he began.

"Thank you," said Beatrice. "I do trust them to you – and Marion." Then she smiled. "Marion's a happy girl to have you, and to have you *safe*!"

The last word was like a sob.

With the flush which came to David's face, and the glad start of surprise to his heart, there came also shame. The warmth of his love made Beatrice's loneliness seem the more pitiful.

"You knew, Mrs. Sutherland?" he stammered. Then all that he wanted to say came out with a rush. "I don't know how I ought to thank you. You've been so kind. Coming here and – and all that has helped me, and I'll bet it's helped Marion too. It's people like you who make life livable… I can't make you understand, but… look here, you oughtn't to be alone just now. Let me order your cab. I – I'll be in town this evening, so I'll look down at the station about the time of your train, and if you want anything…"

She interrupted him, accepting his offer simply. "How good you are, Mr. Grant," she said. "It would be a help." She gave him her hand, and he left her.

That night he saw her off at the station, and did for her all that he could, which seemed but little. Then he went home. He had missed the last train to Castlerig, and that meant taking a tram and walking some distance from the terminus. Out in the country, it was very dark, a night of few stars; but the darkness was in tune with the heaviness of David's heart. "It's a damned shame," he kept saying to himself wearily. "For a woman like her to have to go through with that... why *should* it be?"

The blackness of the war was upon him then far more than it had been even during his own two years of it. It shut him in, foul and suffocating. It was more powerful than the goodness of God – if there was a God. To this desolation came the fairest things; and the more intimate and tender they were, the greater the desolation. It meant nothing but destruction, broken bodies and hearts; the very marrow and centre and meaning of life reft away.

He thought of the girl in her courage, defying death and sorrow. But her courage would not save her; she would go to London through the night and find death, inexorable, at the end. She would learn that there was nothing too bad to be true.

To David, during the months, beauty and hope and the possibility of good had been slowly returning. He had begun to make a foothold for himself, but this threatened to sweep him back to the very beginning. Again he wondered, was anything worthwhile? He had fancied that Beauty was lasting, and love had made life an entirely new and nobler thing for him. But he had been forgetting, like a fool. Beauty was not death-proof; and even he and Marion, love as they might, were only like children wandering hand in hand pleased with the bright things they found on the wayside of the world, but fated to miss the path and lose hold of each other's hand among the shadows at last.

And then a strange thing happened. Looking back, it seemed to David as if a flower of living, rosy flame had sprung out of the darkness. Whatever it was, and he could never explain it, his soul seemed to reach beyond wandering fancies and weariness and all that had ever hindered and baffled him until it touched something sure and eternal. For a moment there was that extraordinary sense of contact; he felt about him a presence definite and real, and not a semblance of his imagination. Then it passed.

But in that moment, David knew beyond all doubting, that in the face of death, in the face of undeniable failure, in the face of a thousand sorrows, one thing alone and always was worthwhile – a lovely life. He knew that though courage and graciousness and a high heart might appear to go down into darkness, the mere fact that they had ever been at all was enough to make them immortal. He knew, then, God.

Eighteen

Will ye gang to the hielands, Leezie Lindsay,
My bride and my darling to be?

—Scots Song

All telegrams do not bring bad news. David received one on the morning after Beatrice went to London. It said: "Unexpected leave; week. Arrive tomorrow, three-thirty. Minnie."

David laughed over the blunt "week". It was like Minnie to economise about halfpennies, and he was so glad of the news that anything served as an excuse for laughter. He had a shopping expedition on his own account before train time, bought chocolates, and a big cornflour cake, which she loved, and a new novel of John Buchan's to delight her heart. And she caught sight of him at once on the platform, and teased him about all the brown-paper parcels he was carrying – he, who hated carrying parcels.

They were just in time for the Castlerig train. Minnie sat at the open window of the compartment in loud delight during the whole journey. "Give me Castlerig in the beginning of May," she cried joyously. "Look at the geans in the Lodge woods; they're finer than ever. And there are those ragged-robins and wee forget-me-nots among the lushy grass. I remember I thought 'lushy' the very word for our dell when I saw it first in a poem. Ah, and there's the Manse at the bend…" She leant out. "Just about here," she confessed, laughing, "I am always seized with a sentimental fit." She drew in her head abruptly, remarking, "They told us three years ago that the tunnel was on the brink of falling in, and it hasn't fallen yet. I always remember just in the middle of it."

Together they went up the brae, and into the Shieling. David disparaged the garden, and laid the blame on doctor's orders, for Ross had vetoed digging. But Minnie was content. Jenny had been baking; the white cloth was set out, with three kinds of scones, white scones, drop scones, and treacle scones, besides crumbly buns heavy with dripping, and a spoonful of raspberry jam buried in the heart of each. There were perkins, gingery and crisp, and dainty round oatcakes, and David set his purchase from town in the place of honour.

Minnie took her old place behind the tea-pot, and as she poured out, she unfolded her great piece of news which had been saved for the occasion.

"I've been promoted," she announced.

"Well played!" said David, with appreciation and proud eyes. "Go on and give us the details."

"There aren't any," said Minnie airily. "I'm as much of a duffer as any of them. I only seem to have developed a peculiar talent for scolding people over the phone. It's been most effective in several cases, and I have made it my special forte. I can't think of any other reason for the honour. Unfortunately, the pay doesn't increase very mightily."

"And what rank have you now?"

"Oh, I'm a full administrator, and none of your assistants! Some swank, eh?"

"There's nothing succeeds like success," remarked David. "You were evidently born to make a name for the family, Min!"

"Are you being sarcastic?" asked Minnie. "If not, you should know by this time that it isn't good policy for a brother to praise his sister to her face. And anyway, I don't see failure written large upon *your* brow, so you don't need to grouse. Ah... um! Jenny hasn't forgotten her ancient cunning in the matter of drop scones. Do you remember when I bagged a whole batch off the girdle, and we went and locked ourselves in the bathroom, and ate them? And had pains and whippings afterwards! But they do melt in one's mouth."

David looked across her, and laughed, with an odd buoyancy in his spirit. Life had become very pleasant of late. Minnie observed his light-heartedness, and wondered. She very soon probed to the chief cause of it. After supper, she drew in her chair, and proclaimed herself thirsty for news. David took out his pocketbook to find her Alicia's latest letter. The pocketbook smelt of tobacco, and was very rubbed, and ready to fall in two; Minnie, remarking its condition, made up her mind about David's next birthday present. Then she noticed a small crooked grey snapshot falling on to the hearthrug, and she stooped and picked it up.

The Sutherland family was not seen to advantage in it. Effie had arms akimbo, and a scowl; Jullie exhibited large stretches of leg; Marion – alack for David – was a hazy blur; Nannie simpered in the very front, and took up most of the picture. But at least, they were all, save for Billy, unmistakably and alarmingly feminine, and Minnie had never seen any of them before, and the snapshot had fallen from her bachelor brother's pocketbook. Minnie prided herself on an acuteness hardly second to that of Sherlock Holmes, and something gave a jump inside her as she studied the photograph with increasing displeasure. It wasn't possible surely...

Then David missed the photo. "Hello," he said, looking round. "Where – oh, I say, would you chuck that over, there's a good fellow! It must have dropped out."

"It did," remarked Minnie, looking at him quizzically, but she did not offer to return it. She realised suddenly, with a queer feeling of loneliness, that he was not her kid brother any longer, but a man whom any woman might be proud to love. She realised, too, how little she really knew of him, of his beliefs and ideals and loves; he had always remained very much shut up within himself in spite of their close friendship. Obstinacy seized her. "I'll make him tell," she determined, and then aloud: "Say please."

"Shan't," retorted her brother. "I'm not a pet Pomeranian doing tricks."

He leant across the table laughing, and snatched it from her.

Minnie watched him steadily. "Friends of yours?" she asked.

David, with annoyance, felt the colour rising in his cheeks. "Some clients of the Uncle's," he said in a grave tone, which was too much for Minnie's sense of humour. He crossed quickly to the piano, lit the candles, and taking down *The Songs of the North*, he dashed into the first ballad he came to. It happened to be "Leezie Lindsay". The note on expression at the top of the page said "Gallant and beseeching". Minnie remembered that, and how they used to laugh over it. Tonight she did not laugh. It seemed to her that this brother of hers, as he sang,

> *"Will ye gang to the hielands, Leezie Lindsay,*
> *Will ye gang to the hielands wi' me?*
> *Will ye gang to the hielands, Leezie Lindsay,*
> *My bride and my darling to be?"*

was obeying the quaint direction not in the letter only, but with his heart. When he had finished, and before he could turn the page, she ran over to the piano, and put a hand on one shoulder.

"Just tell me," she begged with gentle humour in her voice. "It's not the grinning one in front with the blackened eyebrows, Tousle?"

David wheeled round on the piano stool, and sprang to his feet, catching both Minnie's arms.

Gallant and beseeching he looked without a doubt, his

hair pushed back carelessly, a laugh in his eyes and on his lips.

"My dear," he told her, "I loathe the grinning girl with the eyebrows, and you have no business to look at other people's private photographs."

"I thought it was private," mused Minnie; but she got nothing more out of him that night, for he insisted on them both going to bed early, declaring that she must be tired with the journey. David left Minnie the next morning to breakfast in bed, and laze there with a novel till after ten o'clock. He had a long day at the office, but he contrived to visit the Sutherlands' on his way to the train. Nana opened the door to him. She thought Miss Marion was out, but would he come in half a minute and she would see. Miss Anne had taken worse again, and was back in bed, and the doctor coming regularly.

David followed her into the parlour. He found Alison there, seated on a big chair, her legs curled round its legs, her tongue protruding nervously as she laboured with an excruciating old pen, and a penny bottle of ink. She looked at him solemnly over her manuscript.

He smiled. "You're busy this morning," he said. "I won't interrupt, though. Please don't mind me."

Alison's gravity relaxed. "It's quite all right," she declared graciously. "The fact is, this is our magazine – Babs's and mine. And it's just nearly almost ready. You can look; I don't mind."

David stood behind her, and peeped. "How nicely you print," he said, regarding a row of crazy capitals.

"Think so?" said Alison rapturously. "I *am* glad. Mummy wants me to *write* so badly. It's the one thing Mummy and me can't agree about. Why *should* I write when all the books are printed?"

"It's handy, of course, to know how," suggested David. "And what are you at just now? Editorial?"

"Well, no; the fact is, it's the Editor's auto-bogrammy."

Alison indicated a headline with the stump of her much-bitten pen. "It's true as true," she assured him. "Nana told me it."

David read: "MY LIFE. Once upon a Time, I supose I was very small indeed. When I was Borne, I wayed 8 pounds and a haff; now I way 5 stone, 8 pounds and ¹/₂. I am a little girl, the fact is, I am a writer, and rather clevar. I am dark, rather pretty, and of a genrous and afectionette nature, I am fond of parties and all sorts of gayties, but am also a motherly Little Person. Doddles, like myself, is Beutiful and vertuous. Doddles is my daughter. When I was 4 weaks old…" Here the document ended abruptly.

David blew his nose, and was seized with a fit of coughing. "How exceedingly interesting," he said gravely. "Can I be a reader, Alison?"

"Course. Oh, there's Babs. Babs, *have* you got that fronty-spiece ready? I can't wait another minute. Babs is the Special Artist, but it's awful messy."

Babs trotted in, the fluffy Sheep at his heels, and a piece of paper in his hand, very pleased with himself.

"Here 'tis," he cried, with his usual breathless, unpunctu-ated gush. "It's jus' lovully I used all the blue chalk for the sky and I don't know what I'll do 'bout the next it's a lovully naeroplane killing a zepp."

David admired the "lovully naeroplane". "And what do you do all day?" he said next by way of conversation.

"Och it's not nice," said Alison slowly, getting off her chair. "It's horrid 'n' dull. Do play some really fierce game, like 'The Sleeping Lion' or something. We've got to be so horrid and quiet."

"Naunty Nan's so ill, and Naunty May's no time to play," complained Babs. "Hate when people is ill. And they don't 'member to untie your feeder, nor wash your back, 'n' it's so dark."

"It's an awful dark house," added Alison. "The upstairs

stairs are the worst. Babs is really frightened; the fact is, he thinks Satan lives in the place where the hot bottles and dusters are."

David had sudden memories of a nervous little boy long ago, and he swung Babs up into his arms. "Look here, old chap," he said. "Just you take it from me that Satan's far too busy out at the war to bother frightening wee boys at home. He'll never look near you."

"Sure?" asked Babs with relief.

"Mummy's never written," pouted Alison. "And I thought Daddy would have been all right by now. Oh, I wish we was home."

David was about to set the stage for a lion hunt, when the door opened, and Marion came in, out of breath, and flushed. Even then, she remembered their last time of meeting.

"I came to ask if you had any news?" began David.

"Just a wire; he's hanging on, half-unconscious, and they don't know what will happen," said Marion wearily. She could not meet his eyes; she sat down, and pulled Babs to her, tying the bow at his neck which had loosened itself.

"I'm sorry your sister is worse," said David.

"It's most disheartening," agreed Marion. "I thought she was out of the woods."

"I expect it was a great shock to her – about Mr. Wyndham, I mean," said David. He stood by the window, his head turned away from her.

Suddenly Babs who was playing on the rug, fell against the sharp fender, and scraped his bare knee. A wail arose, bitter and uncontrolled. Marion jumped nervously.

"Oh, Babs, shut up!" she said sharply. "You mustn't make a row. It's nothing really… and Nannie…" She ran and caught him up, but David turned in time to see the child shrink from her.

"Mummy!" he roared.

"There… cheer up, old man," soothed Marion, dabbing

the knee with his handkerchief. "I didn't mean to be cross. Oh, Babs, don't!"

She patted his shoulder awkwardly, but he dropped his head, and sobbed with screwed up eyes.

David made up his mind then. "Poor soul, she's all on edge... and the kids are miserable," he thought. "They'll get to hate her in a day or two, and it isn't... of course, it's not her fault, really."

Then he spoke aloud.

"Will you think me very interfering?" he said, hesitating. "I saw Mrs. Sutherland before she went... and... I promised to... if there was anything I could do for the kids while she was away, I would. I'm afraid... it's too much for you. I want to invite them to Castlerig for a week if you'll let me, just till your sister is better again. My sister Minnie happens to be at home just now, and we would love to have them. Eh, Alison? What do you say to it? It's a great place for adventures, and there's hens..."

He spoke to the children to cover her embarrassment and his own, and they interrupted him with gasps of joy. Babs looked up, tears rolling still down his cheeks, and unbounded eagerness expressed in his wide open eyes and mouth.

"Will you let them?" said David again.

Marion stood up slowly, ready to burst into tears. It was such a sudden relief; and there was something in the tone of his voice that seemed to go out to her and encompass her like a protection against the little sharp things in life. She felt that it was not just because of Beatrice, or Nannie, or the children, that he cared and offered, but peculiarly because of her own need.

"You make me ashamed," she said, as she followed him into the hall. "I know I'm no use with kids... just now, at least. They'll be far happier with you and your sister."

She gave him her hand, and he held it firmly for a moment,

so firmly that she shrank back foolishly, her nerves playing her false.

But David kept her hand in his. "You're doing too much," he said. "It's not right. I don't care how ill your sister is. I can't let you…"

"But it doesn't matter to you," gasped Marion, pulling her hand away. "It's nothing to do with you."

"You know it is," he began, taking a step towards her, but he saw she was in no mood to listen. He broke off and smiled. She was too worked up for a proposal; what she wanted was a little common friendliness.

"Well, I'll call tomorrow, and take them out by the three-thirty," he finished, bringing the conversation back to a prosaic and safe level.

"Will that do?"

"It's far too good of you," she answered quickly, regretting her stupid confusion.

"Goodbye," he said, and was gone. And Marion felt that the house was empty without his presence.

Nineteen

You in a garden green
With me were king and queen,
Were hunter, soldier, tar,
And all the thousand things that children are.
                              —R. L. STEVENSON

When David went home that evening, he found Minnie in the garden weeding; it was her favourite form of labour, because, as she declared, one saw the results clearly and immediately. She was in behind the currant bushes, where he had sown peas and beans, and he went round to her, smiling. "I've been rash," he called as he came up.

She straightened herself. "You couldn't have been rasher than me," she told him, leaning on the hoe. "In spite of my hideous past, I actually attempted to make apricot jam today, and burnt the whole hypothec. Jenny won't speak to me; I'm disgraced; I'm branded as a domestic failure, although I was aware of the fact before."

"Hoot, woman, that's nothing," scoffed David. "I've adopted a family!"

She stared. "Good heavens! Belgian babies, or stranded Serbs? I always knew you had a compassionate heart, Tousle, but there are limits."

He laughed. "I knew you'd say I should have asked you first," he admitted. "Now, listen and I'll explain."

She sat down placidly on the wheelbarrow.

"About time," she remarked.

He took out his pocketbook, and searched for the little grey snapshot; Minnie's eyes sparkled, but she waited demurely.

"I spoke the truth and nothing but the truth when I said that these were clients of Uncle's," began David. "As to friends of mine… well, feelings are mixed. Their name is Sutherland. This maiden with the legs is the youngest, a flapper; oh, I believe she's put up her hair now, but she's a flapper in spirit still. This – Effie, is a brick; she's doing war work. I'm a wee bit frightened of Effie, to tell the truth."

"Good for Effie!" commented Minnie pleasantly.

"The grinner with the eyebrows is Miss Sutherland, Nannie by name. I wrote you about the pageant, of course? Well, this is the one that dragged me into it. She's a holy terror. However, her fiancé's just been killed, and she has had the flu, and rather gone to pieces over the whole business, so we must deal charitably with her. This… is Marion. I'm… sorry for her. I don't think she's strong, and she has to nurse Nannie just now and run the house as well. Well, they have a brother who is dying of wounds in a London hospital, and his wife has gone to him, and left the two kids in Marion's charge, I certainly wrote you about the kids – Alison and Babs, the most delightful pair – didn't I?"

"I believe you did," said Minnie. "Yes?"

"They're cherubs, but they're no rest cure, you may depend on it, and they are a jolly sight too much for Marion just now with all she has to do. And, well… I sort of promised their mother to help with them if need be. I wish you could see her, Min – you'd love her; she's one of the best. And the long and the short of it is that I've invited these two children here for a week, to relieve the Sutherlands' domestic pressure."

Minnie said nothing, but examined the snapshot.

"Well," said David, "I'm waiting to be scolded! Have I spoilt your leave?"

"Don't be a boiled owl," said Minnie affectionately. "It'll be great sport having them. Fancy kids in the Shieling! I always thought it ideal for a doll's house. I must get into my old rags, for a change, though; I couldn't dandle infants on a khaki knee."

David put away the photo. "Then that's all right," he said. "I thought you loathed kids."

"Not indiscriminately," amended Minnie. "I take your word for it that these are superior kids. You have good taste in children, David."

He bowed. "Madam is pleased to be complimentary. They are, though – just dears. I found Alison writing her autobiography this morning when I called. She's started in good time!"

"Something like your diary, Tousle. Remember? You kept it up for a week, with long lists of the meals: 'Today we had boiled mutton, beans, roly-poly, etc., etc.,' but it gradually degenerated to 'School as usual.'"

"Well, if I was a wee glutton, at least I was persevering," retorted David. "You never kept a diary at all."

"I was otherwise employed."

"Yes – breaking the few toys we possessed! I've just been thinking what we can give them to play with, and there's not a whole article in the box in the attic. I mind Jenny used to call you a 'damagin cratur'."

She flung a weed at him, which he returned promptly.

"I'll away in and tell Jenny," he said. "It's a comfort to know the kids can't die on our hands while *she's* on the premises."

A shower of weeds followed him down the path. But Minnie did not go in. She sat a while on the barrow, thinking.

"This is Marion – I'm sorry for her," she repeated to her-self. "If pity be akin to love… hmm! It can't be the one with the fiancé, and never the flapper – he loathes them. Effie in-spires awe, not a bad beginning! Oh… there's none of them good enough for him, and what an inquisitive minx I am!"

David called for the children on the following afternoon. He took a cab from Princes Street, and drove down to fetch them, with their belongings. Marion met him in the hall smiling, and delivered them into his hands. "I would like to have come to the station with you," she said, "but I can't leave, as Nana goes out today. Don't spoil them too much. They go to bed about half-past six...

"Me at seven," chimed in Alison.

"And Babs has a wee nap after dinner, and a bath every night."

"And you must come and rub my back!" insisted Babs.

"They eat anything reasonable, but they don't have tea. I do hope they'll not be a dreadful bother," finished Marion anxiously.

"They will be the life of us," David assured her.

"As long as they aren't the death of you!" she laughed back.

David was hardly prepared for the amount of luggage they brought with them. There was a neat little case for Alison, and another for Babs, and a cardboard box, tied with string – "Our toys!" said Alison, with a wave of her hand; and a brightly painted scooter, and Babs's hoop, and Doddles, rolled in a scarf, and an old chocolate box which Babs hugged to his heart and proceeded to open and spill when they started. It contained people cut out from the illustrated papers, each with a name written on the back.

Alison's first act was to dig her hand into her deep coat pocket, and lay the contents on her lap. There was a little black book, which she scrawled in with the stump of a programme pencil, a piece of butter-scotch, Doddles's shoes, and a tangled bit of blue wool, which she called "my fancy work!" A child has a passion for carrying its dearest possessions where they can be seen and felt every three minutes. Once Alison was assured of the presence of all her treasures, she put them away again, and began to inform David on the nature of her wardrobe.

"I have two new purple cotton pinnies, and two new grey ones, and knickers to match," she said. "Mummy embroidered them, *just* like Liberty. And I have a brown straw hat with cowslips, for Sunday, but Nana thinks it's too old for me. Everything nice always is too old. And we have our Coronation Bibles with the King and Queen in them, and Babs says his prayers to someone always, but *I* say them to myself, and Mummy doesn't let Babs read just ord'nary stories on Sunday, but *I* know better."

David was quite glad that they had a compartment to themselves in the train; the engine occupied Babs fully until they left the station, but once they were started, he asked: "What'll we do?"

"Mr. Grant tell a story," said Alison.

"Suppose you tell me a story," said David evasively.

"No, but I'll say poetry. Shall I, Babs? I love poetry; I don't mind learning poetry one bit. I learn lots just to please myself, not 'cause of Mummy. What'll I say, Babs? I can do the 'Pied Piper' and 'Young Lochinvar', and 'Killiecrankie', and... and lots of the *Child's Garden*, and I just love Tennyson."

David looked at Alison with respect; he remembered how "The Lady of Shalott" had opened a magic gate for him some eighteen years ago. "What do you know of Tennyson?" he asked her.

"Oh – Elaine the fair Elaine the lovable Elaine the lily maid of Astrakan!" burst out Alison in one breath.

"Oh, the 'Pied Piper'," begged Babs, "all the rats – do!"

"No, I'll do 'The Heights of Killiecrankie'," decided Alison. She clutched the seat with both hands, and began in a rapid singsong which was yet very dramatic, jigging herself up and down to keep time with the swinging ballad and the lurching train. David watched, fascinated; she was enjoying herself with the utmost abandon. Some words she forgot, many she mispronounced, but the fire of the old story was kindled within her, and when she reached:

"We flung away the scabbards
And we swore to do or die!"

her black eyes sparkled like stars with excitement.

"Now I'll do 'Young Lochinvar'," she said, as she came to the end, and began without a breath,

"Oh Young Lochinvar is come out of the west."

"Thank you awfully," said David, when she finished. "You *have* got a splendid memory, Alison. You're as good as Pet Marjorie. D'you know about her? I have a lovely wee book all about her, and you shall read it."

"Was she preciosus? Mummy says I'm preciosus," Alison informed him. "She doesn't say it to me. She said it to Dad, when I was meant to be asleep. So it must have been something nice, 'cause people don't mind saying nasty things straight at you. She said it was 'cause she liked poetry so much herself and read lots to me."

"Your house isn't dark?" broke in Babs, "like Nauntie May's? No room for Satan, is there?"

"Not a square inch," said David emphatically. "Country houses are always light and jolly, Babs, and much more sensible than town ones."

"Mr. Grant," said Babs anxiously, "who made Satan? It couldn't have been God."

Fortunately, Alison intervened. "It's very nice of you to take us to your house, Mr. Grant," she said.

"Must we *always* call you Mr. Grant?" asked Babs.

"Let's find a name for him," cried Alison in glee.

"What shall it be?" asked David, with amusement.

"Nuncle," said Babs.

"But he's not a nuncle," protested Alison, "and *that* would be acting a lie! And you know, what the Bible says about liarites, Babs Sutherland!" She had coined the word herself, proceeding on the principle that those persons denounced in Scripture, the Hittites, were depraved characters who, in nursery phrase, "struck back".

"My sister Minnie has a nickname for me," laughed David, "but it's a horrid one. She used to call me Tousle, because my hair was always so untidy when I was wee."

"But it would be so rude for us to call you that," said Alison shocked," and you a grown-up gentleman." Then she cried, "I know. We'll call you 'Young Lochinvar' – out of the poetry, you know. It's so pretty. You're not very young, of course" – in a dubious tone – "but we can leave that out. Anyway you're nice!"

And so David arrived home with a new name, and the children with great expectations, and corresponding appetites. Minnie met them, all smiles, and when they sat down to tea together the parlour was more crowded than it had been for a very long time.

Minnie and David had made great preparations. They had looked out the old china which belonged to their own nursery days. Minnie wanted Babs to have her mug with the purple carnations, and "For a Good Girl" on it, but David objected. "Keep that for Alison," he said. "How could you do anything else with that inscription? Besides, I always hated that mug. We got our castor oil out of it, in lemon juice! Don't you mind? Babs shall have my plate and cup with the nice florid apple painted on it. It's not as good as his own plate with the Three Bears, but that can't be helped. And haven't you got those wee brown porridge bowls still, with 'There's Mair in the Kitchen' written on the foot? It's usually a lie, but no matter!"

"At least, he shall have my horn spoon," declared Minnie, and she sent Jenny to rummage out the top shelf in the pantry.

There was also a pepperpot shaped like a mottled bird's egg, which delighted Babs so that he played with it till the pepper all came out, and nearly choked him, at which Minnie frowned on David, who had unearthed the bird's egg. And there were little jam dishes formed like thistles, with a coloured map of Scotland in the foot of them, which had come from Perth, and which Alison fell in love with immediately.

There was much running of bath water that night, and shouting, and splashing, and rushing of small, bare feet along the passages. Alison enjoyed immensely sitting on a high chair to have her hair brushed, by the light of two tall candles in burnished candlesticks instead of gas. "I feel like a fairy-tale now, or a Roman Catholic!" she announced to Minnie.

Babs lost himself happily in the feather bed which fell to his share; it was so very big, and he so very small. And they heard him murmuring happily to himself: "Now I'm Sinbad the Sailor, and I'm buried alive and it's jus' lovully being buried alive an' then I'll escape out through a little little hole and see a... crocodile... eating... Nauntie May..."

The rest was sleep, and silence.

Minnie and David came and stood at the door on their way to bed. Alison was in the bigger room, and Babs in the little one opening off. A breeze sent the ramblers tapping against the window, and below there came the calling of night birds through the spring gloaming.

"I always like that old fellow who had mottoes cut over the doors of all his rooms," said David, musing. "A minister, wasn't he, and put 'Martha, Martha!' in Greek letters over his wife's store-room!

I think if I had a nursery, I'd take that bit of Stevenson to put over its door –

> *'A pleasant place wherein to wake,*
> *And hear the leafy garden shake*
> *And rustle in the wind.'* "

Minnie gripped his arm. "Do you remember our nursery in the basement, Davie?" she said.

Twenty

He to her a hero is,
And sweeter she than primroses.
—R. L. Stevenson

Minnie came down from her room about eleven into the glory of a perfect May morning. She had put on an old, cool, tennis skirt, and a very much washed shirt blouse; and the world seemed a pre-war world again.

David was away at the office.

The children were on the back lawn, playing their favourite game. It was a curious game, invented by their two selves, and no one had ever been able to trace its obscure origin. They called it the game of "Police Offices", and played it in this wise. Alison, a distracted mother, had lost some half-dozen of her innumerable children, and must needs pursue them, going from police office to police office, where Babs, as sergeant or plain clothes detective, or something equally mysterious, took down the names and description of the missing offspring, and looked up details in a ponderous tome which they had stolen from the parlour bookcase, and which was really a German Bible, although they never imagined it. I do not know whether Alison ever found her children. The charm of the game consisted in the police office, in the piles of documents, in scribbling with David's stump of blue pencil, and above all, in turning over the pages of the German Bible with a moistened thumb and an expression of profound wisdom. Alison indeed sometimes rebelled against Babs continuing to play the most fascinating role, but she was quite consoled when the idea came to her of lunching at Macvittie's half-way through her search, and ordering the courses as her own mother often did. She would seat herself at the kitchen table, remark on the heat, and scan an old almanac in place of a menu with a blasé air; after which prelude, Jenny in the character of waiter would furnish her with hot oatcakes from the oven, and jam skimmings in a saucer. Babs always made a point of appearing then, and deserting the German Bible.

This was the game, with variations; and when once they had started on it, they were safe for a good hour.

Minnie knew that, and did not trouble about them; she went into the kitchen where Jenny was making marmalade. The entire household had sat round the kitchen table the night before, cutting up the peel into strips, and messing themselves liberally with juice; and now a delicious, warm, orangy smell hung about the kitchen walls, and penetrated into the hall in whiffs, whenever the door was opened.

Minnie sniffed appreciatively. "I love marmalade time," she said. "Will I be awfully in the way if I ask you for an iron, Jenny?"

"I'll heat ye one in twa shakes o' a sheepie's tail, dearie Miss Minnie," declared Jenny.

"I just have some collars that need freshening up," explained Minnie, spreading a cloth on the low dresser, and sitting down to wait. Jenny set the iron to the blazing fire.

"Ay," she said, beginning to chop suet for the dinner, "It's graun tae see ye in dacent claithes again, Miss Minnie my lamb. Yon uniform'll dae for the men, but in spite o' a' their havers, the lassie's'll never be sic clean gone dottled, Godforsaken fules as tae stick tae it. A wumman's a wumman, I will say. And dinna you forget it, dearie, ye may be a poo'er in the state and a pillar o' the kirk, but a wumman's main job has aye been tae mind her man, and bring up her weans, and will be till the Day o' Judgment. Ma mither used tae say, 'Ay, Jenny,' she wad say, 'ye ken naething aboot life till ye've borne weans, and bred them, and married them – ay, and *burried* them!'" "And she burried fower."

"We can't all marry," said Minnie, clasping her hands thoughtfully, and resting her chin on them. "There's not enough men to go round, you know."

Jenny merely snorted. "There's aye men enow gin the lassie's the richt sort," she declared.

Minnie sprang up, and reached for the iron. "Jenny," she remarked, as the hot surface hissed along the damp muslin, "David's looking well."

"He's weel in boady," admitted Jenny.

Minnie thumped her iron vigorously. "What I want to know," she said, "is – have you been hunting out a wife for him, eh, Jenny?"

"Losh keep us, no' me," exclaimed Jenny. "I wouldna say I'd mind seein' him settled, indeed it wad be a verra guid thing. But he was aye a finicky laddie, and I thocht he'd dae best tae pick yin for himsel'."

"I doubt he's been doing it, then," said Minnie. She came and put the iron to reheat; then remained by the fire, sitting on her heels, and watching the marmalade bubble, and the little bag of pips drift about in the frothy jelly.

"Jenny," she burst out at last, half-laughing and half-crying, "I'm horribly, disgustingly, primitively jealous. I never thought I'd be such a cat. David *is* in love, and I know it's the very best thing possible, and yet I don't want him to be."

Jenny stirred the marmalade with one hand, and laid the other on Minnie's shoulder. "I wouldna think that muckle o' ye if ye werena jealous, my lamb," she said.

"It's natural," said Minnie, "but I thought I had overcome the natural man – the natural woman, rather! I just feel I'd hate another girl here, but it's pure bosh and sentiment when I'm away the whole time."

"But what gars ye think it?" asked Jenny. "Has he tell't ye? Is it no juist yer ain notions aboot it?"

"It is just my own notions," admitted Minnie. "Did you ever know David tell anything of his own accord – though I must say he's been more communicative lately! Oh, but I'm certain. It's one of the Sutherlands – those children's aunts, I'll bet. I just wish I could see her, and if she's the right sort, I'll push the affair for all I'm worth. David needs pushing."

Jenny smiled broadly. "Dinna push ower far, dearie," she said. "Ye were aye for managin' his affairs as weel's yer ain. Mebbe ye'll push him the wrang gate if ye dinna tak' tent."

Minnie got to her feet, and took the iron. "I'll be canny," she said. "Trust me." She set to her ironing with energy to give vent to her spirits. It was like Minnie to take up a disagreeable duty with all her heart. She did not wish David married, but if he wanted it, married he should be, and she would manage the business properly. She loved him too well to do anything less.

The next day, at supper, she began her experiment; it was really David himself who gave her an opportunity.

"I called at the Sutherlands' today," he remarked. "They had a letter from London. The poor chap is just holding his own. He's an awfully strong fellow, and I don't think he'll give in easily. Nannie is better. She's coming downstairs again. Marion is pretty washed out. Jove, she *has* a life of it!"

Minnie looked at him over the coffee pot.

"She's not so capable as the Effie one, is she? Pity all the burden falls on her," she said quite indifferently.

"She's as capable as any woman needs to be," said David quickly.

"But not very strong?"

"She spends all her strength on the others."

"What's she like? I couldn't very well make her out in the photo. She didn't look as attractive as the rest of them."

David laid down his fork. "Some people have all their goods in the window," he said.

Minnie smiled. "Go on, Tousle! You defend her well."

He glanced at her suspiciously.

"I'd like to meet the lady," continued Minnie imperturbably. "She sounds as if she needed a rest and change. If the invalid can be left, why not ask her to come out and fetch the kids home – and stay a day in between. Today's Wednesday – ask her to come on Friday afternoon, and she could get the weekend in. It would be company for me."

David hesitated, biting his lip. "I don't know that she would come," he began.

"I think she would," contradicted Minnie.

"You don't know anything about her," said he impatiently.

"Well, why don't you tell me?" she asked point-blank. "I haven't second sight. You're a remarkably presentable brother on the whole, David, but I wish the fairies at your christening hadn't endowed you with such a stock of Scotch reserve!"

She leant her elbows on the table, and clasped her hands under her chin. "Tousle!" she begged.

David unclasped her hands, and took them in his. "Curiosity killed the cat!" he laughed. "Well, I'll say more for you than you did for me."

"You're the nicest sister any one ever had, and you don't deserve to be kept in the dark. But I didn't mean to keep you in the dark; I've been screwing myself up to telling you. Minnie, my dear, I do love her very much. And I think… she knows it. That's why I don't think she'll come."

He was rather red by the time he had finished, and Minnie coloured too, and drew away her hands. "I'm glad," she said heartily. "But she's got to come, David. The invitation needn't be from you; I'll write. And she won't see much of you since you're out most of the day."

"But it's my house," said David dourly, "and there's Sunday, and the evenings. It wouldn't be fair on her."

Minnie got up with a shrug. "Don't be so dashed chivalrous," she ordered. "You haven't… said anything?"

"Not… no, I haven't said anything."

"All right. She'll be a fool if she's embarrassed. I want to be kind to her, don't you see? The rest will do her a heap of good. And – I want to see her!"

"Truth's coming out. Well, perhaps you're right about the rest. God knows she needs it. Ask her if you like, only it won't be easy for either her or me. And don't you go matchmaking, Minnie, and arranging things all the time, and expecting me to bring it off. I'll be damned if I ask a girl to my house on pretence of kindness and a holiday and all that, and then go and propose to her! It wouldn't be decent."

He met her eyes defiantly.

"You look nice when you're raised," she remarked with coolness, "Keep calm though. You do the just and honourable, and I'll give her a good time, and we'll bide a while for the proposal." She rumpled his hair as she passed him, and then ran out of the room, laughing.

She skipped upstairs breathlessly, and went to her bedroom for paper and fountain pen. This was the letter she wrote:

"I have heard so much about you from my brother that I am longing to meet you. As you speak of having the children back this weekend, could you not come out yourself on Friday afternoon and take them home on Monday? It would give us such pleasure to have you, and myself especially, as I am lonely out here all day while David is in town. I am sure your sister could spare you; we were glad to hear she was keeping better."

Minnie read it over with a chuckle. "Heard so much," she murmured. "What a proficient liar I have become… David, of course, being in town most of the weekend… I've made myself sound quite a pelican in the wilderness!"

But she posted the letter.

Twenty-One

Why should a dog, a horse, a rat, have life.
And thou no breath at all? Thou'lt come no more.
Never...

—King Lear

I
t was on Thursday morning that Marion got the invitation. Post always came at breakfast time; but not knowing Minnie's writing, she had laid the letter aside to pour out Uncle Alexander's third cup, and get Billy away in time, and she forgot it till they had gone and she was alone in the dining-room. She poured the last dregs from the teapot into her cup, and sat down wearily for a few minutes' rest before clearing the table.

It was very dreary now in the Sutherlands' house. Marion was half sorry she had let the children go, in spite of the increased quiet, and lessened work. Without Effie, without Jullie, it was a changed place; Billy was at school all day, and Uncle Alexander at the office. There was nothing to do but make beds, and dry dishes, and darn stockings. At about eleven Nannie would come limply down stairs with a shawl, and take the big chair by the parlour window, and there she would sit without speaking. It was a dull house indeed; and the shadow of Pat's danger was over it too. Fragrance and colour had gone out of life; and Marion's hat with the new ribbon lay unused in her drawer.

She was thinking of these things, and wondering whether they could possibly eat cold mutton for a fourth time that week, when she caught sight of the neglected letter. She opened it. She read down to the first words of the invitation, and no further.

What did it mean? To get away from the sickly, weary atmosphere of this house for two – three whole days, away from Nannie, from cooking… she had not been away since a fortnight's holiday last summer. What bliss it would be to lie long in bed in the mornings! She thought of that first, in the childish ecstasy of joy which came to her.

But could she go? For one night, perhaps, not more. She could not leave the burden of the house for a whole weekend on Nana, who was not her own servant, who had already worked herself tired in her willingness.

That was it; she would have one glorious night of romance, of fairyland; she would be Cinderella running off for a short, enchanted time from the fireside. The fun of it made her clap her hands together as Alison would have done.

Then she realised what this meant, that behind the invitation was David. Perhaps Miss Grant was only being polite. "I'd better just run out for tea," she thought regretfully. But dared she? She cared so much, and she had fancied that he cared too. And yet it was all uncertain; he had said nothing. Nannie's old cruel words haunted her. "I would never push myself forward, or run after a man if I was to die for not doing it," she thought, flushing angrily.

She pondered over it that morning as she sat darning in the parlour. But the spell was too strong. In two hours' time she had reasoned herself out of doubts and false modesty, and her logic was a pliable thing, like the logic of a good many women. "After all the children must be fetched," she persuaded herself, "and I shouldn't wonder if I broke down shortly unless I had a rest."

The children and her health had nothing in the least to do with it. She could not put her reasons into words, but it would be fun and she was going.

It was then that Nana opened the door, and said, "Ladies, mum!"

Mrs. Gerard came in first, jaunty as usual, in a youthful hat, and champagne-coloured stockings. She grasped Marion's hand, and introduced, "My friend, Miss Brixton."

"My friend, Miss Brixton," was a big, plump woman, over thirty, with very fair hair, no colour, and a deep voice; she wore a string of heavy green beads round her neck, and used a small lorgnette whenever she spoke. Her clothes were finely made.

"How entirely nice of you to let us call so early," began Mrs. Gerard, although she had not asked permission.

Marion sighed, and pushed away the darning basket.

"But we mustn't interrupt you," protested Mrs. Gerard. "We really came to see Nannie. I hope the dear child's better this morning. You can't think how all this has distressed me, Miss Marion."

Marion rose. "I'll tell her," she said, "if you'll excuse me a moment."

"She'll probably be expecting us," remarked Mrs. Gerard. Marion was mystified, but she escaped with relief, and sought out Nannie, who when she heard the news, changed her old blouse for a new black silk jumper, and went down hastily.

Marion was busy after that up in the linen press; she heard the door bang, when half an hour had passed, but she paid no heed. When next she came downstairs, she was surprised to find that Nannie had gone out with the other two. She stood, swinging one foot, and frowning. It was stupid of Nannie, for the day had become colder, with an east wind, and in any case, she ought not to have taken her first outing after her illness with mere strangers. It was thoughtless of her; "after all the trouble we've had with her," thought Marion in vexation.

Lunch time came, and brought no Nannie. Marion sat down alone, and felt angry, and not in the least hungry. She prepared a plain speech to be delivered to Nannie on her first appearance; and set aside her vegetarian pie almost untasted, puzzling the while over Nannie's conduct.

Sometime after she had helped Nana to clear away, the front door swung open, and Nannie came in. She had only a jacket over her frock, and wore thin stockings and shoes; her face was rather flushed, and she looked excited and overtired. Marion felt ready to slap her, and equally ready to dose her with quinine. "Where have you been?" she cried, drawing her into the dining-room.

"To lunch with Mrs. Gerard" said Nannie carelessly.

"But you're dreadful," said Marion sharply. "You're a great silly, Nannie, to rush out like this after being so very ill. It's bitter today, and you haven't even a scarf. I don't know what's taken you, at all."

"Surely I can visit my own friends," said Nannie fretfully, Marion saw that she was very tired indeed. "Lie down on the sofa," she said, trying to speak gently. "Do, Nannie." But Nannie sat upright, playing with her gloves, and staring straight before her.

"Why did you go?" asked Marion again. "Was that Miss Brixton there?"

"Yes, of course."

"Why of course? Do you know her? I never set eyes on her before."

"Edith Gerard introduced us," said Nannie. "She's known her for ages. She's very keen on her."

"She seemed to me a queer fish," declared Marion. "I hate women with deep voices."

"Oh, you are prejudiced about everything," cried Nannie crossly. "She's really quite a sport; has a flat out Murrayfield somewhere. She's jolly well off, and has lots of taste. She smokes cigarettes of different colours to match her different frocks, and Edith Gerard told me her bathroom is quite oriental with black and gold tiling. All the flat is nice, so Edith Gerard says. Of course, she can afford to do it. All these people can."

"What people?" demanded Marion.

"Like Miss Brixton. She's a... well, I don't know what you call it; not a medium, but she's quite professional. She knows all about spiritualism, and arranges for séances at her house, and is in communication with all the well-known mediums. Of course, she charges a fee, and I suppose the money pretty well rolls in, especially now."

Marion shivered. "What a horrid woman," she said.

"There you are again," pouted Nannie. "All prejudice. I suppose you think all that's a fraud?"

"I don't care whether it is or not," declared Marion. "I don't want to have anything to do with it. Anyway, you're to come to bed and have your tea there. And for mercy's sake, Nannie, don't go running out again till the doctor's seen you. He's coming tomorrow afternoon, because I phoned."

"But I'll be out tomorrow afternoon" said Nannie quite unexpectedly. "You'll need to put him off."

"Out? Where on earth?" gasped Marion.

"At Miss Brixton's of course. Oh, to be sure, you didn't know." Nannie twisted her gloves, and pointed her neat shoe before her. "I've made an appointment with her."

"But why? What to do?" cried Marion breathlessly. She ran and sat down on the sofa by Nannie's side. Nannie's colour rose high, and she sat up straight, and took one of Marion's hands.

"About – Noël, of course," she answered with a little sob in her voice.

"O Nannie." burst out Marion, "you don't mean you're going to let that horrid, vulgar woman swindle you about... about things like that? I couldn't bear it if I were you. Tell me just all about it."

"Well," said Nannie talking rapidly. "Of course, Edith knew how cut up I was, and she wanted to help me. And she's very gone on Miss Brixton, and has begun to study with her all the science of the thing. She says she has a peculiar talent for it. So she brought her over the afternoon you left to see me, and see if she could help me – if Miss Brixton could, I mean. And she says she can; she says at least she can try and communicate with Noël through a medium she knows about here. Oh, Marion, don't look that way! If you knew how miserable I am… how much I want him. If I could only know he was still really – somewhere – it would help. Anything sure and certain about him… and she says…"

Marion's heart smote her for Nannie. She put an arm round her shaking shoulders, and drew close to her. "But I don't see," she began awkwardly, "the Bible, says, a sure and certain hope of the resurrection of the dead, at least, I think that's in the Bible somewhere."

"But I don't believe the Bible," sobbed Nannie. "I can't."

"Then how can you believe this horrid woman?"

"Oh, but it's different. Think, May, a message really from him supposing he is alive…"

"But it wouldn't be really from him. Nannie, listen! It's all a disgusting hoax…"

"No, no, it's not. You should hear the things Miss Brixton tells, simply wonderful."

Marion sat up again and hesitated. "And have you fixed up definitely?" she asked slowly,

"Yes," faltered Nannie, drying her eyes, "and I've paid the fee, too."

Marion looked at her; she was all unstrung, obviously ill yet, and under the influence of a morbid emotion and a pathetic desire. It was pitifully sad, and very natural; but Marion realised what awful danger there might be in the effect of such an experience on Nannie. Suddenly, impetuously, she slid to her knees beside the sofa, and held out beseeching hands to Nannie, the tears starting from her own eyes.

"Nannie," she cried, "you won't go… you mustn't go! Oh, my dear… promise, promise me. I just shan't let you. It's too great a risk. You won't go." She had caught Nannie's arms as she spoke, and did not realise with what a tight grip she held them, as though by the holding she might prevent Nannie from leaving her and taking the risk.

"Let go," cried Nannie, "you'll make me black and blue. I must go, so don't say another word."

"It will make you worse," insisted Marion passionately. "Nannie, you might think of me… of us if you don't care about yourself. You'll be ill again. I shall tell Uncle Alexander, and he'll positively forbid it."

Nannie flamed scarlet. "How dare you?" she cried. "As if I wasn't of age! Did Uncle Alexander ever prevent me yet from doing anything I wanted? No, and he won't, and you won't either."

She burst into tears, sobbing hysterically. Marion got to her feet; she saw that it was absolutely necessary to keep her own head, and be quiet. Nannie was beyond all reasoning; she could only moan, and declare she would go, like an obstinate child. Marion began to fear that the effect of opposing her desire would be even worse for her than the effect of the actual séance. She stood biting her lip, and wondering helplessly what to do. Nannie had spoken truth about Uncle Alexander; he was ineffectual in spite of his well-meaning kindness, and he had never had the least authority with any of the children. He had rather been inclined to lean on them for support.

Then Marion made up her mind. If Uncle Alexander was weak, she could not afford to be; and if Nannie behaved like a child, she must be treated like one.

Marion sat down beside her on the sofa. Responsibility and authority were things she had always shrunk from, and now her hands were trembling and her voice unsteady. Why did all this depend on her alone?

"Nannie," she said, "whatever you promise or don't promise, and however much you cry, you – are – not – going!"

Nannie looked up from her handkerchief and Marion's eyes met hers steadily; it is an odd thing that people often look most severe when they are sick with nervousness. To the sobbing, excited girl, Marion seemed firm enough.

Nannie's silence encouraged her. She took one of her sister's hands, and began to stroke it soothingly, with a vague idea of mesmerising Nannie into submission.

"You're not going," she repeated more decisively. "And I am going out now to send a wire to this Miss Brixton saying that the doctor forbids it, also a wire to Mrs. Gerard. So the whole thing's at an end. See? Now, I'll get you some nice strong coffee, and when that's warmed you up, you'll lie down in bed. I'm sure you must be tired."

Nannie was tired, completely exhausted with her outing and the excitement and sobbing. She felt all strength to resist ebbing from her.

"You hateful thing," she faltered, but she rose limply, leaning on Marion's arm, and suffered herself to be led upstairs. Marion helped her to undress, and then drew the blankets over her. As she did so, the two came very close together, and Marion bent down and gave Nannie a hurried kiss.

"You'll feel better soon," she said, trying to speak tenderly. "I'll get you a nice book at the library when I'm out."

That kiss moved Nannie. She was like a naughty child when it is forgiven.

"I was so miserable," she sobbed in repentant self-defence.

"I know," said Marion.

Then she went and despatched the two telegrams. Only after that had been done could she feel secure again.

Twenty-Two

Oh! Young Lochinvar is come out o' the west...
—OLD BALLAD

Marion felt very much like Cinderella as she stood before the glass at midday on Friday. She wore her hat with the purple and silver ribbon, and the new grey coat and skirt which Beatrice had helped her to choose; Nannie's grey suède shoes, borrowed for the occasion, were on her feet, and to give the finishing touch, she twisted a piece of fresh lavender tulle round her throat. There might be no glass slipper or satin train, but Marion was well satisfied. She did one or two pirouettes, stood back to inspect herself better, and nearly cricked her neck in her efforts to see whether her hair was quite tidy behind.

There was colour in her cheeks, and excitement enough in her heart to transform the sooty railway carriage which bore her to Castlerig into the most luxurious of pumpkin coaches. She felt at ease about Nannie, now that she had sent off these wires, and she gave herself up entirely to the enjoyment of the story-book world into which she was being carried. From the moment when she arrived at Castlerig she walked in romance; and when David came home at tea-time and greeted her with his quick smile her story-book world was complete. For the fairest dream castle is empty without the fairy prince.

They had supper in the parlour, with the windows open to the garden; it had been a golden afternoon, and the light streamed in more golden through the branches of a great yellow laburnum just outside.

After the dull and lonely meals at home, that supper was a whirl of gaiety to Marion. The little room seemed to be full of people; David, at the foot of the table, helping absurdly large portions, Minnie opposite, pouring out fragrant coffee, rich with creamy milk. Dr. Ross, who had come in for the evening, less taciturn than usual, and given to making bad jokes, Alison and Babs excited and happy. The table shone with its white cloth and bright silver – Marion remembered the yellowness of their own – and there were scones and fresh, sweet butter, and cress in a crystal dish of water, and dainty green-handled knives with which to spread Jenny's homemade jam.

The conversation was a noisy affair, punctuated by laughter, and David's frequent warning: "The next pun will be your last, Ross!" followed by a menacing gesture with the carving knife and giggles from the children, who did not in the least understand what a pun was.

The chief topic, as supper came to an end, was, "What shall we do next?"

"Well, what *shall* we do?" asked Minnie for the hundredth time. "David, pass Miss Sutherland the shortbread again; she only wants pressing."

Alison looked up beseechingly from the folding of her feeder.

"Charades, of course!" she said reproachfully. "You promised."

"I did," admitted Minnie. "They've dressed up for tea every single day, Miss Sutherland. An old kilt of David's, my dressing gown, and a squashy felt hat have assisted at representations of Mary Queen of Scots, Peter Pan, William Wallace, Moses, and a host of other worthies, sacred and secular. I was hoping the craze would wear off before they discovered the beauties of burnt cork, but in vain, and we have been afflicted by the Kaiser ever since, with moustaches rampant. And charades were to be the crowning glory when you came! But we haven't long. Bedtime, you know."

"Aw!" sighed Alison and Babs in concert.

"You don't expect an old, cave-man like me to act?" demanded Ross.

David turned to Marion as he rose from his chair.

"Miss Sutherland shall be queen of the revels," he announced, "and her decision shall be final."

"Yes, yes! Let me crown her," clamoured Alison, pulling two pieces of wallflower from the bowl on the table, and reaching up to stick them in Marion's hair.

Marion stood up, laughing and blushing; there was a spirit of mischief entering into her.

"I decree that we have charades," she cried. "Alison and Babs are to stay up extra late in honour of the occasion, and everyone is to act, including Dr. Ross!" And she gave the shirker a smile, which David, watching, grudged him.

"The Queen has spoken," said Minnie.

"How late?" asked Babs breathlessly.

"Half-past eight; not a minute more," said Marion. "Now!"

They picked sides, Minnie choosing the Doctor and leaving David for Marion. Alison and Babs were to act on both sides in turn, so as to get as much out of their crowded hour as possible. They dashed up to their bedroom at once to search for the acting clothes; Alison found a wreath off one of Minnie's old hats, and she would have been quite happy all the evening strutting up and down in front of the wardrobe mirror imagining herself Queen Elizabeth.

Minnie's side had its innings first; and Marion and David laughed themselves sore over a scene at the Zoo, with Dr. Ross in the rôle of elephant.

"We must do something original," they said to each other, while the actors were disrobing.

"I have it," said David. "You know that plan of taking a

famous man's name, each initial letter in turn, and acting scenes in the life of other famous people whose names begin with that particular letter. Oh, that's confoundedly complicated! Well, suppose we take Paul; first we act a scene from *Peter Pan* – that's P. Then we might give them *Antony and Cleopatra* – that would be A: and so on. Are you absolutely in a fog?"

"Not a bit; that's a splendid notion," agreed Marion. "Let's take Paul; it's not too long."

They did take Paul. The performance went smoothly until they came to L; then they hesitated, searching for a suitable name. Alison seemed to be struggling with something half-remembered; then she gave a delighted skip, and caught David's arm. "I know," she cried. "What we call you – Lochinvar!"

Something made David colour. He looked at Marion. "Shall we?" he asked.

"We'd better; time's flying," she replied.

They made her the bride. "You must be very beautiful," explained Alison, dragging from the wardrobe an old evening wrap which Aunt Margaret had given – second-hand – to Cousin Jessie, years ago. It was woven of green and white and gold thread, yellowed slightly with time and smelling faintly of cupboards and rosemary. Marion drew it round her shoulders, over her white dress, and the wallflower was like a crown.

"I'll be the real offended bridegroom," announced Alison, sketching fierce moustaches on her rosy face with a fragment of cork. "Babs can be the haughty sisters, or the suspicious father and mother." That left the title rôle for David, and it was easy for him to cast a plaid about himself, and clap on an ancient highland bonnet with a feather in it.

The ball opened in grand style; the offended bridegroom twirled imaginary moustaches, the haughty sisters and the suspicious father and mother ogled Lochinvar and flounced their skirts. The hero made a gallant entrance, sweeping off his bonnet with a low bow; the heroine gave him shy glances, then her hand, and then a dance, all with the proper intervals of hesitation. Once they passed the door and danced on, twice – and then, a pressure of her hand, a defiant glance flung towards the rest of the company, and away they went!

It was a pretty thing, and no play-acting to Minnie. She sprang up, clapping her hands as it ended, and Will Ross shouted encores. The applause brought the runaway couple back again, breathless, laughing, and shamefaced as grownups are when they have fallen victims to the fascination of a game. Marion sank down on the window seat to gain breath, and the cloak billowed out around her; she made as though to pull the wallflower from her hair, but Alison stopped her. "You're queen still, you know," she reminded her; and David's heart echoed the words.

He had flung off the plaid and bonnet, and stood near the window. "Did you guess?" he asked.

"I should think so," said Minnie. She looked at her watch. "Hours past bedtime. Come on, bairns! No, Miss Sutherland. I'll officiate. You came here to rest, not to bath Babs." And she carried the reluctant children away with her. Their voices floated down from the stair as they went, planning their dreams for the night; they always planned their dreams beforehand and were never discouraged because the scheme rarely worked.

When Minnie returned, the Doctor was sitting near the table, and David and Marion were on the window seat, apart by themselves. It was a round spacious window, and the seat ran in a semicircle. On the right hand sat Marion, leaning back, her hands folded placidly; on the left was David, in his favourite position, leaning forward a little and clasping one knee. His eyes were upon her, and lips and eyebrows mirrored all his moods as they talked.

The burning gold of the sun through the laburnum blossoms

had passed into a brooding golden haze above the garden and the line of the hills, and that, as the moon rose, into a flood of pale fairy gold, filling the space of night. Dreams seemed to come out of the shadowy lilacs, floating through the air, with the heavy scent of wallflower; and the moonlight made a halo about their two heads. And they talked freely, for there was a spell on them. Minnie sat down by Ross, and listened; she was taking Marion's measure that night.

"I wish I had read poetry," Marion was saying. "I'm so hopelessly ignorant. But I love every scrap I can get hold of."

"Don't you find yourself remembering little lovely bits and saying them over?" said David. "It's a very bad habit of mine! There's that thing of Stevenson's – two lines of it just sing themselves again and again:

> *'Grey recumbent tombs of the dead in desert places,*
> *Standing stones on the vacant, wine-red moor.'*

The very sound of that long sort of line is like the wind down howes of the Pentlands."

"Don't be shocked, please," said Marion, "but what *is* a howe? I'm Scotch, but I don't know that."

David laughed. "I must teach you," he said. "A howe's a hollow, so is a haugh; that's a wide hollow by a riverside. And a hope's a wee glen. I never knew what a syke was till I dipped into Dorothy Wordsworth's journal. It's that sort of nameless trickle that 'creeps tae swell the heids o' the burns,' as John Buchan says."

"There's one piece of poetry I love," said Marion. "It's the only piece I know of, and it's like magic, the way it swings:

> *'Lovely are the curves of the white owl sweeping*
> *Wavy in the dusk lit by one large star.'*

"You know it; it's Meredith,"

"He's great," said David. "His *Woods of Westermain* is the weirdest thing I know. Isn't "Westermain" a lovely word?"

"Funny how one word can be like a whole line of poetry," mused Marion, "and make you think of all sorts of things. Your uncle's name – Traquair, always does that to me. It's a fine old name. It makes me think of the ballad about the gates of Traquair that were shut till Prince Charlie should return, and have never been opened. Isn't there something sad about it?"

"Do you know the Jacobite song?" asked David.

'Hearts tae break, but nine tae sell,
Gear tae tine but nane tae hain,
We maun dree a weary spell
Ere oor lad comes back again.'

"This poetry competition is all very pretty," quoth Minnie to herself, "but we must get something more out of the lady." And when Marion remarked, "I'm sure I should have been a Jacobite if I had lived in the old days," she struck in with: "You may be thankful you didn't – cooped up like a wax doll and made to sew samplers. If I had lived in the old days, I should have felt suffocated. Just think, women had no sort of chance then."

Marion turned her head from the window. "But what difference have all our chances made?" she asked. "Has our education helped such a marvellous lot? I don't see it. I'd just as soon have lived then."

The two men were silent, interested listeners, and Minnie took up the cudgels again. "D'you mean, you think our times are no better?" she demanded.

"I don't think so," said Marion, "in some ways worse."

"But you can't gainsay the facts," retorted Minnie. "Our social life is immensely higher. For example, gentlemen don't lie about drunk under their own dinner-tables nowadays. Things *have* progressed."

"Perhaps," said Marion unconvinced. "I think it's all outward though. I think it was just as possible to be a fine true woman then as now, in spite of no university education, and they had more time to do it in and less rush."

Her eyes had kindled with the keenness of the argument. David's heart went out to her. There was a glorious exhilaration between them that night; even Minnie and Will Ross shared in it. It was sweet to talk of beautiful things to her, it was sweeter to hear her defend herself with such spirit. The conversation and friendship, and the mystery of the night, and beneath them all, his love, were like a strong wine that lightened his heart and stirred his spirit.

A silence fell; then Marion, looking out to the garden, said, "What a perfect night!" David threw open the window; it was so low that he could step out, and after a moment's hesitation, she followed him. They stood together under the huge dome of the sky; the moon was sailing triumphantly, flinging clear light down through the winds, laying bare the fields and garden, and the utmost ends of the vacant hills. A strange, steadfast gladness came to David as he thought how back through centuries of men's lives the moon had shone of nights with the same enchantment for other friends and other lovers. Plato had talked in the groves, Shakespeare had talked at the "Mermaid," and nameless folk from the beginning had gone hand in hand, and loved each other. And it seemed that all the friendship and love of the world had endured, had been saved up that he and Marion might taste it now in its full strength; he knew himself to be marvelously rich, for the experience of every other man was concentrated into his own, and he was heir to all the world's happiness. The time that they stood there seemed like a fragment taken out of eternity.

Then he heard Marion give a long sigh of pleasure. "I don't think I ever saw so great a stretch of night sky all at once," she said, speaking low as if they were in a church.

"Ah, but you should see it from the corner down by the orchard," he answered. "That's the bit I like best. The hills seem to spread out…" He led the way across the lawn; it came back to his mind how he had picked the violets at that corner, how he had longed to give her that beauty for her own. At the fence, he turned to her. She had followed more slowly, not knowing the ground so well; now she came, making her way between the lilac bushes, one hand holding her skirts away from the dew and damp earth, the other clasping the green and gold tapestry of that foolish cloak which she had forgotten to lay aside; most of the wallflower had fallen from her hair, but a bit had caught just above her brow, and beneath its cluster of velvet buds her face showed pale in the moonlight, and her eyes were shining.

Beauty? She needed no gift of beauty. She had it within her. Something began to throb wildly at David's temples, and he clenched his hands to keep them steady at his sides. What had he said to Minnie? Would it be unfair to the girl? "Good God, why should it be?" he cried in his heart. "I've got to speak – now. Minnie can sneer, I must."

Then Marion, almost at his side, tripped over a root and would have stumbled. In a moment he had caught her, and she put her hand on his to steady herself. He held it; this time, she did not shrink away.

"Marion!" he said very low, "you beautiful thing!"

"Don't," she gasped. "I'm not. It's this silly cloak." Then she turned her head suddenly. "Listen! They're calling," she began. David listened too. Across the garden Minnie's voice trailed, very faint, then louder.

"It's me she's calling," said Marion, and she broke away from him, and caught up her skirts to run.

Twenty-Three

Why should we reck of hours that rend, while we two ride together;
The heavens rent from end to end, would be but stormy weather;
The strong stars shaken down in spate would be a shower of Spring,
And we should list the trump of fate, and hear a linnet sing.
—G. K. CHESTERTON

The next minute, the four of them stood staring at each other in the parlour, by the light of two candles flaring unsteadily in the draught from the open window. The anticlimax seemed ridiculous, until Minnie began to speak.

"Your maid rang up, Miss Sutherland," she said. "She says your sister isn't well, and that you'd better go in as soon as possible. I kept her waiting; hadn't you better speak yourself?"

Marion became very white; she tore off the bright cloak with a shaking hand, and pulled the last bit of wallflower from her hair. "Oh yes, please," she gasped. "Where is it? What else did she say?" She followed Minnie to the telephone.

David picked up the cloak and the wallflower. "She's missed the ten-five," he said. "Your two-seater, Will?"

"Surely, surely," said the Doctor quickly. "This is a sad business. I'm sorry for the poor lassie." He looked at his watch, and then turned towards the door. "I'll bring the car round now," he said. "We'll run in in twenty minutes or less."

David stopped him at the door. "I'm taking her in," he said.

"Havers," said Ross. "I'll be back within the hour."

"But I'll not," said David. "She told me her uncle was away

from home for the night – not that he would be much use anyway – and there's only the servant and the kid Billy there. And – we don't know what she's going to."

"I'm the very man, doctor and all," interrupted Ross.

"You're a wearied man with a busy day behind you, and another to look forward to."

The Doctor looked at David, at the cloak over his arm, at the bit of wallflower he was pulling to pieces nervously while he tried to catch the sound of the voice at the telephone.

"Have it your own way, lad," he said, and went out the door.

The telephone rang off abruptly, and David thought he heard a sob. He went into the parlour till Minnie and Marion had hurried upstairs together. Then he came back to the hall for his overcoat. He heard their voices above, and snatches of talk floated down between the rustling of paper and banging of drawers. "I'll pack your case," Minnie called. Then Marion's voice, low and indistinct, gave a long explanation which ended in a pitiful cry, "Why did she? I thought I had settled it quite." He heard Minnie say, "My dear," and then something about the children; and soon after they came down the stairs together, Marion wrapped in her thick coat, with a veil of Minnie's tied over her hat, Minnie carrying the case.

Marion hesitated at the foot of the stairs. "I hate bothering Dr. Ross," she faltered. David saw that she was making an effort not to cry. He went across and took the case from Minnie. "You aren't bothering him," he said with a smile. "I'm going instead." Marion drew in her breath. He felt she was shaking as he helped her into the car.

They left Minnie and Ross standing at the gate, gazing after them till the little red light of the car was eaten up by the darkness.

Again they were alone together under the moon and the night sky; but the romance and pageantry had gone. David said nothing; but stared straight before him into the shadows as he increased the speed, and the car leapt over the miles of road. Marion gradually ceased to tremble; he heard her begin to breathe naturally, and felt her body beside him relax. It was a strange, silent race they rode that night for Nannie's life.

David knew nothing of what had happened; Minnie had whispered to him hurriedly, "The sister's had a shock – mental. It's pretty bad." That was all, and he asked no questions.

They had come in sight of the town with its scattered lights before Marion spoke. Then she asked, "Do you believe in… in spiritualism?"

David had had philosophic doubts on the subject, but this was not the time to be philosophic. He felt her wait anxiously for his answer, and he began to guess at the nature of Nannie's shock.

"No, I don't" he said. "Not in the beastly, morbid frauds that pass for it."

"It *is* morbid; it's horrible," said Marion, and there was fierceness in her voice. "People shouldn't be allowed to."

She tried to make herself clear. David helped her out.

"Has Miss Sutherland…" he began, and she interrupted.

"Yes, that's it, about Noël Wyndham. I was so sorry for her, but I knew anything like… like that would upset her frightfully. It's that woman, Mrs. Gerard, who's got her to do it. I found out that she meant to before I came away, and I made her promise not to, and wired Mrs. Gerard to say the doctor forbade it. And… and I thought it would be all right. Oh, it's my fault… all my fault. I should never have left her. I might have known."

"How could you know?" asked David indignantly. "I think you did all you could. What went wrong?"

"Oh, Mrs. Gerard called after she got the wire, to say she was so sorry Nannie was worse. And they let her see Nannie, and she wheedled her round. Of course Nannie said it was all because of me interfering that the wire had been sent.

This was the very afternoon the séance was to be; so they just went. Nana... the children's nurse, you know... did everything she could, but she's a stranger, and it was no use. I don't wonder she couldn't manage Nannie. I could hardly myself."

"And now...?" David hardly liked to ask.

"She's most fearfully upset... lies and screams for me, doesn't let Nana come near her. The message they got through the medium wasn't comforting a bit, and she's gone all to pieces. She's got a temperature, too, Nana says. I knew she'd get a chill, running out like that yesterday in thin things, and overtiring herself. When she came home first she was sobbing and very ill and shaken, but she let Nana put her to bed. She slept a bit, but uneasily, and she had a dreadful nightmare and woke up shrieking; and the fever's high now... Nana didn't mean to bother me, as she knew I'd be home tomorrow, but it got too bad..."

Marion stopped, her voice shaking.

They were in the heart of the city now; shops and houses flew past, trees in the gardens, lights in a few high windows. Then they rounded a corner, and David brought the car to a standstill at the Sutherlands' door. The little street was very quiet; somewhere an area gate creaked hauntingly, and then slammed with a hollow rattle. Everything seemed to sleep. Above rose the house, with blank, curtained windows and not a gleam of light. It was like a gaunt, dead creature with the life gone out of its eyes; and the bell, when David pulled it, echoed away into emptiness.

He went to help Marion out of the car. She was shaking again, and white behind her veil, and she shrank back into her seat for a moment as if she dared not meet what was within the house. Then she placed a hand on David's arm, and he half lifted her down, and felt her body stiffen in her determination not to be afraid.

"My dear," he said, and she pressed his arm.

"Oh, I'm glad you're here," she whispered, then slipped

from him and went up the steps to the door. It opened, revealing a timid, shadowy figure in the half-lit hall. The figure threw itself upon Marion; it was Billy.

"Jolly good thing you turned up, May," he stammered; he had been crying, and was ashamed to let her see it.

"Don't shut the door," she said. "Mr. Grant's there."

"Thank the Lord," said Billy fervently. "Now we'll do. And the very night old Nunk was away. Nannie was a fool, but she's awful ill. She can scream, you bet."

Marion turned from him to David, who had come after her, and was now pulling off his gloves. "I don't know how to thank you," she said. "But... but you mustn't wait. You must get back home."

"I'll go home when you've done with me," he said. "Doctor sent for, Billy?"

Billy nodded. "He's been."

Marion opened the parlour door, and turned up the light. "Well, if you will wait, perhaps just till I... see how she is," she began uncertainly. "Come in here. I'll go up."

David, left to himself, paced up and down in the dismal little parlour for the longest space of weary time which he had ever endured. He tried to read the morning's paper which was lying on the table, but gave it up; such a lot had happened since that morning, and the war news seemed far away. Then he examined the scant store of books – sermons in dusty covers, for every family appears to have its relics of forgotten divinity, *Good Words* in several volumes, some sentimental novels which had been popular at the end of last century, Dickens complete, and obviously unread, *Treasure Island* with Billy's name on it, and a huge old Bible. The Sutherlands were patently not readers. He wondered where Marion kept her books – he felt certain she read.

He turned impatiently to the fire; the ugly black marble clock told him that he had been waiting there three-quarters of an hour, but it seemed thrice as long. There was not a sound in the house. Once he went to the door, and at the same time a door creaked open upstairs, and he thought he heard a cry.

At last Billy came in. "Nannie won't let Marion go," he said. "She's got tight hold of her hand, and kicks up the dickens of a row whenever she moves. And Nana says the doctor was to come back last thing, so he ought to be any minute now. And Marion says will you wait just till then to hear what he says."

"How's Miss Sutherland?" asked David.

"Awful feverish. They're sponging her all over with vinegar and things to take it down. *I* think she's in delirium, gases in the most awful way about poor old Noël. It's a rotten lookout." Billy flung himself on the sofa and banged a cushion on to the floor. "I say, you know," he added, "it was jolly sporting of you to bring May in."

"Only thing to do," said David laconically.

"I say," said Billy, "have a cig. Go on! They're only Nannie's, and putrid, 'cause the Nunk doesn't smoke, but never mind."

"Thanks, I don't think I will," said David with a smile.

"No? You don't mind me?" asked Billy, and helped himself. "Soothes the nerves. I say, what make of car is that you've got?"

David laughed outright. The air with which Billy stood, legs apart, puffing smoke rings, accorded so ill with his nice, schoolboy face, freckled and stumpy in all the features. They plunged into mechanics; and then the doctor came.

David saw him before he went away, and explained himself and asked for an honest verdict.

"It's serious – very," said the doctor. "First thing they've got to do is to get the temperature down. They're trying all they can. Then I've left a sleeping draught. Miss Sutherland has had a severe shock, and taken a heavy chill on top of it, and after her previous illness it's no joke. I'll call first thing in the morning, and am seeing about a nurse."

"But there's no immediate danger?" asked David.

"Not if the fever goes down and she sleeps. The thing is, she won't let Miss Marion leave her side just now. The nurse is a stranger, and nothing will do but her sister holding her hand. That girl's a brick. I didn't believe she had it in her to do it."

Pride stirred in David as though he had been praised himself. After the doctor left, a message came to him from Marion, and he went upstairs. Nana opened the door to him. Her hair and apron were dishevelled, and she looked haggard and tired. She had had to struggle with Nannie all evening until Marion came, and was still constantly on her feet, bringing fresh supplies of cold water and toilet vinegar. She beckoned to Marion. Marion drew away her hand, and David heard her say soothing words, as one speaks to a child; the bed was hidden from him, but immediately Nannie began to cry out imploringly till her voice rose to a scream. Marion left her to cry for a moment, and came running to the door.

"This is dreadful," she whispered. "She won't get quiet. Her temperature's still at 104 in spite of the sponging. Did you see the Doctor?"

David nodded. "Is there nothing I could do?" he asked.

"Nothing," sighed Marion. "It's just – so nice to know you're here. You have been good. But you must go home now, and not wait any longer. Tell Miss Grant there's no immediate danger at present. We'll let you know how she does. Good night. I *must* go back to her – listen!"

She put out her hand, and seemed to push him away. "Don't wait," she said again, and hurried back to the bedside.

They worked with Nannie for another hour. By one o'clock, the temperature had fallen a little, and she was very worn out and inclined to be quieter. Then Marion persuaded the nurse to go to bed.

"You're dreadfully tired, Nana," she insisted, "and you've had more of it than me. Go and lie down, do. The sponging's finished for just now, and I have the cold milk and potash to give her. I expect the sleeping stuff will work shortly, and she just wants me to stay beside her. If I did need you, I'd waken you. Honestly!"

Nana was tired indeed. She hesitated, with a hand to her aching head, but the thought of rising early in the morning made her give in.

Marion sat on in the low chair beside the bed. Nannie lay very still; and Marion thought after a while that the sleeping draught had worked. Very softly, she slipped her hand away, but at once Nannie started up.

"Don't," she moaned. "Don't go. Don't leave me. Marion, are you there?"

"Yes, I'm here, I'm here," whispered Marion, making her lie down again, and straightening the sheet. "I won't go away."

"You won't, really?" asked Nannie faintly. "O Marion, it was so awful. That horrid woman… and the dark room. And they said he needed help… oh!" Her voice rose sharply in agony. "And then I dreamed…"

It was the hundredth time she had gone over that evening's misery. Marion stroked her hand, and hushed her to silence. "Take some of this," she said, feeding her with the milk and potash. "That's nice, isn't it?"

Again Nannie was silent, but Marion did not try this time to draw away her hand.

She heard the clock strike two. The candle by the bed flickered, and the grease rolled down in shapeless lumps – "winding-sheets" Marion remembered their nurse calling them long ago. She shivered. Suddenly each piece of furniture in the room began to creak, and things rattled in the chimney; then it seemed necessary to glance at every corner and into every mass of black shadow to see what lurked there. Marion felt panic within her; a thousand fears started up to appall her. She knew it was absurd, but that strange atmosphere which comes with illness had fallen round her, wherein are unknown possibilities, a morbid tightening of the nerves and straining of the imagination, and the very pains of hell.

Far away a train whistled eerily through the night. Marion realised that she was very cold, with a sort of dead coldness...

Her brain tried to work. She kept wondering, wondering all kinds of things, and in particular why life was such a sad affair. Nannie's screams, and the wild look in her eyes haunted Marion. Why was such torture of a soul possible? She began to weave a nightmare about it; it seemed that some one had set her that riddle and she could not find the answer. She was conscious of searching everywhere desperately for it, alone, out in the night... then she was in that Castlerig garden, still searching, and David was there, and he was trying to stop her, and she broke away from him... why, why?

With a start, she realised that she had been dozing. How cold it was, colder than before. The candle was choked with winding-sheets... then she felt herself slipping from the chair into a heap on the floor. Her head dropped on her arm. No, she must keep her eyes open; yet they were heavy... just one minute she would shut them. That was comfortable. She drew a long breath. Then she slept.

It seemed only a minute before she was awake again. Light had crept in at the window, and... there was some one in the room. She started up. It was David, rather grey and tired about the face, with untidy hair and his jacket creased; but he was smiling, and he had a cup of tea in his hand. She swayed on her feet, then caught the arm of the chair.

"I didn't know you were here," she gasped. "I thought you went away... home."

"I didn't. I couldn't let you stay alone in case... well. Oh, sit down and drink this, and we can talk in the morning." He made her sit in the big chair, and put the cup into her hands.

"Isn't it morning?" she whispered, sipping the tea.

"It's four, and getting light. I'm going now. You see, I must take Ross's car back. She's all right and sleeping, isn't she?" He spoke low, nodding towards the bed.

"Yes, at last. Oh David... did you make this?"

"Nana left the cup and things out before she went off."

"And Billy?"

"Billy went to bed centuries ago."

"And you?"

"I lay down on the library sofa. That better? What about bed yourself now?"

"It's lovely." She gulped the last mouthful, then lay back in the chair and broke down completely. "I'm such a fool," she sobbed.

"You're not," he contradicted quickly. "You're splendid."

She rubbed the tears from her eyes, and stood up, flushing with pride. The memory of that old bitter day was wiped out now. Together they went from the room quietly, so that Nannie might not be disturbed.

At the head of the stair he turned to her. "I must go now," he said, and his eyes asked a question of her. She gave him both her hands. They were not boy and girl playing at love in a beautiful garden now, but a tired man and woman, who had known fear and sorrow together that night. Then he kissed her. "That was what I meant to do in the garden!" he said. "It's a queer time to propose, but we might as well be original. My dearest, you know I love you without me saying it. Do you care?"

"With all my heart," she answered.

David drew off the signet ring he wore, and slipped it on to her finger. Then he kissed her hand. "We'll get a proper one when Nannie's better and you've had a decent sleep," he said. "At least, that one's businesslike, which is in keeping with your brave, splendid self. Now I'm off, and you must go to bed and rest. Good night!"

"Good morning, you mean!" she laughed.

And so he left her.

Twenty-Four

Good things end, and bad things end.
And you and I remain!

—G. K. CHESTERTON

One afternoon, several weeks later, a family council was held round the Sutherlands' tea-table. Uncle Alexander sat at the foot, silent and patient. Effie was next to him, very gay, her hands reddened with the work of cooking, her laugh louder than ever. She had astonished them the week before by arriving suddenly, with her box, and in one breath asking for Nannie, telling them that she had left the hospital for good, and announcing her engagement to Bob Trotter. But Marion had been glad indeed to have her at home, for Nannie's illness was a long, trying business, and her convalescence more difficult still.

Marion was at the head of the table pouring out tea, and David sat between the two children with Beatrice opposite. It was she who was talking; she had come home only the night before, feeling that the world had become a different place, for the doctors had told her that Pat would live, although it might be months before he could walk again.

Nannie, the subject of the present discussion, was not there; she lay upstairs, very thin and fretful, with a pile of novels on her bed, and the room sweet with flowers sent by the Grants from Castlerig.

"It would be the very thing," Beatrice said, looking round at them all. "You see, I'll need to be with him up there for ages, so this cousin of mine, who is doing matron's work in a war hospital, has offered me, like the saint she is, her little house out in the country, but quite get-at-able from London. I'll establish the bairns there, and Pat shall come to it to convalesce whenever he's out of hospital. The house is on the right side of London for escaping air raids, and I don't believe there's a more ideal place for a rest cure. And Nannie can bask there in the sun and grow fat. If that's not a complete change…"

"We would have had her at Castlerig," said Marion, looking at David, "if the doctors hadn't wanted an absolute change, away from Scotland and all of us here."

"It is immensely kind of you, my dear Beatrice," said Uncle Alexander gratefully. "You relieve my mind…"

"Your poor old mind!" laughed Effie. "I don't wonder it needs relieving. Bea always is our good angel."

As they rose from tea, Alison drew from the bulging folds of her sailor blouse a small leaflet like a tract and presented it to David. It was covered with rows of printing at an acute angle, and its substance was Beatrice's best notepaper.

"Is this for me?" asked David, bending down.

"Just a little engagement present," said Alison in her penetrating whisper. "Why shouldn't there be engagement presents as well as wedding ones? Anyway I couldn't wait till the beastly old wedding."

David unfolded the pamphlet with a perfectly grave face. It was entitled "The Seaside, and Other Poems: Illustrated by the Awthor." There were four poems in all, an illustration to match the title with a many-rayed lighthouse springing like a chrysanthemum from the bed of ocean, and a foreword headed "To All who read This Book."

The foreword said, "It is to be hopped that all who read This Book will like it very much. With best wishes to My readers, I close."

David handed Marion the production.

"Thanks ever so much," he said to Alison. "Look here, as soon as we're settled in the Shieling will you come and have tea with me, Alison?"

"And Babs too? Yes rather. Thank you exceedingly. And I'll recite you *The Ancient Mariner*. I've learned three parts of it, and it's nawful long. Would you like to hear it now?"

"Oh, preserve us," cried Effie, and proceeded to monopolise the conversation. Beatrice joined in. The subject was Effie's trousseau, and ways and means; Uncle Alexander was constantly appealed to anent the means. While Effie was getting under way with hats, David caught Marion's eye, and she nodded, and went out quietly. Five minutes after, he found her in the hall, dressed as she had been on her visit to Castlerig, with the best hat and the piece of lavender tulle.

They looked at each other.

"You won't be ashamed of me, David?"

"You're perfect. I love that gauzy thing. But will I do? This confounded suit shows every speck."

She picked off some bits of fluff. "I like you better in grey than navy," she said reluctantly. "But this is awfully braw. It ought to satisfy Aunt Margaret. David, I'm horribly frightened of your Aunt Margaret."

"So am I," he laughed. "But it's our duty, May. She sent a command through Uncle Duncan. 'Why hasn't he brought her round to see me?' We've got to obey."

"Well, if we must… only, you do the talking."

"Aunt Margaret will do the talking," said David with conviction. "Didn't you like our engagement present, May?"

"It was lovely," cried Marion. "'To all who read This Book' left me helpless. Aren't they dears?"

Aunt Margaret and the spaniel received them in state; Isabel was out, for which David thanked Heaven. The call lasted a bare half-hour, and when they came away, Marion was hot all over.

"Oh it was awful," she breathed, on the doorstep.

"But, dear, you were beautiful," David pointed out. "You managed it so smoothly. Girls always seem to be able to make so much of the weather and the rations. I fairly envied you."

"Don't be silly," said Marion. "My cheeks were burning, and I found a hole in my glove half way through. *You* looked so much at home. I felt like a new housemaid being interviewed. Oh, it's horrid to say it about your people, but why do some women make one feel less than a worm?"

"Sheer snobbery. I shouldn't have asked you to go," said David remorsefully.

"No," she interrupted. "We had to. I quite see, I'm not a fool. Only... I think I'm glad we aren't very rich; it doesn't spoil things, and it's so much freer. We can do so much more what we like. I don't mean being poor... just half and between. What do you think about it, David?" Her voice grew a little shy. "I don't know a bit what you think about things like that. Are you a Socialist? Most clever people seem to be nowadays."

He laughed. "Thanks for the compliment," he said, "but I'm neither. I think you might call me a progressive Conservative or a conservative reformer, May, if there can be such a hybrid!"

"I don't understand a bit about politics," she said, wrinkling her brow. "I hate reading the papers, and I shan't be able to ask you intelligent questions at breakfast. You'll need to tell me heaps of things. I get muddled. Nothing seems to be certain just now, not even religion, and I don't see how one can carry on without something definite and sure in the centre of life."

David looked at her. "I know," he said. "I've felt that too. It's difficult, but then this is a difficult time to be living in. We've got to be adventurous."

"And not comfortable," she finished. "I see. Life wasn't meant to be enjoyed."

He wondered if she had read that bit of Chesterton too. "No, but it is glorious," he said gaily. "Dearheart, you've helped me to find that out. Can't we go on being adventurous together?"

"Of course we can," she said.

They had been walking in quiet side streets, and now Princes Street opened before them, and all the wide space of the city. The Castle, and the tall houses of the Old Town, the towers and the spires, shone like gold in the sun of the late afternoon. Below, up and down the street, the crowds passed and sounded, with tramping of feet, and voices, and laughter. The shop windows were full of fine wares; jewels glittered, silks and ribbons flaunted their brightness. At the street corner, a lame man in a wheeling chair played a lilting, sobbing tune on his fiddle.

Marion gripped David's arm. "It's quite different," she said. "It's like a magic city. Is it the light? I feel as if..."

"As if we were going into Bagdad and the Arabian nights," he suggested.

"As if we were going into fairyland," she finished.

"We are," he said confidently.

"We only need the wishing ring!" she laughed up at him.

"We're going to buy it," he answered her.

They passed the fiddler; David gave him a silver sixpence, and he struck into a medley of Scots airs.

To the music of the reel, they left him, and entered Princes Street. And the mass of hurrying life, as it swung past, surrounded them, and drew them along with it.

Afterword

—ALISTAIR McCLEERY

We hope that you have enjoyed this book, and that in reading it you have been provoked into thinking about its themes and characters. Perhaps too, you will wonder how it was planned, designed, edited and produced. As with any book, it is the result of a collaborative effort by a large team, in this case the staff and students of the postgraduate publishing programme at Edinburgh Napier University.

There is a particular appropriateness in this. Edinburgh Napier has strong connections with the literature of World War One through its campus at Craiglockhart, used as a hospital for officers during the conflict and the place where Siegfried Sassoon encouraged Wilfred Owen to write a more direct form of poetry reflecting his experiences at the Front. The Craiglockhart library now houses the War Poets Collection and permanent exhibition. This novel contrasts with that more familiar war poetry. The war provides the background to the novel but Christine Orr focuses on the home front in Edinburgh.

The Glorious Thing fits well within the fiction list developed to date by postgraduate publishing students for Merchiston Publishing. While Christine Orr may not be as well known as many of her contemporaries, she deserves her place, on the basis of this novel alone, alongside Catherine Carswell, Willa Muir, Nan Shepherd and others. She was also a contemporary of Edward Clark, the prominent Edinburgh printer and publisher, whose generosity in establishing the Edward Clark Trust we must acknowledge. We would like to thank the current Trustees for their continuing willingness to support our students' work and, in doing so, to bring neglected classics like this back into public awareness.

—Alistair McCleery is Professor
of Literature and Culture,
and Director of the
Scottish Centre for the Book

Pictured above is the tin sent to every soldier at the Front for Christmas in 1914. This was the idea of seventeen-year-old Princess Mary, who organised a public appeal to raise funds to ensure that "every sailor afloat and every soldier at the front" received a gift. The contents varied, but included tobacco, chocolate, a Christmas card and a picture of the Princess.

The tin you see here was given to Thomas Rimington Laycock (Northumberland Fusiliers), the soldier who appears on the cover of the book, who fought and survived four gruelling years of war. He was the father of ten children and the great-grandfather of one of the students involved in this project, and his tin has since been passed down through the generations.

This illustrates just one of the deep connections we had with this project. The collage used in the cover design was created by the Production team, and was compiled entirely from family heirlooms, photographs and mementos from the time, all of which were brought in by members of our group.

Edinburgh Napier University's links to the First World War through Craiglockhart campus were what first led us to search for a work with this subject matter, and we quickly adopted the poppy as our "brand" as an instantly recognisable symbol of the First World War. We are also donating 100 copies of the book to Poppyscotland and the Scottish Veterans Residences.

Finally, Christine Orr was an Edinburgh author who has largely been forgotten, publishing her is therefore not only relevant to Merchiston Publishing, but it has been a real joy to know we're helping in some small way to bring her work to a wider audience.

—MSc Publishing Postgraduates
Edinburgh Napier University
2012/13

About the Author

—SALLY PATTLE

C hristine Orr is a somewhat enigmatic figure in Scottish Literature. She was certainly prolific during the inter-war period, and seems to have been involved with the Scottish Renaissance – C.M. Grieve published one of her poems in his third and final edition of *Northern Numbers*. Her obituary in *The Scotsman* described her as "the last of the New Town Literary Group", whose most famous son was of course Robert Louis Stevenson. However, despite leaving a large volume of work behind her, very little is known of Orr's personal life.

During her writing career, she published 14 novels, numerous volumes of poetry, and several plays, including *Miss Scott of Castle Street*. It is for her poetry that she is primarily remembered, "The Atholl Road" still appears in many collections, although it seems the theatre was her main passion. Orr worked for the BBC and held the position of Organiser of Scottish Children's Hour until her marriage to the journalist Robin Stark in 1936. In addition, she was also editor of *Greatheart*, the Church of Scotland's children's magazine, for many years. It is telling that the most affectionate scenes in *The Glorious Thing* deal with Beatrice's two "darling children", Alison and Babs, and yet we have no information as to whether Orr herself had children.

Along with her husband, she was instrumental in founding *The Unicorn Players*, the company based at the Princes Theatre in Edinburgh, as well as *The Makars*, one of Edinburgh's most influential amateur dramatics groups. With all of these attributes it is even more astonishing that apart from these scant details so little is actually known about her life, and that her undoubtedly valuable legacy to Scottish literature has all but been forgotten today. Her contemporaries include Catherine Carswell, Naomi Mitchison and Willa Muir, yet while they are now recognised as pioneers in the field of feminist fiction, Orr, who in many ways preceded them, has been almost entirely neglected.

All of her novels have been allowed to go out of print, although copies of each can still be viewed in the National Library of Scotland, and both the Scottish Poetry Library and Central Library in Edinburgh each have a volume of different work. It is hoped that this special edition of Christine Orr's 1919 war novel, *The Glorious Thing*, will stimulate a long overdue revivial of her work.

—SALLY PATTLE, MSc PUBLISHING
ON BEHALF OF MERCHISTON PUBLISHING

Discussion Questions

1   "What shall Cordelia do?
    Love, and be silent." *King Lear*
    Consider the portrayal of women. Did their roles
    affect the way they interact with one another?

2   "War is not romantic nowadays."
    Compare the different attitudes towards war
    presented by Orr in the novel.

3   "Why should a dog, a horse, a rat, have life,
    And thou have no breath at all?" *King Lear*
    How is personal bereavement presented
    throughout the novel?

4   Consider the setting of the novel: to what extent
    are urban and rural settings opposed to one
    another? Do these divisions hold true today?

5   "They were not boy and girl playing at love
    in a beautiful garden now, but a tired man and
    woman, who had known fear and sorrow together
    that night."
    To what extent is *The Glorious Thing* a "coming
    of age" story?

6 Which character do you most relate to, and how do you think you would have acted when faced with the same circumstances?

7 "From the moment she arrived in Castlerig she walked in romance."
Of all the love stories depicted which is the most believable?

8 Do you think *The Glorious Thing* conforms to literature of the period?

9 To what extent is the author's voice subsumed into the narrative?

10 How are men presented in the novel? What difficulties do they face and how do they cope with them?

Also by Merchiston Publishing

Detective McLevy's Casebook

The New Road (also as eBook)

Lilith (eBook)

Treasure Island: A Play

Peter and Wendy

The Kelpie's Pearls

Travel Light

Imagined Corners

Sunset Song (also as eBook)

The Thirty-Nine Steps

The Private Memoirs and Confessions of a Justified Sinner

The Hound of the Baskervilles

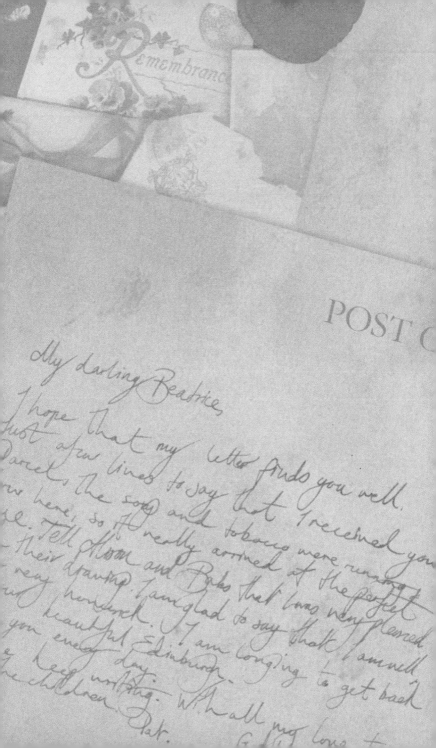

My darling Beatrice,

I hope that my letter finds you well.
Just a few lines to say that I received your
parcels the soap and tobacco were running
low here, so it really arrived at the perfect
time. Tell Mom and Babs that I was very pleased
with their drawing. I am glad to say that I am well
but very homesick. I am longing to get back
to beautiful Edinburgh.
Keep writing. With all my love to
the children. Pat.